To Margaret with Love
Joyce X

Past Lives
-
Fact or Fiction

Joyce Stableford

Visit us online at www.authorsonline.co.uk

An AuthorsOnLine Book

Copyright © Joyce Stableford 2005

Cover design by Siobhan Smith ©

ISBN 0 7552 0231 7

19 The Cinques
Gamlingay
Sandy
Bedfordshire
SG19 3NU

This book is also available in e-book format, details of which are available at
www.authorsonline.co.uk

Dedication

I would like to dedicate this book to my three very special children:
Brian because he is my special first-born son, Andrea because she is my special only daughter, Christopher because he is my special third-born, second son.
All of whom I am sure have been neglected in some degree whilst pursuing my many-faceted career.

Acknowledgements

I would like to thank my husband for his patience whilst I was writing this book and my long-time mentor Ray Keedy-Lilley for his encouragement over many years. All the members of the Torrevieja Writers Group who have patiently read chapters, and particular thanks to Neil McNeil, Pauline Levis and Rex Ellis for their constructive comments and criticisms. I would also like to thank Dr May Taylor for challenging me to write the book in the first instance on such a controversial subject, and Wendy Lake for helping me to get it into print.

Contents

PREFACE

This is the story of Jan who, over a period of one year in therapy, persistently re-lived and re-experienced what seemed to be mainly three past lives in traumatic circumstances.

During our therapeutic sessions she reported that in one life in France she died in Versailles under the guillotine, in another life in London she died by the axe on Tower Green.

Ironically, in her reported third life in London, she was the executioner and axe man in the Tower of London. She later decided that this life was prior to the other two.

Initially Jan was confused and scared, because the last thing she came to therapy for was to participate in any past-life regression. From the very first session she did not know what might be metaphor for present problems, what might be fantasy or indeed what was real, but the experiences became more and more REAL for her as time passed.

She came to believe at the end of our journey that reincarnation, although it made no sense, was the only explanation that made every sense.

Most published accounts of past-life experiences are anonymous because of a code of ethics inherent in practice, which prohibits clients from being named. Jan is an exception to the rule as she is proud to have her story told.

Midway through our sessions she began to question each "self". Was she, Jan, the same self as Juanita or (Gianetta) – a young companion to royalty at the time of the French revolution? Jan writes after a session:

I looked down, and my shoes had changed, so had my skirts, my hair, my age, but it was me. There was a wind in the trees and a sense of impending doom. The atmosphere changed, and I felt fear in my heart. The noise that then occurred was a howling mob, filthy and foul smelling. I was terrified and stayed that way until my death on the guillotine 2 years later. I was so young and innocent of any crime other than being who I was and where I was. I was at the start of an unravelling that has no equal in my experience.

... there was a dream ... in car... driving ... walking, escaping ... young man forcing a pillow on the back of my neck ... pushing ... voicing of many dreams since childhood ...(**Jan threw a small pillow from behind her neck here**) *I DIED on the guillotine ... point of death ... light ... coming in from one side ... praying ... place I don't know ... I'm praying, coming through a valley ... of tears ... part of the journey ... ongoing journey ... dark into light ... can't separate them ... part of the same experience ... warmth ...light ... millions of candles ... what's happening? ... Other people around me ... like shapes ... in a church ... gowns ... hoods ... long dark ... between life ...*

clothes are different ... still the same person ... before ... to help me ... feel a presence... heavy brocade ... in a dress I couldn't stand ... praying ... kneeling ... have a book ... contemplations ... comfortable people ... reverence ... I think ... masses of candles ... comforting people ... kind of light when the evening draws in ... I've been neglectful l... picking up a piece ... before I died ... I was quite scatty ... didn't give a fig about others ... two halves ... both me but different ...

As a therapist I believe that memory is always laid down together with sight, smell, hearing, touch, taste and emotion – and Jan's regression sessions elicited detailed evocations of times past.

Whether or not she was the innocent, but doomed, Juanita, or the nameless young girl who lived and died in London – for what crime we may never know. Whether or not she was Richard, the small boy who was too much like a girl, and had to grow to manhood and become the axe man like his father? These past lives provide a fascinating and very believable story.

Jan writes after a session:

I was in awe of my swaggering father who thought nothing of death, his own or anyone else's. People were a profession to him, and as his son I was expected to follow him, and indeed I did. I hung around the Tower for years as a young boy. I managed to avoid everything unpleasant – I learned to stuff my ears with material so I could not hear. I put a stupid smile on my face and took to the river whenever I could. I was not a simpleton but I behaved like one. I dressed in the required black and grey and sat with my father in taverns and I drank to forget what I was expected at some time to do.

... I hear the noises of people ... shouting and yelling ... but I will not look ... I am in position ... .I raise the axe ... and I have done it ... .that's the end of me ... I hear the sound ... I see the blood ... around my feet ... .and the bile rises in my throat ... and I am sick ... I see skirts ... I have killed a woman ... I take off my hood ... and I know I am done for in this life ... I am down the stairs ... .and I am so clearly disgusted that I can only make amends with my own life ... the people who knew her know me now and they will kill me ... and that is how it should be ... I cannot live knowing what I have done ...

Jan always attended for therapy wearing a neck scarf. I thought perhaps this was her particular fashion statement – but I was wrong! It became clear as we worked, that it was part of a deep-rooted unconscious fear. Jan says:

There had always been this big thing about me ... I've always worn high necks a lot ... .even in summer ... people laugh at me because I always wear high necks ... and I always have the cover up around my neck in bed ... and there's always been this cold thing up here, something I couldn't possibly explain because I was a lot younger ... but it was always that kind of thing.

Jan writes at the end of our sessions:

As I worked more, (in therapy) the line between yesterday and today lessened and I could feel myself being drawn backwards in time until I felt I could turn a corner and be in another place and time. My reality was not as secure as I had considered it to be. My dreadful father from my young days as a boy in the Tower stays with me. I cannot explain the images or the places I have seen, I have never read anything of this nature. What has come to me has come to me. I had no special insight, and it has never happened before. I have had dreams since I was small, but they have never linked or been so much part of my waking days. The people who I AM or HAVE BEEN are in a stream of consciousness that makes no sense, yet makes every sense.

I have no doubt that when the powers that be are making the guidelines for training therapists they do not have in mind what Jan endured in her 50 hours of therapy.

INTRODUCTION

This book initially began with an idea that a spontaneous past-life experience was something very different to a hypnotically induced therapeutic process to a past life. This was because I felt that an induction by hypnosis could make suggestions that might facilitate anything from a forgotten memory from childhood, to imaginative fiction. I have always been fascinated by neuro-science, this book therefore, was to be my search as a scientist into one client's unexpected and unasked for journey into the past. It was never my intention merely to describe, but to speculate, explore, and tentatively interpret.

I began with no desire to diminish the belief in reincarnation, neither did I have any wish to add to the theories which appear to uphold the fact that we have lived before.

However, in the course of my investigation further questions arose such as, who are we, where do we come from, what are we here for, and where are we going? Then, as the journey unfolded, I found myself immersed in the complex mysteries of mind, brain, and consciousness. This included more research than ever before as a psychologist. The questions multiplied and the search extended from hypnotherapy and differential trance states, into questions about the "self", reality and reincarnation. My knowledge of reincarnation was minimal and extremely sceptical at this stage, but because of the many sessions that I had witnessed over the years I was intrigued.

Eventually my journey took me further on from neuroscience to eastern and western philosophy, astrology, geometry, quantum physics and the incredible universe of Stephen Hawking. Then this led me further to legends, channelled writings and clairvoyant predictions. This path was quite a departure for me, as I always needed to be on the accepted, conventional side of therapy and research.

In the end it was not about trying to show how any one theory is more acceptable than any other, because I can offer no proof for my findings. Proof belongs to mathematics and I cannot apply statistical methods to data that assumes that the said data is as exact as the method of treatment. In any case psychological research is too easy to describe with facts, figures, tests and statistics, but the vital question always remains – of what significance is this to an individual?

I am a psychologist who has specialized in therapeutic strategies, a qualified healer and an astrologer, but I can make no claim to being a philosopher, mathematician or physicist. All I can claim is a thirst for knowledge that can access and understand basic questions, and transcend in some way, technical proficiency.

1

My personal conclusion at this stage in my search is that, everything began with Unity and will end with Unity, so there is for me an underlying purpose to this dynamic wholeness of being which creates and destroys in constant change based in number. How this will manifest I do not know. I like Arthur M. Young's (1975) definition of Unity which is that it is projective potential, and as such is the first cause of effect that necessarily divides further into aspects. These aspects create relationships, which then are the foundation of everything, relationships between people, situations and "things". I also warm, like many psychologists, physicists and medical researchers, to the energy theory of living things, "where electricity and the electromagnetic forces are the basic powers of the universe and human life". Quote from *A Search for Truth* by Ruth Montgomery (p. 114).

I am no nearer any definitive explanation of HOW a spontaneous past life experience occurs except that it seems to be a "quantum leap" of the brain/mind/body, which might show that a person has lived before. Neither have I any definitive findings that state that reincarnation is a fact, but there is much evidence to show that it is. If it is a fact, there is certainly little evidence to date to show HOW this might occur. But then we do not know everything about ourselves or the universe, we are but babes-in-arms in this quest.

All I can offer at the end of my search are more theories and such evidence that I have put before you, the reader. One publisher, rejecting my synopsis, told me that there were too many "ifs and buts" and as a therapist I know that "but" means there is still a problem waiting to be resolved.

I would offer you life eternal if I could, or even the certainty of reincarnation, *but* ... I rest my case.

What I like most about the belief in reincarnation, is the hope for the future in that if I "mess up" this time I could choose to have another chance. No-one fails and nothing stops us from making our own judgements based upon our own spiritual insights.

What I can say, with some confidence for me personally, is that the symbolic language and energy approach of personal Spiritual Astrology best explains the answer to even the most inexplicable of questions by any other means. Based upon a faith in reincarnation, it tells us who we are, what we are here on earth to do and points in the right direction if we wish to save our souls. Taken even further, Hermetic Astrology represents an extension of traditional astrology by taking account of previous civilizations. It attempts to explain how approximately every 2160 years (an astrological day) the consciousness of the whole of humanity gradually changes. Hermetic Astrology based upon the cosmology of the ancient Egyptians, presents a new world to the reader who seeks to find the self in relation to the universe. Legend backed by some research suggests that buried below either the Sphinx or one of the great Pyramids of Giza lies the Hall of Records which could tell us who we are, where we came from and where we are going. Hermetic Astrology is first and foremost a Christian astrology for all those who are interested in the deeper existential questions of life. In astrological terms, our life span on earth is but "an hour in school" and not enough time to learn all the lessons.

Jan's experiences of spontaneous regression into what seemed to be the re-living of three past lives, in which she maintains that she was the same person as she is in this life, were not my first experiences of sharing. Mostly they have occurred whilst therapists have been in training, as well as some working with me professionally, so none have been recorded except by me. Not all people appear to have access to these "lives" although many would dearly love the experience for a variety of reasons. This may have much to do with susceptibility to trance states rather than suggestibility, although suggestibility can play a part. From my own research I found that some people are more susceptible and therefore more suggestible than others.

In the past, the words "I wonder if you can go back to the very first time" spoken by a training therapist during his final diploma examination, elicited a past life experience in his client which totally threw the poor man from his obviously prepared script. His client wanted to explore the feeling of unease that she always felt when she had to drive to a new place. As she went into a relaxed state, she recounted an episode in a park, which she described in some detail through the eyes and voice, of a small child in what seemed to be Edwardian times. She was lost and could not find her way back to her parents. After some imaginary work to help the child in the past situation, her therapist brought her back to this life and to some extremely pertinent questions about what had happened here. This episode made me very aware that during training, therapists should be made cognisant with the fact that clients will sometimes go into these apparently "past lives" with no specific instruction. Whether the would-be therapist's own faith or beliefs accept or reject the concept, it is worthy of discussion and they can be given some suggestion as to how they can deal with it.

On one occasion many years ago I also used the words "I wonder if you can go back to the very first time ..." when immediately my client began to speak in a very childlike way saying that "she wanted a grape". I was really taken by surprise at this sudden regression. She told me that she was three and was in a neighbour's house, she could just see on to the table where there was a bowl of fruit. I suggested that she asked the lady nicely if she could have a grape. The answer came back that she could not do that because her mother had told her that she must never, never ask for anything. She then "flipped" to age seven to yet another story about her mother where she was told that a painting that she had brought home from school was not right and her mother had proceeded to change it. When my client was back to her present age, she could not believe that all this had taken place. The problem that she had brought to therapy was that she wanted to apply for promotion in her present career but found it difficult to go to her boss and ask.

She thought that her reluctance was because she lacked confidence, after the session she realised that it was a conditioned reaction to a command that had been laid down at a very early age, forgotten but still buried there. It is a well-known fact amongst psychologists, that instructions given to children under about five-years old remain in the unconscious mind. This is because before children learn to read and write and solve problems, the right brain is in control, there is no left brain "interpreter" to question. I asked this client if she would volunteer to take part in my research into susceptibility and suggestibility. This she did because she was quite convinced that she was never hypnotized, "under" as she understood it. She turned out to have the highest susceptibility score of my 46 volunteers.

Some Past-Life Therapists say "I want you to look down at your feet" and although no suggestion was made by me, Jan did always look down at her feet. Others such as hypno-therapists who utilise dream-work make the suggestion, "I wonder if you can go back into that dream and know what it means". There are many instances that I cannot discuss in full because the students are long gone and permission to recount their stories is unavailable. However, here is discussion in brief, with apologies to those students.

One young lady participating in an automatic writing exercise which is a therapeutic process based in Classical Hypnosis, for unearthing deep-seated problems, produced page after page of "cuneiform" writing, whilst in a deep trance state with eyes wide open. The lady in question when alert and awake could not believe that she had written them, but as the whole session had been witnessed by at least another six students she had to be convinced. No-one, as far as I know, ever did attempt to verify the fact that the writing was a real language. Another student spoke in a language with which he was not even familiar, another re-lived through being injured on two separate occasions during the American Civil War, and continued to limp after the sessions were over. These two occasions where the same past life was re-lived, were a month apart, and as he cursed and swore he named names of generals as well as places. These may well have been verified by historical research had my interest then been as keen as my interest since.

What I can say is that some of these students were quite distressed about their experiences, which came unasked for and unwanted. One student, setting bones in a pyramid during the session, kept telling his therapist to "go away" he was interrupting his work, and afterwards, kept repeating "I don't believe in past lives, but I was there, it was so real." I spent hours of telephone counselling with this particular student over the next few days after the course. It has been verified by archaeologists today that in Egypt at the time when the pyramids were built, medical practices were of a high standard. There is evidence that bones set with splints healed well and even brain surgery had been attempted in those times. Indeed, Imohtep the designer of the Step Pyramid, was said to be the father of modern medicine long before Hippocrates.

The purpose in retelling the experiences of Jan, and explaining them from the different perspectives, attempts more than description alone, which is the failure of many books on reincarnation. There are many such books, which give word by word details of people who have been induced into trance states by psychotherapists and hypno-therapists but none go beyond this description.

These descriptions of so called past life stories are ridiculed by sceptics, who maintain that so many clients claim to have been the same famous person in the past. However in my experience, most people who report past lives have lived very ordinary lives, some of which have been verified by research. The sceptics maintain that all the information that is produced from these sessions is the result of dialogue between therapist and client, suggesting that the client has been led to the answers. They maintain that under hypnosis subjects are only too ready to accept all kinds of distortions of his or her reality. This can be true but it was certainly NOT true in the case of my sessions with Jan. One view that sceptics put forward as an alternative theory to those very young children who convincingly tell of past lives, is that of contacting external spirits though channelling. Another view even more bizarre, is that these children are possessed by entities who control their consciousness.

A more recent story is that of a family member of my own, who was in intensive care, suffering from a pulmonary embolism which shattered in her lung. She was unconscious and on life support for six days and the family was told that it was most unlikely that she would live. At age 30 years this was indeed of great concern and we were told that she had momentarily "died" and been resuscitated. The only help that we could give was prayer and meditation and faith in the medical profession. Her friends lit candles and prayed with us and after six days she began calling for Robbie and regained consciousness. My sister – her mother – was called and she asked who Robbie was, and what was happening as she came back. My niece replied that she was being born and Robbie was her twin who had died. My niece is not a twin in this life, and in conversation with myself later in her recovery, she said that she believed that it had been a past life experience. She also told me that when she "died" her father had told her that she must come back – it was not her time. Her father had been dead for some two years.

Theories are all we have for now, and explanations can be found for all manner of what we see, hear and feel, but I like the optimistic stance that gives ordinary people hope in the future of mankind. Spontaneous regression comes in a flash, with no prompting or suggested scenarios, so it has to be different from a guided hypnotic session.

BACKGROUND

At around the age of ten or eleven, I was convinced that I was here for some purpose and that when I died I would know all about everything. Where these unconscious thoughts came from I have no idea, except that they were a "knowing" that I could not have explained. In the meantime I was convinced that I had to gather all the knowledge that I could, and teach! It took me many years before I actually became a teacher. My parents were not well educated and saw no reason why I should be, therefore all my education was as a mature student.

Then, perhaps it was because I became an undergraduate student of Psychology and Sociology at a more mature age than most and already a trained teacher, that I questioned more the assumptions of both. In fact I suppose I was quite a pain when it came to regurgitating the conventional wisdom of psychology in order to gain my degrees.

I could never understand the long running debate about nature versus nurture in Psychology, as to which was more important with regard to brain development, IQ and personality – genetic inheritance or cultural conditioning – surely they both had their contribution to make. Genetic inheritance sets the scene with potential, characteristic ways of responding and talents, and then exposure to the environment and conditioning together with life events inevitably encourages or discourages that potential.

Every developmental psychologist will tell you that providing there is no pre-birth damage, we are all pre-programmed to see, but we have to learn to make sense of shapes and colours in our own particular environment. After much experimentation over many years, we know that if this learning does not take place at the critical time of visual system development after birth, then the individual will never be able to recognize certain aspects of that environment. Hubel and Weisal in the 1960s showed how the undamaged brain comes with its hardware already established but that early environmental differences in visual stimulation can modify the neuronal wiring in the visual cortex. They also found evidence of "activity-dependent" development, and even the quality of bonding and initial social relationships can have a significant effect on potential. We also know from many years of experiments that we are pre-programmed to hear, but must learn to discriminate between the sounds of our own language and others in order to facilitate language development. In fact babies at only a few weeks old can recognize their own mother tongue from other languages. We must learn that whatever we feel has meaning for us in terms of our cultural beliefs, and what, from what we see, hear, taste and touch, is important to our survival.

I could never understand how, if you were a follower of Freud or Adler, you rejected the Behaviorist theories of Skinner and his compatriots. It always made sense to me, that once again the theories were merely the different perspectives from unique individuals in their interpretation of human behaviour, which is never-endingly complex. Babies develop from birth, physically, intellectually, socially and emotionally. They have to learn how to integrate all these stages within themselves, and externally, they must learn how to respond and relate to their parents, siblings, other relatives and eventually teachers and friends. This is one big learning curve, but what was wrong with all these "so called psychologists" with only one perspective? Then when testing student perception with ambiguous pictures I realized that no matter how one person tried to explain the second picture of two, some students just could not "see" the other.

When it came to Social Theory I could never understand the long running argument between the German philosophers Georg. W. F. Hegel and Emmanuel Kant, about reality. Kant (in a nutshell) maintained that we human beings could never know "reality" or what he called "noumena", because we must necessarily filter what is out there through our five senses. Therefore all we could ever know from the information was the re-presentation of reality, "phenomena". Kant meant that what is out there, only supplies the crudest sense data, and we human beings, with the total of our available senses supply the properties of substance, causation, time and space. He maintained that nothing could enter our experience without acquiring the characteristics and learning of the observer. This has been a fact well accepted in the world of Classical Physics although more recently it has come under some criticism and scrutiny. The world is, however initially unlabelled, so categorization and discrimination is a necessary process for human beings in making sense of the diversity of incoming information. All these things together with language, obviously become that filter through which our individual reality is formed.

Hegel on the other hand argued that if that is all we will ever know that IS our reality, which is a stance, normally taken by modern day psychotherapists and makes practical sense. Hegel was essentially mystical, rejecting the theory of separate objects and minds in space and time and embracing a philosophy of unity with the whole.

Why the big debates I constantly asked?

Are they not only different perspectives of the same thing?

Are not all ways of seeing and thinking valid as long as we know that these are always biased towards the individuals who provide them.

It can now be shown scientifically that brains and minds develop idiosyncratically in both structure and software, because of genetics, adaptation through evolution, and different life chances.

Now I dare to pose the question – are our brains pre-programmed to experience spiritual knowledge about who we are, where we came from, and where we are going when the time is right for us to know?

Furthermore do our brains constantly monitor not only our internal reactions and our responses to external happenings, but even the wider cosmos?

Perhaps the only reality is that we are immortal souls in relation to God, but this fact is not yet conceived by humanity in our present state.

CHAPTER 1

IN THE BEGINNING

My first undergraduate dissertation was "An Historical and Sociological Analysis of the Concept of Self". This told me a lot about how the children in a large inner city school and those in a small country school differed in attitudes, interests, beliefs and values. It told me that family, friends and teachers all aided in the construction of a child's concept of self, but common sense told me that we knew that already.

My MSc dissertation was "How Neuro-Linguistic Programming Constructs the Social Self". This added the fact that language, and the neuro-linguistic programming of a child's brain in the early years, has a further enhancing or inhibiting effect on the way in which a child becomes a person with a good, poor or indifferent sense of self. I had joined the run of the mill research of what scientific Psychologists want to know and Social Scientists need to know for educational, political and sociological planning. What I did not know at that time was that psychology as I knew it was dying, or that psychology grew out of philosophy. Neither was I aware that the basics of meaning and reality are to be found in mathematics, in geometry and algebra which scared me in my younger days.

The research into astrology for the final dissertation of my counselling course, done in-service whilst lecturing in psychology amazed and intrigued me. I discovered that an astrological birth chart told me far more than a psychological personality profile. In correspondence with Michel Gauquelin, the French astrologer who for many years has done research into time of birth and predisposition for certain professions, I pursued further research with some very willing students. My mind became more open to other than traditionally academic sources of knowledge. Then however, I faced the incredible question, "what is a nice psychologist doing dabbling with astrology?"

Many years later my dissertation on "Susceptibility in Hypnosis" told me how the programming of individuals can continue through susceptibility and suggestibility. I also came to the conclusion that programming continues throughout life, not only through counselling, psychotherapy and hypnosis but also through theatre, art, music, religion and politics. It continues through the clubs and societies that we join and most importantly through our significant others, partners, relatives and friends, and above all through all aspects of the media. We may abhor the word "programming" but programmed we are! Hence the rise in popularity of courses in Neuro-Linguistic Programming for all manner of persuasive management and selling to the public and a

9

therapeutic "quick fix". The "Stepford wives" of science fiction is not a myth, it is fact.

Not until I moved, quite by accident (literally), from lecturing in Psychology and Sociology into training Psychotherapists and Hypnotherapists, and dealing with clients face-to-face, did I learn what individuals seeking therapy really want to know. **They want to know who they are, how to deal with relationships, how to cope with everyday problems of fear, fear of being alone, fear of the unknown and most importantly, fear of death itself. Many are seeking some meaning in their lives and some belief to which to cling, that will make living worthwhile. They yearn for some security and stability in this world of fast and stressful change.**

I never intended to become a psychotherapist, lecturing and teaching was my profession, and my life. I once asked a member of the clergy, why, if God had wanted me to become a therapist did it have to be at the mercy of a double-decker bus? The bishop replied that perhaps He had tried a single-decker bus and it had not worked!

As well as the initial aim of this book to seek explanations for spontaneous past life regressions, another aim was to explore whether or not we live in the world of the scientist where we can only perceive reality through our senses, and which apparently is separate from us or do we live in the world of the mystic, the artist and the poet, where it is the inner world that constitutes reality?

The conclusion must inevitably be that we can inhabit both worlds, moving easily from one to the other. All this we can do, through the power of our brains and in spite of our central nervous system which only recognizes differences. The way into the world of the mystic is through trance states, hypnosis, meditation, prayer, or other means, during which we can seek a higher level of consciousness.

The book also aims to show that although change is inevitable, change is not always slow or indeed continuous. Sometimes there is a discontinuous leap, which a physicist calls a quantum jump, and this change cannot be tracked. In one instance before the jump, a particle is occupying a given region of space, then an instant later with no intermediate state when the process is taking place, the particle is somewhere else. No duration of TIME separates them and no physical process connects the two physical states. **"a miracle happens." This for me explains in some way a spontaneous past life experience, a quantum leap of neurons in the brain, and I also believe in what appear to be miracles.**

As scientific research continues to find perfectly normal explanations for what were once thought to be miracles or psychic phenomena, the more I believe that the Central Nervous Systems of human beings act as receivers, transmitters and transformers.

I have found through my research that Quantum Theory blurs the distinction between subject and object, cause and effect, and introduces the holistic element into our particular world. So, not only is it possible that we live in both worlds simultaneously, the most important fact for me is that the most recent research shows that **human beings are capable of CREATING that reality both inside and outside themselves and therefore have far more power than ever they thought.**

If this is true and the outer world is something that we create with our minds, on this level, the future is in our own hands – or should I say minds?

CHAPTER 2

FUNDAMENTAL QUESTIONS

"Tell me not in mournful numbers,
Life is but an empty dream!
For the soul is dead that slumbers,
And things are not what they seem.
Life is real! Life is earnest!
And the grave is not its goal;
Dust thou art, to dust returnest,
Was not spoken of the soul".

From *A Psalm of Life* by Henry Wadsworth Longfellow.

One of the biggest mysteries for science today is still the question of the nature of consciousness.

It is difficult, especially from my own dissections, when "becoming" a psychologist, to contemplate that all mental life and consciousness emerges from the mass of tissue that makes up the brain. However from the neuro-scientific perspective, at the present time we think that it does. In our western culture particularly, it tends to be the assumption that consciousness is produced by the activity of the brain, so consciousness is seen as identical with brain activity. This is the psycho-neural identity thesis based on the wider theory of a materialist community. This theory maintains that because the universe itself is made up of matter and energy of a purely physical nature, consciousness must be a result of physical activity of some kind. I cannot argue with the fact that each of us is a subject of experience, of sensations and perceptions, also the entertainer of ideas and deliberations. I have no quarrel with this, except that it may not be as simple as it sounds and must be a more complex activity than just the patterns of firing neurons in the brain and nervous system. Dane Rhudhyar in his writings always maintained that consciousness has to be the relationship between objects that are constantly changing and a subject (I) who can maintain a distinct identity.

We live in a culture today which mainly believes that we do what we do consciously, but research as well as practice, can show that what we do best, we do unconsciously. We would never remember how to walk, drive a car, play golf or any other sport, if the programme was not somehow based in what we call the unconscious mind and in the physical pattern in the body memory. In fact the very concept of conscious and unconscious mind is central to our model of learning, where according to Jung "unconscious processes stand in a compensatory relation to consciousness." What, in the beginning, was practised step by step with much concentration and selective attention, eventually becomes internalized and automatic and requires no attention. So we move from conscious effort to unconscious control. Jung also believed that the two parts of psyche, the conscious and the unconscious complement each other in the "Self".

Jean Piaget, a Swiss psychologist, many years ago expressed his theory of intellectual development as beginning with a spontaneous act then what he called *assimilation* through to *accommodation*. What he meant was, that we must necessarily look, touch, taste and smell so that we "experience" until we understand and know the meaning of any object. He maintained that intellectual development had to go hand in hand with physical development of body and brain, so that more complex learning had to wait until the brain was mature enough to cope. Many students have asked HOW this switch from "not knowing" to "knowing" occurs but it is a question not easy to answer. However it has to do with the brain changes, electrical and chemical which come about through the very act of repetition and learning, and perhaps a "quantum leap" that we cannot measure or explain.

What we do know is that we as individuals, consciously learn for as long as it takes for information to become unconscious knowing. So for me, brain functioning must be a complex feedback system involving many changes in neuronal structure and chemical processes, as well as an integral part of body memory.

But what exactly is consciousness?

From the point of view of a psychotherapist, healer and astrologer I believe that individual consciousness must vary in degrees that correlate with different degrees of neuronal activity. This degree of neuronal activity is constantly monitoring everything within the body, and responding to what is happening outside the body. Your body/brain monitors temperature changes. Your Central Nervous System deals with external shock through internal means. Your Sympathetic system puts you into "fight or flight mode", your Parasympathetic system calms you down. Experiments many years ago where volunteers were locked away and deprived of sensory stimulation showed that the subjects soon became distressed and prone to hallucination. So it seems that constant monitoring of the internal and external environment is not just sufficient but a necessary condition of normal life.

In the wider sense, the Hermetic view of history is what they call "the schooling of consciousness". They see the consciousness of man as a generic term changing every 2160 years naturally through evolution or by way of following a spiritual path to reach the higher states of consciousness. So for them, individual consciousness must be part of a wider consciousness.

The next question is what is Reality? Is it a fact, as opposed to fantasy, fiction, or even illusion, as some physicists would have us believe?

Realism as a philosophical term refers to the doctrine that objects exist independently of sensory experience, however, others will continue to argue that nothing exists until it is observed. One of the most famous realists of our time Albert Einstein, said that reality is the business of physics where what appears to be REAL can always be seen as two aspects of a single entity, like the wave and the particle, but never at the same time. This makes sense to me as a psychologist because when two forms are present in what are called "ambiguous pictures" individuals can usually only see one picture at one time. (see figure 1 below)

They learn to switch spontaneously or when the other picture is explained, and although perception can switch in a flash, it is rare to see both at the same time. This takes us back to the limitation of the human senses, and so it is totally pointless to ask even a physicist of today questions about reality because there are still only a variety of theories and physicists are only human after all.

So what is reality?

As a psychotherapist I would argue that reality, like beauty, is in the eye of the beholder, because it depends upon the individual MEANING that we assign to it. Arthur M Young, a mathematics graduate who set up a Foundation for the study of Consciousness and Reality, takes the stance that all meaning is a relationship based upon Geometry. This reasoning gives credence to my faith in Learning Theory and Astrology, both of which are based in mathematics and angular relationships. Maybe the number 42 is the answer to life, the universe and everything!

Astrology as well as being based in mathematics and angular relationships also proposes an underlying assumption that life on earth has purpose and a belief in reincarnation.

Hans Ten Dam refers to Reincarnation as "the no man's land between religion and science". I disagree, belief in any religion whether it is Buddhism, Christianity or any other is only a belief based upon the evidence that people are given, and that evidence can change from generation to generation. Christian beliefs before AD 553 (cited in Young) were that evolution took many lifetimes. Bodies had spirits and souls, and after death, souls had to move through four levels, first "down" then "up" with each change being a rebirth or self-determined growth to a higher status. This theory further suggests that when the "SELF" has made use of what it has learned and mastered about the laws of matter, in order to extricate itsSELF it will turn around and go the opposite way, just like learning theory generally.

Then the pre-existence of the soul was declared to be a heresy and religion has been reorganized and changed over many years. Much religion today is based upon hearsay and almost certainly biased written information, which has been re-written, and passed on for thousands of years. Only Islam claims that the Koran today is the same as the first transcripts written thousands of years ago. All religions however, preach of life after death and the resurrection of souls.

Science eventually became the new religion in the western world, because it was based upon observation and experimental evidence, which could be verified or not according to probability. However we must remember that scientific research is also biased in favour of those doing the experiments. There is no such thing as value-free observation or experiment, because they always involve the attitudes, beliefs and values of the experimental team plus all the inevitable intervening variables such as time, place and environmental conditions.

Both religion and science then, are subject to inconsistency, omission and embellishment, and even deliberate distortion.

Now carefully recorded research in the present day reveals many stories of Past Lives told by children, which cannot be accounted for in terms of fantasy or imagination. Some can even be verified without resort to experiment. There is the recorded evidence of past life stories of children by Dr Ian Stevenson. Then there are the recordings of past life regressions by American psychic Sylvia Browne and psychiatrist Dr Brian Weiss, both of whom believe passionately in the eternal survival of the soul. Certainly these people are no lightweights when it comes to qualifications and years of careful research.

For thousands of years reincarnation has been the underlying assumption not only of personal Astrology, but also of many religions and sects. Hermetic Astrological theory has also been based on the assumption that during the great years of astrological time, *the consciousness of man has changed levels according to "what is out there".* So if brains, minds and consciousness are fashioned by what is out there, then brains, minds and consciousness can change what is out there, all things are possible.

If there is such a thing as Reincarnation, how can this happen?

CHAPTER 3

JAN'S STORY

"Scientific discovery is impossible without faith in ideas which are of a purely speculative kind, ... faith which is quite unwarranted from the point of view of science, and which to that extent, is metaphysical."
Karl Popper, *The Logic of Scientific Discovery* (cited in Szanto)

Jan did not seek help with any belief in past life therapy, far from it, she came initially for her own therapy as part of her own ongoing supervision and training programme. Jan was already an accredited counsellor, but doing more training to become a psychosexual counsellor. She was neatly dressed, in her late 50s, obviously highly intelligent with an enquiring mind, but exhibiting a nervous tension in her body language. Initially the presenting problems were headaches and high blood pressure and the outcome that she wanted was to understand herself better so that she could work more effectively as a therapist. All fairly standard requests from a person who is conforming to present regulations of "own therapy". She did however eventually admit to a persistent feeling of fear and what she described as "dread", for which she could not account, and I later learned that she had suffered from nightmares and what she described as "night terrors" from an early age.

She had been married and divorced previously and brought up two children unaided, yet she hated being alone. She described her childhood as unhappy because her mother had made it quite clear that she would have preferred a boy, and there seemed to be little affection from either parent. Feeling unwanted and a nuisance, of no value, "plain Jane", she felt herself to have been a dependent child with no confidence or self esteem. Her first marriage had been an abusive relationship and she must have had tremendous courage to extricate herself and her children from it.

Now, in her second marriage and her children grown up, she had trained as a psychosexual counsellor, but had many issues of her own. These issues were about anger and resentment or so she thought, however, it turned out that the issue of the deep-seated fear and dread was to dominate our therapeutic sessions.

Although neither Jan nor I, initially had any preconceptions as to where therapy would eventually lead, it certainly led both of us to the conclusion that the memory of feelings, sights and sounds, can be brought from the experience of what appeared to be past lives. In her case as with many others, the consciousness of emotion in far memories was relived and re-experienced as if it was "real" and "now". These far memories were to invade her waking life as therapy progressed. They became more confusing, more distressing, more insistent and pressing as time passed.

I present the unedited, descriptive transcripts of feelings and thoughts, not as much to question what happens during a trance state for some people, but to speculate on HOW it might happen.

Are the memories and feelings elicited by stimulation of different parts of the brain through my way of working with Advanced Hypnosis or might they be part of a wider scheme of things for humanity as a whole?

Indeed the answer to the question is that it might possibly be both. In the end event, what happened over the year that Jan and I worked together, changed both our lives significantly.

SESSION 1, 31st October 2001

For many years I have been practising my own interpretation of Advanced Hypnosis, which does not need the lengthy induction that many Hypnotherapists utilise. In the beginning we agreed to work with what in Neuro-Linguistic Programming terms is called a "Visual Squash" in order to establish how Jan saw herself in the present and how she would like to be in the future. A Visual Squash is a conflict resolution exercise where different negotiation skills can be imaginatively used between the multiple parts of an individual's personality. This would be followed by Yoga breathing, relaxation and finding a "safe place". In further sessions we would work with Mnemodynamic therapy, a therapy based upon the theory that memory is dynamic and therefore still alive, even though buried. In this way past memories can be retrieved, confronted and dealt with in a therapeutic way. This is a "child within" disassociated regression therapy which is a fundamental part of the training course of The Centre Training International School of Hypnotherapy and Psychotherapy, and designed initially by Sue Washington. It is a way of dealing with the perceptions of the past, deep-seated memories of childhood in order to confront and change the meaning of issues such as fear, rejection, resentment and anger in a more mature and understanding way.

Mnemodynamic therapy is based upon the myth of Mnemosyne, the cross-cultural seeds of which can be found in an ancient Mayan story. The Mayans thought that individual memory comprised of basic patterns of resonance which together formed a huge memory circuit moving like a great figure of eight connecting past, present and future. It has been said that the path to self knowledge is the quest of myth (Szanto 1985). Szanto maintained that the path itself leads nowhere, and that we human beings end where we started – with ourselves, but along the journey we come to recognize ourselves. If memories are always present and available in the figure of eight it can be likened to a "moebius" strip, so that past and present may be available both together at one time. The moebius strip is a geometrical curiosity whereby if a narrow length of paper is given a half twist before the ends are joined we now have one surface and one edge (see figure 2 below).

Could memory be one such geometrical curiosity outside the normal laws of classical physics but amenable to quantum theory?

If this is so, then this might also explain Carl Gustav Jung's idea of a collective unconscious, higher sense perception, telepathy, precognition and clairvoyance. It may also lead to the recognition that individual consciousness is within a multidimensional, all-embracing, all-unifying memory "field", that links human beings with the universe itself.

Our therapeutic journey began with Yoga breathing, relaxation, and a check to establish Jan's predominant sense or lead mode, whether it be visual, auditory or kinaesthetic, and the establishment of a safe place. We all have what is called a more dominant way of understanding and interpreting the world, for some, seeing is the most used mode, for others it is hearing, for others it is touch and doing. If we listen to another person's conversation this lead mode can easily be detected. "Look at it this way", or "I hear what you are saying", or "Let me show you how". For teachers as well as therapists, or indeed anyone wishing to establish a rapport with another person, this knowledge of an individual's predominant way of perceiving the world can help people better effect a good result.

Jan's "safe place" was a garden in Paris, Versailles to be more specific, which she described in vivid detail at the end of the session. The reason I use a "safe place" is so that if any trauma becomes evident during a session, the client can be immediately, returned to their own place of safety, comfort and security.

Jan's safe place where she had initially chosen to be, turned out to be not the place of comfort and security that she thought it might be.

SESSION 2, 8th November 2001

On Jan's second visit I had a plan of what I thought might be a fruitful session, but it soon became evident that Jan had her own agenda. Well, perhaps not Jan's conscious agenda, but it was a session that neither of us expected. There were no preliminaries, the minute that she sat down in my client's chair her head went down, as if she could not wait another second to go back to her garden in Versailles. I did nothing other than write down whatever she told me was happening, no intervention except to occasionally let her know I was still with her. So she had no authoritative guidance as to what to concentrate on or what to leave out. She finished the session eventually herself. This is what happens in a spontaneous past-life regression, no induction, no suggestions – just a fast switch to another time and another self, a quantum jump, perhaps, a different consciousness, a different reality, but real nevertheless.

Transcript from notes:
I'm sitting outside ... it's September ... there's a fountain ... and music ... Handel's water music ... I'm back in time ... different clothes ... a skirt with a pannier ... shoes with little heels and square buckles ... it's about 1700. I have to practise ... I'm always being told "do it by yourself" ... I'm frivolous ... deliriously ... joyful ... happy in the water ... kicking it up my feet ... now I'm running along ... through enormously long corridors ...

There was a change of state here, noted by a change in facial expression, gross body movements and rate of breathing.

... feel physically sick in the pit of my stomach ... like scrabbling about in sea ... tossing up and down ... swirling ... looks like a figure of eight ... water ... blue ... grey ... white horses in the middle ... relentless ... not stopping ... nauseous ... pulls a plug ... (state change here again) *changed colour now ... sea green ... blue ... warmer ... Greece ... can see the bottom ... can see feet ... clear ... calm ... hear the pine trees ... water moving ... lapping ... pleasantly quiet ... like breathing ... light came back ... relief to be there ...*

The atmosphere in my therapy room was tense to say the least. Jan was quite shocked at what had occurred, and totally bewildered by the feelings and images. She said that when she looked down at her shoes they were different, but hers, they "belonged" to her. I asked if she had any idea what the images meant, but she could not explain where they had come from. There was little coherent description here that might make sense except the description of the clothes, her personality and the year in question. The fact that she was "frivolous" occurred again and again in our future sessions as well as the phrase "do it by yourself". It almost became a pattern, a lesson to be learned perhaps? Jan persistently admitted that she had always been a very dependent person to date. How clients can be so specific about dates is still a mystery to me, and I can understand the scepticism when someone mentions something like 550 BC!

CHAPTER 4

SOME SCIENTIFIC EXPLANATIONS

Neuroscientists today can explain all manner of experiences in terms of brain activity, from past memories through creative expression to near-death reports.

Even many years ago in the very first exploratory brain surgeries, patients told James Papez of forgotten memories recalled with the stimulation of a single brain cell. So is it possible that memory can be triggered by the stimulation of just one brain cell through a trance state?

More recently Ramachandran (1998) writes that in many cases of his brain research findings, that he is able to find a clear neurological basis for much seemingly mysteriously phenomena. He tells the case of a man aged sixty who started having epileptic seizures arising from his right temporal lobe. The strange thing was that, apart from the distress that those seizures brought, the man began thinking in verse, he became fascinated by poetry and began to produce his own. Another story Ramachandran tells, is that of a patient who stimulated his own temporal lobes for research purposes, and told how he experienced God for the first time. Under these circumstances of "altered consciousness" everything is imbued with cosmic significance, suddenly everything makes sense during these deeply moving spiritual experiences.

The question is, are these experiences real, genuine or pathological? Are they fact, fiction, or sheer fantasy? Or is it a natural state of the brain, natural in the biological sense, as suggested by Ramachandran in that extraordinary faculties might be "programmed" in the brain like the specialized ability to learn language. He wonders if it might be possible that we human beings have evolved a specialized neural circuitry for the brain to reactivate forgotten memories, initiate new creative processes or even to respond to the patterns of the wider universe. If this is so, not only does it make for a better understanding of ourselves and the world in which we live, it also gives us the power to interact with and influence those universal patterns as they influence us.

Papez initially reasoned that the limbic system of the brain must be intimately involved in human emotional behaviour. Then Maxwell Cade and Nona Coxhead (1979) suggested from their experimental evidence that it definitely seems to be the limbic system that appears to be responsible for some of the phenomena of altered states of consciousness. They found that the limbic system can elicit feelings of euphoria, divided consciousness and loss of awareness of body boundaries, as well as feelings of floating, flying and strange visual experiences like white or golden light. It is possible then, that as the limbic system evolved, the pre-programming may well have always been there. In the light of this reasoning, the consciousness of human beings may well have changed according to what is "out there", namely the ever changing planetary positions which surround our small part of the universe as part of the wider cosmos.

Although Ramachandran thinks that emotional changes cannot in themselves be responsible for religious experiences, he does consider that there may well be links between the sensory centres of vision and hearing with the amygdala. The amygdala is part of the limbic system, and it seems to be for the purpose of recognising the emotional significance of events in the external world. Hunches appear to start as a function of the nerve pathways via the amygdala's related circuitry to the viscera, where we get a somatic response to the choices that we face in daily life. These choices are linked to "risk" (a gut feeling) of what is right or wrong, dangerous or not. The amygdala is the site where the emotions of an experience are stored, the repository of everything that we feel about what we experience. It is a web of connections which stretch to the prefrontal lobes just behind the forehead. The amygdala has been identified as especially concerned with anxiety and fear. Research shows that damage to the amygdala causes loss of fear, and as the frontal lobes play a major part in personality, in some cases frontal lobe injury leads to dis-inhibition.

If this is the untapped potential of the brain, then perhaps visualisation, together with auditory and kinaesthetic cues, can stimulate the right temporal lobes in anyone to unleash any latent ability such as story telling without the seizures? Or perhaps the prefrontal lobes can be stimulated to elicit memories of anxiety and fear?

I was as surprised as Jan at the outcome of our therapeutic session, but I assumed that it could not have been my methodology, because I had made no suggestions, nor asked for any visualisations or imagery, or followed any plan whatsoever.

It could, of course, be what psychologists call crypto-amnesia, a memory of something Jan had seen or read at some time and then forgotten, or merely a metaphorical sorting of some present problem.

Jan herself asked, "could the images be some kind of metaphor or Jungian images?" She had no idea. The answer to the question of metaphor is yes, probably and will need to be explored to uncover her particular structure of mind, which undoubtedly underscores her individual reality.

Metaphor therapy has been part of my working life for many years because of my Ericksonian training. Metaphor therapy assumes that there is a neuro-psychological explanation of the brain mechanisms which mediate between the linguistic and cognitive-affective processes i.e. language and thinking. This way of working proposes, that individuals structure reality metaphorically because they have no other way of describing it. Words depend upon definitions, which depend in turn on other words and end in a closed circle.

Jungian images they may well have been from a psychological perspective. Carl Gustav Jung was a Swiss psychologist influenced initially by Freud but definitely with his own wide ranging theories about the mind and personality. Sigmund Freud believed that we human beings were always at the mercy of our instinctive, sexual but unconscious mind. He provided us with a concept of the instinctive, unconscious development of mind and the conflicts inherent in that development. This in hindsight would have been elicited by the "old" brain, which contains the basic desires for survival in all species. Then evolution and development provided the other layers of the limbic system and later that convoluted layer for thinking and reasoning of the cerebral cortex.

Jung at a later stage always referred to the "psyche" rather than the mind, which for him was a dynamic system in constant movement and at the same time self regulating. In Jung's view the unconscious mind is different from, but compensatory to, the conscious mind. He believed that the conscious mind grows out of an unconscious psyche. Furthermore in contrast to those psychologists who maintained that mind was a secondary manifestation of the brain – "a ghost in the machine" – for Jung the psyche was real with its own structure and subject to it own laws.

This would make sense if we take into account the theory that as far back as the beginning of time even in the primeval phase of the universe, there began a cascade of self-organising processes triggered by gravity that led eventually to us. People as living organisms are active matter and life itself is characterized by a whole host of unusual properties. There is a complexity all around us, within and without, which is organized and harmonised by a network of feedback mechanisms that control every level and between levels. Physicists theorise about a self creating universe and a cosmos that erupts spontaneously like a sub-nuclear particle which "pops up" from nowhere in certain high-energy processes, so why not self-creating brains and minds where "quantum miracles happen"?

Jung also gave us the concept of the "collective unconscious", that realm of the psyche common to all mankind. He theorised that the collective unconscious contained the whole spiritual heritage of human evolution which would be born anew in the brain structure of every individual. **A kind of reincarnation by any other name!**

He believed that the collective unconscious was a deeper part of the personal unconscious from which our personal unconscious emerges. Jung also gave us "archetypes and complexes". An archetype is an image or motif that recurs in myths, fairy tales, dreams, fantasies and delusions such as the hero, the witch, demons and dragons. Archetypes are the "a priori" inborn forms of intuition, of perception and apprehension. They are unconscious and therefore we only become aware of them through certain typical images, which recur in the psyche. A complex on the other hand is a group of associated ideas, which may be conscious, partly conscious or unconscious. If a complex is unconscious it can behave like an independent person and a person can be heard to say " I was not myself". If the images were Jungian images then these would need to be analysed by depth psychotherapy.

On the other hand if Jan was working metaphorically on present problems, perhaps she needed no guidance or an exploration of her particular structure of mind.

There is much evidence from some of the new therapies and indeed from meditation, that if allowed to do so, the brain responds automatically to the natural order of "polar opposites". So there is no need to apply any external pressure through suggestion to reach a prearranged solution, because change is inherent in nature and the "this" becomes "that" over time.

I had recently found great faith in Dr Ernest Rossi's deep psycho-biological model of a four-stage creative process in psychotherapy which enables a client to work through a problem without any suggestion from the therapist. After working with Dr Rossi over an intense weekend workshop, I found his method another secure way of avoiding any suggestion at all. In his work, Rossi maintains that this process is one of mind-body information transduction and healing. In the first stage that Rossi calls "Initiation", normally the therapist would ask if the client has the courage to stay with any overwhelming feeling or pain. Because Jan had moved from her place of safety into pain and stayed there for a while, I wondered if Jan had managed to do this without any initiation from me. He then suggests that there is a stage of "Incubation and Arousal" where the process is developed, merely by the therapist quietly asking the client if she can allow it to continue. His theory is that during this phase the client is going through an intense state of sympathetic arousal whereby the stress proteins and hormones produced at this time, are the same as those produced during the real life trauma whichever life it may be.

Based on his earlier theory of "state-dependent memory", this results in what has been traditionally called emotional catharsis. After this follows stage three, "Illumination and Insight", where Rossi maintains a transition takes place, involving private creative work towards a solution. Finally in stage four "Verification and Reintegration" where the client becomes aware of how the solution can be achieved. Although Rossi's therapies appear "as new", the four stage creative process follows Young's fourfold explanation in *The Geometry Of Meaning* (1976).

This session had not followed exactly the process because there had been no offered solution, still I wondered if it had all the elements of beginning therapy and I resolved to continue to work in this way.

Dr Ernest Rossi began his career as a Jungian therapist, after which he became a friend, follower and then collaborator with Milton Erickson. Rossi is very convincing in propounding the validity of his idea that there is a direct link between psychological factors such as thoughts and emotions, and

25

biological factors. In his book *The Psychobiology of Gene Expression* (2000) he maintains that it is novelty, physical exercise and those constantly new experiences which enrich our lives, and can activate what he calls "neurogenesis". By neurogenesis he means new growth in the brain, he further maintains that this can take place throughout life. This far reaching claim means that within minutes, these experiences can turn on gene expression in both brain and body to facilitate new growth, development and healing whatever a person's age.

Inevitably then, my ways of working have been firmly entrenched in Jung and Erickson, and more recently Rossi.

It is an intriguing fact that I find that for many years in teaching and lecturing I have been working in terms of polarization, continuums and learning cycles based on a fourfold process without realising. Young states that all meaning is a relationship, oppositions are represented by an angle of 180 degrees and all other relationships are contained within the whole of 360 degrees.

He maintains that there are four types of action, four relationships, four acts and four states. Faith and fact are opposite, so are purpose and form. Conscious action is opposite unconscious reaction and unconscious action is opposite to conscious reaction.

Jung also proposed his fourfold theory of the personality as sensation, intuition, thinking and feeling. He described these as the four basic functions or forms of psychic activity present in every individual, which provide the primary ways of "knowing".

Thinking and Feeling are based on data from the external world that he called the "rational conscious".

Sensation and Intuition are based on perceptions without evaluation or interpretation and this he called the "irrational unconscious".

So! On this basis, only four aspects are necessary and sufficient for the analysis of any situation, therapeutic or otherwise, if we know three then we should expect to find a fourth. From the theories of Piaget and Young and the beginning of learning, through Jung, to Rossi and his therapy, all work according to the natural laws of learning. Nothing can arise that is not already there.

CHAPTER 5

WHO IS THIS SELF?

SESSION 3, 16th November 2001

Jan reported that she had had a huge number of images for days after our last session and her dreams were full of death and destruction. Jan was scared of a side of her personality she described as vengeful. The fountain though, was a safe place, non-judgemental, and she was a "self" there who was devoted, always patient, a listener, respectful and able to enjoy life. I asked Jan how she felt about past lives, but she still did not believe in reincarnation. She preferred to think that what she was experiencing was metaphorical, pure imagery to deal with present problems.

Yet Jan talks about a "self" that is somehow split. This is not a new concept, Gestalt therapy is based upon the theory that the self is many-faceted, whilst other psychologists have argued the point – one or many. Jan describes herself with a personality of parts, one of which was vengeful, yet another part that was patient and respectful. So who is this "split self" spirit or soul who remembers in such detail and dreams still of death and destruction in the depths of the dark night?

The search for the self/soul has been the subject of debate like any other in psychology. What do we mean when we say "myself". The dictionary definition is "an individual known as the subject of his or her own consciousness". It is a relationship between the "I" and the world, the subject and the object. The "I" constantly notices the changes in the world from a relatively stable "I" position. Rudhyar as stated previously, says that if the subject or "I" cannot keep a sense of distinct and characteristic individuality or identity then the "I" can freeze and split and disintegrate. This theory tends to put the "Self" squarely within the brain but where the seat of consciousness is, has been the subject of debate for many years.

Descartes thought the seat of the soul was in the pineal gland at the base of the brain. But whether or not he was using the term soul as equating with self I am not sure. Many people use self/spirit/soul interchangeably but I prefer to make some distinctions. Self for me is consciousness of individuality, which makes it particularly "earth bound", to do with brains and complexes. Soul is eternal and therefore belongs to cosmic consciousness, and spirit is what links the two. Cynthia Bohannon in her book *The North Nodes and South Nodes – The Guideposts of the Spirit* (1979) says that the Soul is a separate entity from the Spirit but that Spirit is a product of the Soul.

The Soul is the giver of life to the Spirit, which in turn is the energy source of life. The Soul she maintains is the entity that reincarnates and the one that will return to its original destination in the fullness of time. Thomas Moore also sees soul and spirit as separate, but says that soul and spirit work best when they are connected, linking the energy of everyday life with that of contemplation. My interpretation of the original destination would be the source to which all life returns.

In scientific terms, the consciousness of self as a body can be located in the brain, as my hand, my foot, my shoulder, because stimulation of different places in the brain will elicit feeling in those parts. (Consult any Psychology text book.) The somato-sensory cortex is the strip of cerebral cortex lying immediately behind the central sulcus which represents the body surface. The size of the region of the cortex devoted to a particular region of the body is highly negatively correlated with the sensitivity of that region. Research in this area, shows that if one area is damaged, then another pathway is forged which can give false information to the cerebral cortex. Because body sensation is mapped on the somatic surface of the cerebral cortex, and the different correspondences are so close together, when one body part is missing, sensation from one part can be felt elsewhere simultaneously with the missing body part. The body however does not contain the self any more than the brain, body image is a construct of the mind like everything else. Many body parts can be removed, even parts of the brain, by accident or operation without the loss of the self and self-awareness. Recent research by Antonio Damasio a neuroscientist, puts the brain at the centre of the human mind but thinks that the brain and body form a total indivisible organism. For him as well as many other scientists, the brain constantly and continually registers the state of the body so that we have a body-minded brain. Damasio maintains that every change in the body, is initiated by the brain. This is usually without conscious deliberation, so the brain must be pre-programmed to do this. He states that the brain reconstructs the sense of self as a moment-to-moment process, so it is not a "thing" but a biological state. However, when scientists who work with "phantom limb" patients record that the brain thinks that a severed limb is still there, and even registers pain in that limb, so the moment-to-moment theory of reconstruction does not necessarily always apply. Perhaps an intact "self" remains, as a memory, even through loss? If we look at Kirlian photography we can see pictures of leaves that have been cut or torn, but the surrounding "aura" is still intact. Healers can see many bodies outside the physical body, which they describe as mental, emotional and etheric bodies. Many healers and mediums can detect illness and pain in the visible "aura" which surrounds the physical body. Much of modern science now concludes that the human organism is made up of at least two bodies. There is the physical body, which all of us can see, then there is an invisible body that is the electrical energy force which follows the contours of the physical body. This human energy system is the electromagnetic field of energy that creates the auric glow of light around a person, which healers can feel and many can "see".

Mystics and metaphysicians have always believed that all the information a person needs is contained within this energy system to link the physical self with the spiritual self. It is within this complex energy system that we maintain a sense of balance by constantly adjusting and re-adjusting to both internal and external influences. So the energy force is dynamic and constantly changing, pure energy, a multitude of wavelengths which have their own individual frequency.

Eventually one can conclude that the self is not located in any specific part of body or brain, but is distributed throughout both. It is, some think, a product of the whole rather than a sum of its parts. Michael Gazzaniga (1998) suggests that the self is the "interpreter", an interpretive synthesis of information in the left hemisphere of the brain, which allows us to know how contiguous events relate to one another. From the evidence to date, we have to conclude that the self is not an organ but a state of organisation in the brain that helps to keep our personal story together. It is the string that ties events together and allows actions and moods to appear as meaningful, purposeful and self-directed. Dr Brian Stableford (1977) describes it as "not in itself material but a pattern within matter ...". He further maintains that the fact that the self remains, when body parts disappear, cannot prove that the self is not in those parts. What it does do, is illustrate the extent to which the self can sustain itself against the erosion of the material structure on which it is superimposed.

Does this mean then that the self/spirit/soul is really a diffuse thing, which is not confined by the structure of bodily matter? Carol Ritberger (1998) describes the energy system as "energy plus information", and she suggests that every situation and event that we experience imprints as a cell memory throughout our entire being.

Furthermore if the immortality of the human soul in relation to God is a reality, then electricity and/or electromagnetic forces must be the basic powers of both human life and the universe.

In Shamanic terms a "soul" would be described as the energy part of our being and that which connects us to whom and what we are. Shamanic healers will talk about loss of this energy as "soul loss". From this perspective, all disease is believed to be due to the disconnection from spirit. In the process of reconnection, the shaman believes that when they heal the individual, they restore the community and the whole of creation to harmony. They believe that when we lose the connection to the soul through trauma, and when everyday events that are hurtful, life will lose its purpose and symptoms will arise eventually. In the Shamanic perception of reality, the soul parts that we lose can be retrieved because they have only gone off to wait in other worlds that exist in parallel to ours. Shamans work therefore in the realms of extra-psychic forces where our psychotherapeutic logic does not apply. This is based upon the underlying belief that all things are interdependent.

Edgar Cayce – hailed as the world's greatest psychic, through his many "readings" in his sleeping trance state – maintained that the soul is already there when a child takes its first breath. He had a vision of the soul as a creation of God, which contains a minute particle of Him at its core, and said that all mortal sorrow comes from the soul's own misuse of the free will given by the Maker.

Edgar Cayce was a devout and orthodox Protestant, a man who had read the bible once for each of his 46 years. During his early years he lost his voice and doctors could not find any logical cause. He eventually healed himself through self-hypnosis, and from then on his latent psychic talent rapidly developed. He discovered that in a self-induced trance he could diagnose illnesses, and correctly prescribe successful treatments for other people. He did not even have to meet the person for whom he was asked to diagnose a treatment. All this was in spite of his total ignorance of medicine when awake. One day, having awakened from a self-induced trance state, he was shocked to learn that whilst in trance he had stated that the law of reincarnation was a fact. His doubts conquered eventually, he came to believe that this concept neither challenged nor denied the teachings of Christ, but laid the foundations of a powerful spiritual philosophy. He told his listeners that karma was a universal law of cause and effect here on earth, which provides the soul with opportunities for physical, mental and spiritual growth. Cayce called souls "entities" and said that each entity's task on earth was to make use of successive rebirths to balance its positive and negative karmic patterns. He further maintained that Karma is memory, and as each person dies, "to be continued" should be written at the end of each life.

Edgar Cayce also claimed that during each life on earth, the reincarnated soul would bring the memory of what learning has to be completed in that life, even though it would be unconscious. Karma he says is the law of balance, not punishment, just debts to be repaid for wrong doing in past lives. Cayce also said that the body is an atomic structure obeying the laws of nature just like the universe. Each cell, he told his colleagues, in the atomic force is like a world of its own which can construct and reconstruct the body. He said that the structural forces are made to conform, and to rely upon or to be one with the spiritual activity.

It cannot be denied that our conception of self is strongly rooted in the memories of past experience. The concept of self is in part what we know we can and cannot do, and what significant others tell us we can or cannot do. Early messages of failure, stupidity and lack of confidence, or of achievement, confidence and cleverness appear to mould our personality. So it is through memory that we achieve a sense of identity and recognize ourselves as the same person from day to day. Our physical body changes considerably through the years as cells die and are replaced on a regular basis, and our personalities can change over time – but we believe that we are the same "self" throughout this continuing metamorphosis. When people lose their memory they do not know who they are. When Jan claims that she is the same self in different lives, the only evidence we have to prove a point is her memory of events. So! Is memory the key and can it re-run in another body at a later time? If it can, it leads us to question HOW.

CHAPTER 6

MNEMODYNAMIC THERAPY

Because Jan was so concerned about drifting back into the painful images, we decided to stay with Mnemodynamic therapy in order to deal with some of her buried feelings of anger and resentment in early childhood.

Karol Kuhn Truman (1991) believes that buried feelings in this life are very real energies, which are alive and constantly affecting the person. In spite of all the evidence for the unreliability of actual memories, he believes that memories are alive in the physical energy field (the body). He also believes that at some time those feelings will have to manifest in some form, because they remain a source of unresolved conflict. Truman believes that even feelings from long ago may still be registered at and within the cellular level of our being, and that they govern not only thought patterns (memory) but also underlying beliefs and attitudes. If this is true, then far memories might well be passed on genetically, although any biologist or geneticist, would probably argue vehemently against this proposition. Another explanation would be that from birth, past memories from another incarnation could still be resonating in the energy field because energy is never destroyed.

A Mnemodynamic Therapy Session begins by the therapist asking the client to visualize a television set in the corner of the room, complete with a video recorder. This is to make quite sure that the client is in total control of the situation, then he or she is told to imagine that they have the remote in their hand. The therapist explains that the video in the recorder is the client's past life to date, and when they are ready to switch on the video to do so. They are instructed that when any significant situation comes on to the screen or into mind to "freeze" the image and tell the therapist, by raising a hand.

I always ask the client, when any images appear, to refer to the child as "he" or "she" to keep the image disassociated. I only allow the client to associate with the image of the child as parent or sibling or significant other, to heal the child when feelings have been dealt with.

Transcript:
What do you see on the screen?

She's in a cot ... there's a noise overhead, flurrying round, she didn't understand ... hanging on to the edge of the cot ...

How old is the little girl in the cot?

She's about 18 months old ... she's waiting for someone to come.

How does she feel whilst she's waiting for someone to come?

Panicky, empty, sicky feeling in stomach, abandoned, vulnerable, powerless, out of control, nothing to hang on to.

I wonder if you can imagine going back to that child as if you are the mother now, and tell the child that it was all right to have those feelings because she was very young and did not understand.

Jan says she can do this. After she had reassured the child that it was all right to have all those feelings because she was only very small and did not understand what was happening I asked Jan if she could imagine in some way taking the feelings away from the child. "I don't know how you are going to do this ... but I know that you will find a way ... I want you to take all those feelings away from the child one by one," and I guided Jan through this procedure.

After this had been done I asked Jan how the child looked now?

Peaceful, smiling, just wants to be held ...

Is there anywhere you would like to take the child so that she would be happier still?

Down to the kitchen by the fire ...

When there was no more to be done I asked Jan to thank the child, and then, if she was happy to leave the child in the past where she belonged?

Yes.

I brought Jan back to her present age and asked if she would like to go to her safe place for some relaxation. The intention was purely relaxation, but the switch came almost instantaneously.

It's the same image ... same ... but different ... I know that I am privileged ... frivolous ... I'm 19 or 20 ... there's some yellow stuff in my hair ... I'm paddling in the fountain ... but there are people calling to me ... in and out of stone urns ... something troublesome ... can't last forever ... waiting for the storm to brew ...

Again I brought Jan back to the present, because this is not where she had wanted to be. In the discussion that followed we discussed the "sicky" feeling of the child and compared it with the feeling of fear and dread that had always been there. We decided that these were issues that needed to be dealt with because the images and feeling were recurring and repeating. It seems that buried feelings do not die in this life, so it might be possible that feelings, or memories of feelings never die from one life to the next however they are passed on. In between sessions, Jan had relaxation tapes to listen to, which she said helped her to relax. Obviously her "safe place" was only a safe place some of the time!

Many psychologists think the recall of images of death and destruction mimic the trauma of the birth process as reported by therapists who practice re-birthing. Jan obviously does not think that this is the case, she mentions a time well in the past, she describes clothes and shoes, places, and emotions. Other psychologists would liken what has happened to a dream, but there was nothing to reassure either of us that it had been a dream. The detail, the sensations, sounds, thoughts and emotions were too vivid and the sequence of the events too rational – unless we take the stance of Winson, cited in Rossi (2003) p.188, that every dream, or in this case an altered state, is a natural experiment which offers self-reflection, and self-creation towards healing. We could also take Winson's evolutionary theory of dreaming to explain Jan's nightmares throughout her life. He states that REM (rapid eye movement) sleep and dreaming is nature's way of confronting mind and consciousness. This in turn would be a way of promoting inner growth, change and personal spiritual evolution. Dreaming is for him a survival mechanism, which might explain the difference between rapid eye movement sleep and other types of sleep, although physiologically the two are indistinguishable. Somehow for me this does not fit the circumstances of Jan's experiences.

SESSION 4, 24th November 2001

Jan reports that lots of sifting and thinking is going on between sessions. She is getting, quite unbidden, lots of images that are scary, together with the sickly feeling of dread, that something is about to happen. The name Juanita or Juanetta keeps coming up, and I ask Jan if she is ready to look at some of the images. Jan decides, yes it needs to be done, because these images are beginning to interfere with Jan's day-to-day activities. Jan begins with breathing, but quickly looks down, and she is once again with her own agenda.

I'm sitting on the side of the fountain ... turning pages of my book ... looking up ... watching people ... they want me to play hide and seek ... I'm reading ... white lace round my neck ... folded edge ... jewellery round my neck ... skirt is different ... there's an apron with a fichu ... hair is not as fussy ... .white cap with lace ... not formal as it usually is ... fancy shoes ... dark blue

... odd ... copies of heavy shoes ... but light ... buckles in front ... glittery ... pleased with myself ... hair is brown ... down ... unusual ... usually covered with white powder muck ... I have a brother and a sister ... younger than me ... spend a lot of time together ... I'm responsible for them ... I chase them round corridors ... lots of laughter ... with them ... there are lots of lovely mirrors ... pictures ... beautiful surroundings ... parents are not around ... I call him father ... but he's not ... he's dark ... darker ... mother is fair ... siblings are fair ... I'm dark ... he works in diplomatic situations ... mother goes with him.

Jan always bring herself back when she is tired or the images are getting too much for her. Then follows counselling to establish some meaning of what has just transpired, and then some healing and relaxation. No meaning yet for Jan from what seem to be far memories, but the sessions are becoming more coherent and descriptive.

There may be underlying unconscious processes becoming conscious at work here, because according to Larry Weiskrantz "the essence of consciousness is the rendering of some sort of ongoing account". Jan certainly uses commentary during therapeutic sessions and appears to be more conscious of the facts, and more rational in her descriptions.

If she is at last, making her unconscious conscious, for what purpose?

CHAPTER 7

IMAGES OF PAST LIVES

"We do not become enlightened by imagining figures of light, but by making the darkness conscious."

C. G..Jung

Dr Roger J. Woolger, author of *Other Lives, Other Selves* (1987/90) maintains that whether or not a client believes in past lives or reincarnation, the reliving of what seems like a past life is cathartic, beneficial and therapeutic in the transformation of present problems. Dr Woolger is a Jungian Analyst and past-life therapist He was born in Britain but has lived and lectured for many years in America. His interests range from myth and meditation to dreamwork and Buddhism. He believes that in order to understand the primary, deep-seated patterns that make up our present life, we need to look at the patterns which seem to be seeded in past lives. He works mainly with Jung's method of "active imagination" in order to allow an individual to enter a level of consciousness that vividly recalls memories of other eras through an ego consciousness quite different from our present identity.

Woolger only maintains that the mounting evidence in psychotherapy suggests that some people can benefit psychologically from working from the standpoint of a previous life, and can show dramatic improvements in their mental health. He does not claim that his way of working validates in any way a belief in reincarnation, it may merely provide more evidence for the complexity of human consciousness and memory.

As an example, reincarnation therapy has been utilised for many years by a Russian in Moscow, Dr Vladimir Rikov. His patients were regressed to supposedly past lives so that in one way or another they themselves would find release from both mental and physical problems. These he maintained were methods to help open out what he calls wider memory.

Woolger himself did not initially believe in reincarnation, but a colleague asked him to participate in an experiment to access past lives through self-regression. Although sceptical he agreed and was amazed to find himself in France in the midst of the Albegensian crusade. These visions were of the kind that his training had told him were impossible. The fact that he had been asked to review a book called *The Cathars and Reincarnation* some time previously would have made him more suspicious of these past life visions except that they were nothing like the story that unfolded for him in regression. He found himself a very crude, peasant mercenary soldier in the midst of hideous massacres where whole French cities were hacked to pieces and burned in huge pyres in the name of the church. It took Woolger two further three-hour sessions to finish the story which at the time of writing his book he said he was still loathe to look at. He did say however, that the re-living of that past life did begin to explain disturbing fragments of dreams of torture and killing that had come unbidden over the years. The way in which his story ended, being burned at the stake, also explained a phobia, a fear of fire that he had had all his life. As he reflected more on this experience, more and more of his personal history seemed to fall into place. He asked – like Jan – why did such a painful past-life memory come, and not something more reassuring or glamorous. Critics who criticize revelations of past lives tend to make jokes about many people claiming to be Cleopatra or someone equally famous. This in truth is not the case in therapy, most clients experience rather humdrum lives most of the time with only a few exceptions. Even the name Cleopatra was commonplace amongst the populace of Egypt, so it is probably the client who wishes that she had been someone famous.

Woolger thinks that part of the answer comes from self-examination. His self-appointed mentor Jung, insisted that all would-be analysts should undergo analysis themselves so that they would not project their less acceptable qualities onto future clients. It may be that Jan is experiencing the past lives as some kind of preparation for her own work with clients as well as "searching for her own soul". Woolger thinks that most people, less versed in meditation or therapy, do not initially get such dramatic memories because the unconscious in its wisdom does not allow more than a person can deal with.

He also maintains that there is a powerful learning to be had from these extraordinary processes. There are some clients for whom their whole life has been changed by only one or two past-life sessions. He says that having the opportunity to confront one's true self, naked and unadorned, in which one can see the essence of their own "stuckness" is unparalleled in any other psychological discipline that he knows. He re-iterates once more however, that past-life therapy is neither proof nor disproof of reincarnation, and suggests that this is the province of parapsychology.

Although the last session with Jan had contained much description, as on previous sessions there have also been many accompanying emotions. If this was Jan confronting her true self, she was not coping very well with the revelations, nor was it yet making any sense.

As a psychologist I base much of my work upon the assumption that past events are always remembered with the emotions which accompanied them. Memories are always state-dependent, and traumatic memories even more so. This is why when psychotherapists are dealing with regression, many believe that re-living and re-experiencing is essential in addition to remembering in order to reach a resolution and clearing. Jan seemed at this point far from reaching any solution to the images that were surfacing now by day as well as by night, and I took my position as a psychotherapist very seriously.

Psychotherapist means "care of the soul" although some would doubt this from a variety of therapeutic practices.

Woolger says that not every client goes immediately to the kind of dramas that Jan is experiencing, but when they do there seem to be two ways in which past lives seem to be being acted out in this life.

The first is that the characters are recognisable as the clients "other selves" – other parts of their multiple personalities that have always been there in the background of consciousness. The second is that the characters' life story is somehow being acted out in this life because it is "unfinished business". Both could be true from the perspective of reincarnation. The second explanation could be true because it could mean that this is the soul's journey through different incarnations to fulfil the laws of Karma, or it is not meaningful at all. The first might be true because the soul brings with it memories from past lives which make up the unconscious "multiple personalities". A third explanation may be that past-life stories really are past lives, and are remembered in order to explain present life fears.

There are two stories from my own experience that I do have permission to tell. The first session many years ago was with a colleague who believed in past lives and used to access her experiences by going through a door at the end of a passage. This particular day as soon as she was through the door, she began to sniff and snuffle wiping her nose with the back of her hand and sleeve. I asked her where she was. In a very young child-like voice she replied, *in school but I'll be going home soon.*

What are you doing?

I'm writing on a slate ... I can read ... I don't like school ... I like to be at home.

Where is home?

On the farm ... I'm on the way there now ... but the cows are in the wrong field ...

And what happens when you get home?

I don't get home ...

So I wonder if you could go forward to the happiest time in that life?

Can't go forward ...

Can you go back then to the happiest time?

I'm riding on daddy's shoulders ... I'm at the fair ... there are roundabouts ...

How old are you?

Three ... and my brother and sister are here ...

Then the voice changed in a flash.

I'm being asked to tell you in language that you can understand how beautiful it is here ... the colours are like nothing I have ever seen before ... blues ... greens ... so beautiful ... and the power of crystals ... so important.

My client stopped here and she became quiet – resting.
What happened to the little girl?

She got killed in the field by a cow ...

After the therapeutic session was over, my colleague said that session explained for her the reason why she had always been scared of black and white cows, for no reason that she was consciously aware of, no others, just black and white. She also felt that the change of voice and place was a flash of life between lives, and that it was quite incredible.

Dr Brian Weiss, psychiatrist and author of *Many Lives, Many Masters* (1988) worked with a client named Catherine for many years. Catherine had 18 months of intensive psychotherapy twice a week with Dr Weiss and was still plagued by anxiety and panic attacks and had vivid recurring nightmares. She was a laboratory technician at a large teaching hospital in Miami, and had no history of mental illness. Dr Weiss was facing what he described as a brick wall with all the therapeutic sessions nothing much had changed. Then one day she told him about a strange happening when she and a friend had joined a guided tour whilst visiting an Egyptian exhibition at an art museum. Although Catherine was interested in Egyptian artefacts she had never studied that time in history, but somehow she reported that the pieces seemed familiar. When the guide was describing some of the artefacts she found herself correcting him, and to the guide's surprise she turned out to be right. Catherine was more than surprised – how did she know. This opened up a new line of therapy, which had been suggested many months before, that of hypnosis. Catherine at the time had been afraid, but now because of the experience at the museum, she reluctantly agreed. Dr Weiss gradually relaxed and then regressed Catherine back to childhood and eventually beyond. When he finally said "go back to the time from which your symptoms arise" he was totally unprepared for what came next. She described where she was, what she was doing, the year, her name, and what life was like at that time. The concept of past lives and reincarnation was alien to them both in the beginning but there were so many, so vivid, so convincing details. Catherine told of many past lives under hypnosis and in between gave messages in different voices when she was between lives. These messages were from people she described as the Masters, about the purpose of life and the lessons to be learned. Catherine had never read anything of Elizabeth Kubler-Ross or Dr Raymond Moody or even heard of books like the Tibetan Book of the Dead and yet she was relating similar near-death experiences that all of them had written about. Like me and countless other scientists, Dr Weiss was not a believer in reincarnation, and he admitted that his experiences with Catherine were not scientifically valid. However, at the end of their time together – as it was with Jan, and me and all the others – their minds were more open and are no longer sceptical of spiritual happenings. Masters are described as highly evolved souls who are not presently in body and they could only speak through her. Dr Weis wrote that, week by week Catherine shed more of her neurotic fears and anxieties and became more confident, more serene and more patient. Dr Weiss admitted that Catherine's experiences had changed him as much as it changed her and now although still very scientific he "straddles two worlds".

Another client who came for therapy for problems she was experiencing in this life also went into what she thought was a past life. Because she wishes to remain anonymous she is happy for me to tell the story as recorded.

She was a serving girl in Egypt around the time of the Romans and told horrendous stories of being abused by the soldiers. She eventually committed suicide because she could not bear that life any longer. She felt let down by her mother who knew what was going on and did nothing to stop the abuse. She saw this as not protecting or loving her enough, and she felt that she had carried that anger from the past through to this life. After the regression my client now saw that her mother had been powerless to stop the soldiers. It also gave her the opportunity to understand so many of the other struggles, which were physical in nature that she had experienced in this life, particularly with the opposite sex. She told me that whether a person believes in past lives or not, the experience was for her immensely powerful experience which released many feelings from the "here and now". She herself does firmly believe in past lives, and she is hoping that this release will have a positive effect on any other incarnations that she is sure will come. She describes her experience by saying *it is like a light coming on in the mind's eye and helps to make sense of unexplainable things that affect present lives.*

Yet another story that illustrates the difference between an induced past-life therapy, and a spontaneous one is told by another client of mine. She was a client who used to make up Bach flower remedies for people as part of her therapy. Although she had trained to do this, she told me that when she mixed the essences she always had this peculiar feeling that she should not be doing this ... it was not right! The feeling was in the solar plexus – a "gut feeling". She decided that she would like to explore the feeling in the hope that that she would find out what it meant. The following description is the client's own, recorded after the session:

Initially I found myself floating above a beautiful mountainous region and gently seemed to get lower and lower, until I was in a valley. There were hills all around me and it was wooded and remote. I felt that I knew the place well, although it was nowhere I had been to in this lifetime. I was on a steep, rocky hillside. When I looked to the left I could see a large city or town shimmering in the haze and sunlight. Rooftops glinted in the light and brilliant sunshine. I appeared to be connected to a youth, he was dressed in a short tunic, no shoes. He carried a pouch slung over his body to leave his hands free. The pouch was made of linen, and the tunic was whitish, with a belt around it in which he carried a knife. I felt that I was seeing me in a previous existence, but was having some trouble getting close into the feeling of being inside him.

(This was how the session began, with description in a detached way. At this point, as a therapist, I intervened, and asked my client to describe what she was seeing and doing, and this brought about the change to subjective awareness because she associated with the boy and she began you use the word "I".)

Transcript:
I'm climbing down some rocks ... I have to get down into the valley ... there's a stream running through it ... it's steep and wooded on the other side.

I asked what he was wearing and what was the reason for going down into the valley?

I'm looking for a herb.

What kind of herb?

It's called rue.

Can you tell me your name?

It's Antoine ... the herb is for the master.

Can you tell me his name?

It's something like Tochinelli ... I am an orphan ... and I was taken in by this master Tochinelli when I was quite young ... he is using me as his apprentice ... in return for food ... he is a very powerful man ... I feel a lot of darkness

41

*around him ... he makes up poisons and potions for other people ... I saw
pieces of gold in his hands ... he lives on the outskirts of the city.*

Do you know what the city is called?
(In her writing after the event she realised the master was an alchemist and
when I asked what the city was called, she was struggling to translate the
name.)

*I can't remember the name ... but it's called the city of the sun ... there's a
doe near the stream ... the animals come to me ... they trust me ... I have to
pick the herbs during the full moon ... this is very important ... am in the hills
for about three days ... because it takes me so long to journey ... I am more at
ease with nature rather than in the city ... I 'm frightened of the master's
power ... and what he can do ... I feel very upset as he uses these herbs often
to harm people and not to help them ... this bothers me a great deal ... but I
can't do anything about it.*

I asked what happened when he grew up, but was told that in that life the
youth did not grow up.

When we had completed the therapeutic session to deal with the feeling, my
colleague still did not know what the herb was, that she had mentioned. She
went away to find out and rang me later to say that it was a herb used in very
small doses to regulate the menstrual flow, but that large doses were toxic
bringing about abortions. In discussion we thought perhaps the place was
somewhere on the French–Italian border as she pronounced "his name" in
perfect French and the name of the master sounded like Italian. We also
thought that it was possible that the distress (state-dependent memory) caused
by using the herbs in a harmful way could have carried over into her present
situation. My client was a believer in past lives, which might have provided
the right conditions for a self-fulfilling prophesy to furnish an answer to her
problem.

Whilst living in Spain, it came to my notice that Lorca in Spain was
referred to as "The City of the Sun" . On checking some facts on the internet
about the area, which has a lot of history, I found that there were stories about
alchemists who came to the area, mainly Arabs but some Italians. Apparently
in the area around Lorca the rulers changed many times over the centuries, but
most courts had their alchemists. In the Guevara palace built by the Guevara
family in 1689–1705, they actually have a chemist's shop in the palace which
has been opened to the public, like a museum. The original jars of medicines
and ointments made by the local chemist are on display. On checking with my
client she said that the photographs of the mountains around were similar to
the terrain that she saw ... she also said *the picture in my mind is still very
clear which is strange when I can't remember what I was doing two weeks*

ago. On the other side of things, I do feel that it could all be explained metaphorically, and more to do with what was going on at that time.

Having spoken to this client some three years later, she tells me that she has just read a book which she knows that she has read before when she was much younger. She tells me now that the book is almost word for word the story she recounted as a past life regression.

So, is this a past life or the brain metaphorically sorting a problem from the present life, or perhaps cryptomania? My client is obviously still sceptical.

My own experience was a workshop with Roger Woolger who asks his audience to think of a country where they are very happy to be, or if they are very brave, one where they would never go. I was torn between Italy and Greece as places that I like but eventually chose Greece because the very first time I went there, I felt "at home" and could strangely find my way around places where I had never been before. After a short reading, a Tibetan bell and an instruction to "look down at your feet" I was really there in a body that was mine but not mine ... a strange feeling. My feet were large, in sandals, thick legs of a male. The experiences I had I would not have believed, had I not experienced them first hand, the sensations, the feelings of happiness, sadness, relief and memories of a family. I knew exactly where I was in Athens. I was a very ordinary Roman soldier who did not want to be there, and hated what I had to do there. When it was suggested that we went to the happiest time of that life I was back in Italy sharing a meal with a very large and close family. (something I miss in this life and wish I had) Then we were asked to go to the moment of death and beyond. I was killed on the battlefield with a spear, after which I was looking down at my own body, but at peace.

There was a high degree of suggestion inherent in this session of guided regression, but the experiences were very real. I do have a horror of wars as a waste of young lives and I am thankful that I have lived in a generation where my two sons were not required to fight. However the significance of the past life to any problems in this life was not apparent. A colleague and I used to meditate and put ourselves into trance in an attempt to access past lives, but I only experienced flashes of pictures and moments of being in another body. These could easily have been the process of a vivid imagination – but, Roger Woolger asks "where does the imagination come from?"

So many people are scared of hypnosis and regression therapy in particular, but for me they are natural states of altered perception. The fault lies very much with the media – films, television and books – who exaggerate the state of hypnosis to that of magic and mysticism for financial gain and publicity. They speak of controlling minds and wicked take-over by external forces. I will admit that hypnosis can be dangerous in the wrong hands, but is an enlightening and healing process with a caring therapist

CHAPTER 8

PERSPECTIVES ON CONSCIOUSNESS

"The source of all creation is pure consciousness ...
... seeking expression from the unmanifest to the manifest ...."
Deepak Chopra (1994, 1996)

The process of mind, brain and consciousness, have been the subject of both Science and Philosophy long before Psychology and Neuroscience took over the search. Evolutionary theorists assumed that consciousness evolved during natural selection in the animal kingdom. Others assumed that consciousness is everywhere and always has been.

These are the two main competing philosophies, but there are many theories.

Hinduism believes that all matter is a manifestation of spiritual reality. Consciousness for them is immanent within form! Consciousness as universal, suggests the existence of different levels of consciousness or mind. Each level has its own qualities and universal function, with the higher levels permitting abstract mental functions and the lower, denser levels carry the instinctive drives and memory functions. Personal minds, brains and consciousness, are part of the universal mind or consciousness.

Buddhism offers a similar theory that the universe itself is nothing but consciousness that is divided into nine levels and individuals are part of the whole. Hinduism and Buddhism assume that future lives are a fact, the round of births and deaths is real. One major function of these religions is to get off the wheel of life and constant learning and return to the source through enlightenment.

Deepak Chopra – a best selling author who blends physics and philosophy, with the practical and the spiritual – states that Eastern wisdom and Western science both explain consciousness in terms of spiritual "laws". He maintains that in our essential state, human beings are pure consciousness, and pure consciousness is pure potentiality. It is for him, the field of all possibility and creativity and our spiritual essence, and when we discover our essential nature then we shall know who we really are.

There are, for me as a hypno-psychotherapist, many forms of "consciousness": waking consciousness, this being the state of awareness, which presumably is a function of the complexity of the living brain and its integrative power; then there is the trance consciousness and dream consciousness of personal experience, and meditative consciousness, which can lead to transpersonal consciousness. It also appears that individuals can move between these "states" easily and effortlessly. The next question that arises is WHAT is the difference between these states, are some more REAL than others? I think not.

From a scientific point of view the problem of consciousness can be approached in two main ways, by studying conscious *events* and conscious *experiences*.

Considered within an evolutionary framework we must ask, HOW did consciousness evolve? Popper and Eccles (cited in Blakemore & Greenfield (1989)) suggest that consciousness, of necessity, does not begin with man, but that man is the end result for the present of a long evolution of primitive neural systems. They further believe, along with other scientists that the rudiments of consciousness must have been present in the very early existence of a neural network

WHAT survival value does it give to organisms? Certainly those species that are consciously aware have a better chance of survival. As far as evolutionary theory is concerned, it would seem that consciousness is a useful product of a selective process that confers an obvious biological advantage on those species that have it.

The main advantage given to these species, would be that of reflection, consideration and comparison of events separated by space and time. This endows the species with the power of choice and therefore of free will rather than stereotypical behaviour.

HOW is consciousness linked to the physiology of the brain?

Some scientists claim that nothing we know about physiology or behaviour to-date would help us to hypothesize about conscious experience. As an example they suggest that we can look at the two types of sleep which can be recorded in sleep clinics. These two types of sleep alternate with each other and appear in most, if not all mammalian species. It appears that the two types of sleep differ on physiological indicators but we cannot say that one kind of sleep is to do with consciousness and the other not. Only by asking people when they are awake have we found that one is accompanied by dreaming – rapid eye movement (REM) sleep – and the other is not. So to-date we have no answer to the question unless we accept once more the theory of J. Winson that REM sleep is more than just for rest and recovery. He thinks that it could provide a memory storage function at night in order to leave the brain free to deal with the problems of the day.

Any theory of consciousness will always reflect the prevailing scientific and cultural philosophy and much of current western philosophy still equates consciousness with brain function, indeed we know that damage to different parts of the brain results in injury and often "unconsciousness". However, brain function alone – based upon computer models of the brain and mind – is not sufficient to explain consciousness. We still have not discovered what consciousness is and how it arises or if there perhaps some threshold of development at which consciousness comes into being. Some scientists believe that consciousness arises at the point of sensation, but then we need a scientific account of how conscious experiences at the point of sensation arise out of brain events, to alter behaviour.

According to the theories of Danah Zohar, there is a physics of consciousness that can link the individual with physical reality. She believes that consciousness, which she defines as the general capacity for awareness and purposive response, must come initially from some primitive physical mechanism like the old brain. Then the mind/body/brain consciousness, which eventually arises, is just a more complex form of the early neural network. She takes this further by suggesting that human beings are essentially made of the same basic "stuff" as the universe and held together by the same dynamics as everything else. This is very much like the explanation given by Edgar Cayce. Zohar believes that we are quantum beings in a quantum universe. She goes on to say that our consciousness appears to have the character of unbroken wholeness that is rare amongst the dynamic processes of nature. However she suggests that if we demand a scientific explanation, the physics and physiology of "condensed phases" is worth investigating, for an explanation of how consciousness could arise in brains. The Bose–Einstein condensate is the one that she puts forward. She maintains that "the crucial distinguishing feature of a Bose–Einstein condensate is that the many parts which go to make up any ordered system like the neurons in a brain, not only behave as a whole, they "BECOME whole". This wholeness arises because the single identities merge or overlap in such a way that they lose their individuality entirely in the process. She suggests that in her model of consciousness, there are two interacting systems. As well as the Bose–Einstein condensate associated with consciousness, there is the computer-like system of individual neurones. The Bose–Einstein condensate would provide what she calls "the ground state" of awareness, then what goes into that awareness would be supplied by our unique genetic code, memories and learning in the brain. This theory closely equates with probability theory, which states that when chaos reaches a certain stage based on number, it changes spontaneously from chaos to order.

Early psychologists equated consciousness with mind and defined Psychology as "the study of the mind and consciousness" and used the introspective method to study it. The problem with introspection of course is that we are trying to connect the workings of our own brain to a subjective experience.

One of the earliest theories of consciousness was the psychoanalytic theory of Sigmund Freud. Freud maintained that consciousness was only the tip of the iceberg of the mind, and that human beings were always at the mercy of unconscious animal instincts, urges and feelings. He believed that the unconscious mind was full of memories, impulses and desires that were not acceptable to the conscious mind. Libido for Freud was aggressive and together with sexual energy was necessary for the survival and reproduction of the species. He gave us a metaphorical name for the demanding child the ID full of selfish needs and wants in order to survive. He gave us the SUPEREGO to represent the conditioning of the child by parents and the significant people in their lives with the "shoulds" and "oughts" that make up the rules of society. He also named the negotiator, the go-between these two, the EGO. His theory and practice brought much criticism over the years but it has been shown that his theory, although not all there is, may well have a factual basis in the brain.

Many years later than Freud, the psychologist Paul Maclean (cited in Susan Greenfield) proposed his scientific theory, which was akin to Freud's instinct theory. Maclean's research of the brain stems of different species, supported the finding that the primitive brain stem was the source of driving power and energy that underscored everything that every species did, and that these were the building blocks of human behaviour. He maintained that brain stems were similar in all species, and thus were responsible for the basic urges of sex and aggression, creativity and destruction.

Freud drew attention to the distinction between what we want to do (the ID) and our final censored actions (the SUPEREGO) and then Maclean pointed us in the direction of specific brain regions responsible for our emotions and our thinking. In human beings the limbic system describes the many brain clusters round the brain stem, which appear to cushion and channel the basic urges, then, the limbic system is in turn suppressed by the cortex, the thinking, decision-making part of the human brain. It is too simplistic however, to compartmentalize brain regions in this way, because neuro-scientific research and clinical observation studies to-date show that there is no one-to-one matching between particular parts of the brain.

We must never forget however, that biological evolution and social change all reflect that bodies and brains, and necessarily minds, all have taken place on a revolving planet in a solar system so there are many and varied complex variables to disseminate. Brain research is still in its very early stages, therefore neuroscientists cannot even begin to formulate any unified theories. However the research today, with the aid of computer imaging of the brain, has upheld many of the "hunches", beliefs and theories of psychologists through the years.

Consciousness can be defined from the perspective of quantum psychology, as an ability to know contrasts or distinctions, and self consciousness is consciousness of oneself, the distinction between the subject (observer), and the knowing object (self). Consciousness is where the distinctions of what is called the explicate order takes place. It does not take place at the implicate level because that is where consciousness "just is" and the unity cannot be seen.

If the function of consciousness in the Central Nervous System, is to see contrasts and differences, then this means that what we call the individual self can never know the underlying unity whilst here on earth. This is because the underlying unity does not have a consciousness of a "you", as separate from, something to be known. So Kant, in his way and of his time, was right

Consciousness is the observer and the observed, the knower and the known. Without the ability to know distinctions there would just be the implicate order of ISness. If consciousness then, arises spontaneously when conditions are right for it to do so "Consciousness itself creates reality" Herbert (1985). For me, that means that the consciousness of what constitutes reality, is individual and unique.

Astrological theory also has a dual expression of consciousness, or what is called its Esoteric and Exoteric points of view. Exoteric Astrology is content with the effect, the practice and the concrete outer expression, and begins its study from the side of diversity and separateness shown in a birth chart. Esoteric Astrology deals with the abstract cause, the philosophy, and the inner, more subtle, point of view. This view once again, looks upon the whole expression of life as proceeding from one central, primeval source. It seeks to understand the subject or person as one flowing forth from the ONE into the many.

Esoteric Astrology teaches that human beings like the universe in general, are essentially consciousness or spirit surrounded by matter. Matter for them is always without and is manifest, whilst consciousness is always within and is hidden. Human beings can be regarded as consisting of consciousness or self/soul which is always within, and a body which is made of the matter of whatever world they are functioning in. The inner self is brought into touch with the physical environment by means of a physical body, to affect it and be affected by it. This theory is, like many others, based upon the belief that there is only ONE substance in the universe – primordial or root matter whatever that might be, and according to this theory, force, life, soul or consciousness are only different names for varying aspects of the same reality.

Consciousness in astrological terms must of necessity be active and outgoing, or it could never affect the world by accomplishing change, or manifest itself outwardly. Then, where there is manifestation there is always duality – force and matter, body and soul. However, consciousness must also be capable of becoming relatively passive and receptive because if it were not, the outer world could not affect it in terms of the five senses. In its passive receptive state it is inward turned and therefore unconscious. If consciousness can be both active and passive, it cannot be wholly so. There must be some neutral mode in which the two are held in relation to each other, without identifying exclusively with either.

So consciousness is within and without, and in terms of human personal consciousness the three aspects are action, desire or feeling, cognition and thought, and their unity is the SELF. All this is explained beautifully in Astrology but it brings together the theories of psychology, in particular the theories of Carl Gustav Jung, hypno-therapy, Eastern religion, philosophy and quantum physics.

From the quantum psychological perspective, every act of consciousness is a focus of effort that actualizes (collapses) a quantum wave function into an experiential part of REALITY. **It is individual consciousness then that creates individual reality, uncertainty and infinite possibility.**

THE MAYAN PREDICTION

According to a Mayan prediction made many thousands of years ago, consciousness, whatever it is, and however it occurs, by the year 2000 at the beginning of the third millenium, will be about to "blow its amnesia circuits". The Mayan mathematicians, astrologers and astronomers who had an excellent reputation for having a tremendously high degree of knowledge about the universe, calculated that by now – in this our time – the evolutionary pattern of our world would be out of balance and in need of memory correction. With most of the world at war with one another at this time, it could well have been seen by those making astrological predictions as the " abomination of desolation" as stated in the bible. The Mayans predicted that because by this time, the beginning of the twenty-first century, there would have arisen some very sick societies, there will be a "jolt of Galactic energy" which will bring about the creation of a new universal energy of consciousness. It could be conjectured that the destruction of millions of people for power and the greed for resources must stop. The Mayan scholar Jose Argelles said that because everything proceeds in cycles, this state of being would eventually "unlock even deeper levels of memory". Individuals will begin to remember who they are, where they came from, how they got here, and why. The culmination of this correction, they predicted, would occur in the year 2012, because if this correction does not take place, there will be no next phase of evolution for the raising of consciousness. It is only peace, love and consideration for one's neighbour, together with a sense of individual responsibility that will change the social and physical world in which we live. The disaster, whatever that might be could be sufficient, but the necessary condition would be the Christ principle in the hearts of men and women.

The recorded history of mankind to-date leaves us nothing of which to be proud, and we apparently have to find another way. Even after all the teachers who have come to earth in order that we know the way to reach our ultimate salvation, the human condition of only seeing differences through our five senses still apparently holds us back. If we see only differences which lead to prejudice then there is no hope. We need to see beyond difference and categorization. If this is not possible through education, then perhaps it is necessary that we fight our way back through meditation for the mind to reach the heart and so promote physical helpfulness and kindness towards others. Even the early Egyptians evidently thought the brain was of no consequence in the after-life because they drained it out of the body during embalming, but maintained and preserved the heart which they thought was a necessary requirement for eternal life. The Mayan prediction appears to be based upon the Hermetic Astrological theory of the slow changes of consciousness over thousands of years which now cannot keep pace with the circumstances of global survival, because the rate of external change is too fast.

CHAPTER 9

HERMETIC ASTROLOGY

"… the experience of higher states of consciousness is necessary for the survival of the human species."

John C. Lilly (cited in Cade & Coxhead)

Most individuals today are not aware of the great cycles of time which embrace generations, centuries, and millennia. These periods are said to vary in quality and each is like a wave, having its own peaks and troughs.

According to the Law of Hermes Trismegistus, man is a fundamental part of the universe with all man's problems reverberating from the infinitely small to the infinitely large. In Hermetic Astrological theory, life is like a river that flows and at any stage can be followed back in its history. If we focus on the spiritual tradition of Hermetic Astrology, the science of the stars becomes a source of divine revelation. In the Hermetic Astrological view, the location of the vernal point in the Zodiac indicates the particular spiritual influence of a particular age, and is a primary marker in the evolution of human individuals and different levels of consciousness. The Zodiacal ages are specified by the location of this vernal point, and are determined by the precession of the equinoxes. The average length of an astrological age is 2160 years which corresponds to the length of time required for the vernal point to regress through 30 degrees (one sign) of the sidereal zodiac. This is referred to as an astrological day, and even I can believe that the earth was symbolically created in 6 days on these terms. The complete cycle of the precession of the equinoxes lasts for 25,920 years and is an astrological year. Along with the astrological ages, running parallel on earth, there is a sequence of cultural ages coinciding with the rise and fall of successive cultures. However, although the astrological ages and the cultural ages run parallel, they are not identical with them. There is always a time lag between the beginning of an astrological age and the corresponding start of a cultural age.[1]

This time lag points to a gradual transformation that begins subconsciously and then breaks into consciousness only after this time has elapsed. The passage of the vernal point through the signs of the Zodiac is connected with a transformation of human consciousness, whereby new states of consciousness arise associated with each sign, just like a personal horoscope. The time lag is 1199 years and is measured by what is called the Venus pentagram. As this

---

[1] The dates of the astrological ages can be found on page 56 of *Hermetic Astrology* Volume 1 by Robert Powell, published by Hermetika, Kinsau, West Germany, 1987

cosmic history unfolds, it manifests as the rise and fall of such cultures as the Egyptian civilisation, the Greek, the Roman and so on. We only have to look to archaeology to find the essence of an age in art, literature, science and religion.

There has been much discussion about the "Age of Aquarius" for many years now, but in fact this does not even start according to Hermetic Astrology until the year 2375 and will last until the year 4535. There is also the mistaken idea that "The New Age" movement can be identified with The Age of Aquarius, because we are still in "The Piscean Age". However, The New Age movement has had a genuine spiritual task in our time, to awaken the impulse towards true "community" in a way commensurate with human freedom and cultivated in the spirit of Christ. The urge for the Aquarian age will be the balance of masculine and feminine energy and balance between one's own internal energy forces so that the transformation of consciousness can be expanded. From the standpoint of Hermetic Astrology this is the new Christ impulse that has begun in this century but will lead eventually into the Aquarian age. The new impulse is called for to save mankind from dangers threatening the course of evolution or so we are told. The new Christ impulse is here present now, but only for those who choose to take it up. Unlike the first coming of Christ, which was a physical manifestation, the second coming is of a spiritual nature in the hearts and minds of individuals. The search for self-knowledge is at the same time a search for a higher self. If people want a deeper understanding of what the "New Age" means, they can find it in the nature of the relationship between Christ and the Buddha impulse. The fundamental concept here is that of Christ as the central guiding being of mankind – the spiritual SUN at the centre of a circle of teachers. Teachers are known in the East as *Bodhisattvas,* highly evolved human beings, far advanced on the path of enlightenment. These human beings, because of their advanced spiritual status, have been entrusted in the past with special tasks here on Earth. Before he became Buddha, Gautama had been a Bodhisattva, and in his incarnation as Gautama had the special task of founding a new religion, Buddhism.

It is the Egyptian system which appears to be the basis of Hermetic astrology because it is relevant to both reality and higher consciousness. It was feared that with the introduction of the Copernican heliocentric system, the whole of mankind had lost touch with the spiritual reality of the cosmos. The Egyptian system related to the "heart centre" and for them, consciousness had to descend from head to heart in bodily terms, in fact it is a bridge to higher spiritual reality.

It is through the Egyptian system that the individual is placed at the centre of experiential reality. It further engenders a new conscious awareness of the individual and the cosmos.

This is the "as above, so below" of Carl Gustav Jung, and mirrors the beliefs of many of mankind for millennia. Apparently according to some great minds, when Tycho Brae and Johannes Kepler introduced the modern astronomical world conception of the Copernican system because it explained physical appearances so well, this became the basis for what we call "materialism". To those of a spiritual nature it becomes the "desolation of the soul", and it is time now to return. If we assess the historical development of individualism, there are two possibilities ahead of mankind. Either the new impulse of community heralded by the New Age, must come to balance the impulse to individualisation, or individualism will develop further. Balance, is the law of the universe, as well as human beings, this is Nature. If individualization continues and the time comes of "every man for himself", then the prophesies of old will surely come to pass.

The Egyptian system was a reflection of the Egyptian mysteries, and the worship of Horus in the Sun was said to be a preparation for the coming of Christ. Egypt is said to be an image of heaven, and the nineteenth century Astronomer Royal of Scotland, Charles Piazzi Smyth, believed that the Great Pyramid was linked to the prophesies related to the coming of Christ. The Pharaohs and the priests of Egypt were then seen as guardians of accurate records of the wisdom of old times. Robert Bauval after many years of research thought that the Sphinx pre-dated the pyramids by a very long time.

If we see a computer generated picture of the sky over Giza in the year 10,500 BC we find, just before dawn at the Spring equinox, we would see the Sphinx pointing in the direction of the constellation of Leo on the Eastern horizon. Then at the moment of sunrise, in direct alignment with the Sphinx, the three stars of Orion's belt culminated at the meridian in the same pattern of the three great Pyramids on the ground. According to this theory, the great Pyramids appear to be an architectural representation of this unique celestial conjunction. This was called "the first time" of Osiris, and I see as no coincidence that "the last time" will be at the Autumn equinox in the year AD 2450 in the constellation of Aquarius – the time of the Humanitarian Age of Community when the skies will have completely reversed.

The monuments then of the Giza necropolis could be said to be the site and marker of the genesis of our civilization. There is a theory, backed by the clairvoyant readings of Edgar Cayce, that either within the Great Pyramid or beneath the Sphinx there is concealed, "The Hall of Records" which contains the entire knowledge and wisdom of lost civilizations such as Atlantis. This triggered much excavation in Egypt, some of it funded by the Edgar Cayce Foundation, because he maintained that those records would be found somewhere towards the end of the twentieth century. None of this has yet come to pass, perhaps the time is not right or we yet have not found the key! One idea is that the knowledge may be in some form of crystal deposited in a central chamber underneath an island called the Island of the Egg, which echoes the legend of Atlantis. This central chamber is flanked by twelve more chambers in a circle, each representing one division of the duat, which will have to be negotiated in various rituals before the central chamber can be accessed. Jan talks about completing the circle?

One speculation about the Great Pyramid is that it was not solely built to be a mere burial chamber. A certain Tom Danby thought that the Great Pyramid may have been built to correspond to the size of the earth itself with its purpose connected to the vibrations of the earth and a receiver of energy. The earth has a resonance to its own frequency, which is the result of electromagnetic activity between itself as it spins on its axis and the upper atmosphere. If this is so, then the ritual needed to activate the secret chamber may be to do with sound. Tape recordings show that the pyramid was designed to reflect a whisper at one side around the walls like a sounding box, but why, we do not know. All researches lead us to believe that Ancient Egypt preserved the knowledge of earlier civilizations but no-one yet has found the secret chamber

So the search for self-knowledge has been with mankind for thousands of years particularly in Eastern thought. One reason has been to expand self-awareness into self control, the other to experience higher states of consciousness. The search for higher states of consciousness is believed to be the gradual transformation of one's being where one's level of awareness is of both internal and external reality. The gradual transformation is through meditation, which takes the form of diligent and continuous effort.

This search for self-knowledge in the Western world has been sought more recently through the external observation of others, experiment and reasoning. After all the reasoning however, many return to the Eastern mode.

The Eastern mystic seeks to empty his mind through meditation so that knowledge can arrive directly through intuition and insight, and meditation practices can be divided into two kinds: concentrative meditation is where one gives one's whole and undivided attention to a single or repeated perception or idea; mindfulness, the other practice, gives one's whole attention to the changing content of one's awareness without choosing, so that the person becomes aware of everything of which one is aware. It is a deliberate switching off of external stimuli and "looking within" to find **"enlightenment"**.

The Egyptians said "the light is within thee";

The Buddhist says "look within, thou art Buddha";

Christ said "I am the way, the truth and the life"

The aim of yoga meditation is to remember, and recall more of one's past life so as to clear the past and relate it to the aims of the future.

Dr Bucke (cited in Cade & Coxhead) said in his book *Cosmic Consciousness* that the supreme experience for individuals has many characteristics in common. There is inevitably an awareness of intense light, being immersed in light, light beyond all description, feelings of intense joy, assurance, and salvation. He states that in an intuitive flash the person has an awareness of the meaning and drift of the whole universe and a merging with creation. Together with these experiences the fear of death just vanishes and a sense of immortality prevails.

Jan has experienced all of these in the course of our therapeutic sessions and now hopes that she has become more enlightened. These have not occurred through slow meditation practices but through "spontaneous" regression to what appeared to be past lives.

Perhaps the current interest in therapeutic practices and past life regression is speeding up the process of enlightenment because we are running out of time!

Carol Ritberger PhD maintains that a new energy force is emerging supporting this desire towards self exploration and spiritual awakening. She thinks that this new energy force as we slowly approach the Aquarian Age is influencing our thinking, feeling and behaviour.

All manner of phenomena such as individual near-death experiences, electric shocks and accidents all seem to be contributing to these changes, as well as larger disasters.

CHAPTER 10

BACK TO THERAPY

SESSION 5, 7th December 2001

Once more Jan spends very little time in talking about her previous week. It is almost as if my therapy room now has become the trigger for her to immediately "go to work". A trigger, is something which elicits a certain state, and hypno-psychotherapists and neuro-linguistic practitioners make good use of them for a desired effect.

Transcript :
Spoiled ... not spoiled ... splitness ... resentment ... count and breathe ... looks at books ... what stops me ...

(she pauses and I intervene, "remember a time when you were motivated")

*I'm sitting in a garden ... reading ... surrounded by an arbour of roses ... smell ... sun ... Pink ... English ... brother and sister ... Cheapside in London ... well dressed ... Walking ... people talking ... Garden ... Shade ... warmth ... people playing tennis ... someone calls ... for me to be with them ... young ... man ... Waistcoat ... ruffles ... takes my hand ... come on you ... you have things to do ... learning French ... back in panelling ... do the work ... doing what you have to do ... instead of what you want to do ... can't avoid duty ... .same issues now ... I have responsibility ... duty and onerous issues ... as a young woman didn't want to be ... it's about accepting more readily ... myself ... Feeding ... clothing children ... don't need it ... who is it that I'm hanging on for? ... me or them ... a lot of religion hanging around ... place I felt safest in was a church ... there was a dream ... in car ... driving ... walking escaping ... young man forcing a pillow on the back of my neck ... pushing ... voicing of many dreams since childhood ...(****Jan threw a small pillow from behind her neck here****) I DIED on the guillotine ... point of death ... Light ... coming in from one side ... praying ... place I don't know ... I'm praying coming through a valley ... of tears ... part of the journey ... ongoing journey ... dark into light ... can't separate them ... part of the same experience ... warmth ... Light ... millions of candles ... what's happening ... other people around me ... like shapes ... in a church ... gowns ... hoods ... long dark ... between life ... clothes are different ... still the same person ... before ... to help me ... feel a presence ... heavy brocade ... in a dress I couldn't stand ... praying ... kneeling ... have a book ... contemplations ... comfortable people*

... Reverence ... I think ... masses of candles ... comforting people ... kind of light when the evening draws in ... I've been neglectful ... picking up a piece ... before I died ... I was quite scatty ... didn't give a fig about others ... two halves ... both me but different ... told so many times ... to read prayer book ... make confessions ... eaten what I shouldn't eat ... wore different clothes ... rebellious...

Jan was silent now, obviously tired so I brought her back to this life and to her present age. This once more seemed like a past life ending in death, and then a time between lives, then back again. Jan always liked to leave in order to digest what had happened in the session without too much discussion. As long as she was feeling all right to drive, calm and back to "normal", I would let her go, otherwise she could sit, have a drink and gather her thoughts. She is still confused and worried about our sessions, wondering HOW and WHY she was reliving these times. Jan is a "down to earth" counsellor who has never come face to face with startling revelations like these.

It seemed here that Jan was mixing two lives, flipping from one to the other, London to Versailles. If however, the natural world is full of complexities, with no regular shapes and where nothing happens in sequence but all together, this is in keeping with the natural order of things, of incoming information where time has no meaning.

We have memories now of death, prayer, religious experience, Jan wonders again if she is going out of her mind perhaps? Jan talks about "before I died, I died on the guillotine" and then talks about religious experiences. She also talks like someone of a high privileged class, and it is a fact that decapitation by an edged weapon was only granted to the nobility as execution. Common criminals were hanged, drowned or burned.

And what of the self or soul, is Jan one and the same self, soul or essence as Juanita or Julietta?` and can this self or soul travel through the ages? And if so how?

Jan writes near the end of therapy :

It's four o'clock in the morning and I wake to know that my life today is free because of the experiences I have had the privilege and pain to work with. I could not have held those on my own and I would never have known the sure and certain hope of life after death without your ability to keep me safe when I felt I was at such risk. I constantly see myself sitting in the chair, bathed in the golden light with that dreadful scar around my neck, whole, complete, and redeemed. That life ended before it had run its course, unfair, unjust. I know my name now Gianetta, I can identify now that for me what happens is not about fine details, and only a few facts feel certain. It's about a compelling intensity that was magnificent but deeply disturbing at the start as it was so far away from when I first entered therapy.

I have once again to dismiss the idea that Jan's experiences during therapy are anything to do with my way of working with Advanced Hypnosis, because no suggestions or hypno-therapeutic metaphors were used that might elicit specific images. I rarely speak during the session, just write, and Jan speaks slowly enough for me to be very sure that I am accurate in my notes.

The sessions almost take the form of what could be described as "channelling" in parts. Channelling or "mediumship" is not new, it has occurred in many cultures in a variety of forms such as automatic writing or art work and sometimes where the voice of another mind can take over. Channelling can occur in light trance where the channel is aware of what she is saying, like Jan, or in deep trance where speech, language patterns and tone of voice are completely different like Edgar Cayce. Neither institutional psychology, nor research into hypnosis, seem to be capable of producing a scientific explanation of channelling so it tends to be "sidelined" or ignored as a hoax by manipulative people.

The idea that external influences can come through an individual begins to question things like reincarnation, the soul, the possible spiritual roots of the psyche and even the very meaning of life. This communication process puts the individual "at risk" and Jan was wise to be scared of channelling when I was not around to keep her safe.

The difference between Classical Hypnosis and Advanced Hypnosis is to be found in the therapist's way of working. Classical Hypnosis does make suggestions through commands and is very direct, it also utilizes the therapist's "reality". It is Classical Hypnosis, which has come under scrutiny in the past few years for planting "false memories" particularly with regard to sexual abuse cases. The procedure itself can be off-putting at times. I used to do some examining for The Royal College of Nursing for basic hypnosis and one day witnessed a session that went far from well. The therapist suggested that his client went into a garden for relaxation as an induction, which appeared to make the client uncomfortable. Questioning the nurse after the session I asked, "what made you suggest a garden," "because I like gardens," he replied. On asking his client where she would rather have been to relax she replied "in a cave". This is the difference between working with the client's own reality and that of the therapist. Curiously though, it has always been through the therapeutic way of working with Classical Hypnosis in training sessions that elicited many of my unsolicited past-life experiences.

In contrast to Classical Hypnosis, Advanced Hypnosis follows rather than leads, it is a combination of Ericksonian Hypnosis and Neuro-Linguistic Programming which is more subtle, metaphorical and vague, leaving the client to make their own interpretation of what is said by the therapist.

My own unique blend of Advanced Hypnosis as practised, involved Mnemo-Dynamic Therapy, Neuro-Linguistic Programming, Milton Erickson's naturalistic trance states and Metaphor Therapy, together with the practise of Ernest Rossi's concentrated focussing and attention on a movement or sensation.

Neuro-Linguistic Programming is effectively a process of attempting, by a variety of means, to inhibit certain mental connections between neurons and forge new connections through learning. The process is achieved through the use of visualization and language often in the form of metaphor. Hypnosis is often defined as an "altered state of awareness", for me a hypnotic trance is nothing more than concentration and focussed attention, a normal function of the central nervous system. Anyone can be said to be in a trance state when focussing on a piece of work, painting, listening to music.

Milton H. Erickson, the foremost practitioner of hypnotherapy, defined it as a state of readiness to utilize learning and abilities, as part of a normal process during which perceptions and conceptions can be changed. Milton Erickson formulated his own "Milton Model" which is widely used by advanced practitioners. The Milton Model is a particular way of using language to induce and maintain a trance state in order to contact what he saw as the hidden resources of one's personality. He believed that this method of trance induction followed the way that the mind works naturally. For him it was not a passive state, as some critics might suggest, nor is the client under another person's influence. The Milton Model uses language to pace and follow only the individual's own reality; the client would be asked to go to a place of safety, thus leaving the choice of place to them. Whilst the client is using their right brain in creative visualization and the voice of the therapist aims to distract the conscious mind, so that the unconscious mind and resources are accessed. **Advanced therapists follow – they do not lead!**

Whether a long relaxation is used or not, focussed attention allows the individual to block out external information in the way of noise or other distractions. The therapist taps the normal functioning of the central nervous system, and the voice, using pitch and tone, provides the blocking of other channels to the cerebral cortex. Sound itself elicits a response to listen and become attuned. Concentration, through story telling or guided imagery as contextual clues, will then sometimes elicit a physiological response to suggestion. Brain wave activity as recorded on computer has shown that eye closure alone can elicit an alpha rhythm. This together with language patterns, pitch, tone and pace of voice ensures that the brain waves of most people go into alpha rhythms in order to bring about the parasympathetic response of relaxation. It has been claimed that alpha brain waves are nothing but a kind of scanning or waiting pattern produced by the visual centres of the brain. Alpha per se is not by itself associated with inwardly directed attention or relaxed awareness. It requires the additional simultaneous presence of beta and theta to achieve this. When this state has been achieved then repetition of words and phrases should inhibit the activity of the Ascending Reticular Tract, which only responds to novel stimuli.

The Reticular Activating System (RAS) is enormously important because of its role in arousal and awareness, as it determines arousal level and states of awareness. So it has a special significance in hypnosis when attention needs to be narrowed, and meditation where a subject modifies his/her own attention in special ways. Research would have us believe that the cortex, together with the reticular system, operate in a feedback mode, in order to maintain an optimum level of stimulation. The function, then, of the RAS appears to provide the gateway to all forms of meditation, creative reverie and higher states of consciousness. Parallel processing of information using both hemispheres of the brain simultaneously then allows the client to move easily between states of awareness, thus accessing conscious, preconscious, subconscious and unconscious thoughts, sensations, and memories of emotions and feelings. (See figs. 3 & 4)

The brain, however, is a complex organ concerned with systems where both evolution and history have played an important role, and a theory is only as good as more repeated evidence becomes available. The most important fact is that therapies based upon the established theories do not always provide the answer for everyone, because people are individuals and require idiosyncratic treatment.

Figure 3

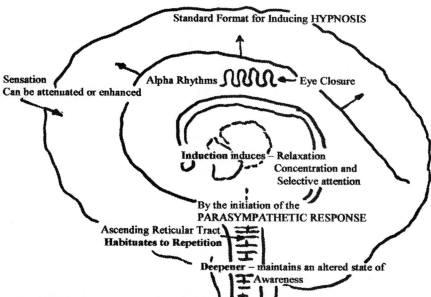

Standard Format for Inducing HYPNOSIS

Sensation
Can be attenuated or enhanced

Alpha Rhythms

Eye Closure

Induction induces – Relaxation
Concentration and
Selective attention

By the initiation of the
PARASYMPATHETIC RESPONSE

Ascending Reticular Tract
Habituates to Repetition

Deepener – maintains an altered state of
Awareness

This **MIND/BODY** Transduction System maintains a closed circuit of communication.

Psychotherapy – utilises visual,
auditory and
kinaesthetic
Imagery as contextual cues

Through a variety of methods:-

        Guided imagery
        Ericksonian stories/metaphor
        Mnemodynamic therapy
        Regression therapy
        Gestalt work
        Cognitive therapy
        Dream analysis
        Neuro-linguistic programming
        Hypnopictography

All methods explore feelings, thoughts and state dependent memories so that perceptions can be evaluated and thoughts and feelings changed.

Termination – restores to normal
Consciousness.

The word "trance" is often misused, in Hypnosis is can be defined as a
"NEUROLOGICAL PHENOMENON WHICH RESULTS FORM EITHER THE STIMULATION OF THE SYMPATHETIC OR PARASYMPATHETIC SYSTEM"

Figure 4

THE BRAIN, CENTRAL NERVOUS SYSTEM & HYPNO-PSYCHOTHERAPY

HYPNO-PSYCHOTHERAPY – utilises the **NORMAL PROCESSES** of the **CENTRAL NERVOUS SYSTEM (CNS)** by working with:- **MEMORY**
LEARNING
& BEHAVIOUR
on **COGNITIVE, EMOTIONAL** and **SENSORY PERCEPTUAL LEVELS.**

HYPNO-PSYCHOTHERAPY – employs methods which serve to evoke:-

SELECTIVE ATTENTION
Selective attention allows an individual to block out extraneous information. The therapist's voice provides the blocking of all other channels to the **CEREBRAL CORTEX.**

CONCENTRATION
Elicits a physiological response (IMR) using guided imagery as contextual cues, visual, auditory and kinaesthetic, Ericksonian techniques of story telling and metaphor.

RELAXATION
Eye closure ensures that brain waves go into **ALPHA RHYTHMS**
The use of voice, pitch, pace, tone, volume and language patterns, elicit the **PARASYMPATHETIC RESPONSE of the CNS.**

REPETITION
Repetition of words and phrases inhibits the activity of the **ASCENDING RETICULAR TRACT** which only responds to **NOVEL STIMULI.**

PARALLEL PROCESSING OF INFORMATION USING BOTH HEMISPHERES OF THE BRAIN SIMULTANEOUSLY
Allows the client to move easily between states of awareness, accessing the conscious, pre-conscious, sub-conscious and unconscious thoughts, emotions and feelings.

THE INDUCTION and its maintenance by **DEEPENING TECHNIQUES** of the trance state, serves to promote that special **PHYSICAL** and **PSYCHOLOGICAL** state called **HYPNOSIS** in which clients can become aware of their own **INNER COMPLEXITIES.**
During Hypnosis:- **PLANFULNESS CEASES**
REALITY DISTORTION IS ACCEPTED
SUGGESTIBILITY IS INCREASED

PSYCHOTHERAPY
Allows exploration of feelings, emotions, and thoughts as **STATE DEPENDENT MEMORIES,** through:- gestalt therapy, cognitive therapy, regression therapy, Mnemodynamic therapy, dream analysis, hypno-pictography, neuro-linguistic

JAN'S BIRTH CHART (see figure 5 below)

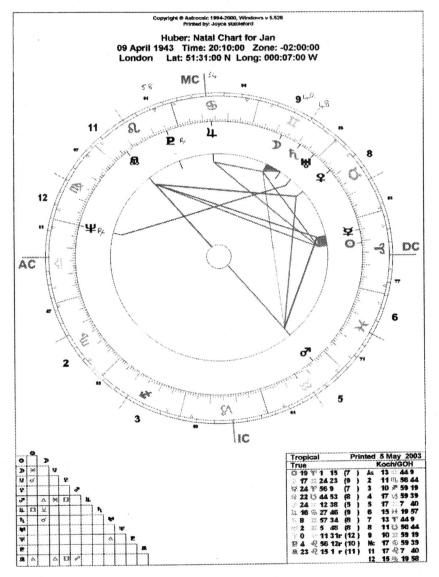

FIG 5

Because a birth chart for me is the best pictorial explanation of personality and character, I asked Jan for permission to erect a chart. My training as an Astrological Counsellor also provides the opportunity to make a clinical diagnosis as to what is happening at any particular time.

Spiritual Astrology, based upon the theory of reincarnation and karma, states that each soul chooses the parents and time and place of birth in order to fulfil the work of cleansing the soul ready to be returned eventually to his or her rightful place with God.

> "… [the] birthright given each soul [is] that it may know itself and by choice become one with the Creator …"
>
> Edgar Cayce Readings (No. 2571-10)

Jan's birth chart is based on the Huber method. The circle in the middle of a Huber chart represents the soul and therefore no line crosses the centre circle.

My introduction to astrology was through the Astrological Society in Manchester many years ago with teachers who studied the Kabbala. Not many people know that there are teachings about reincarnation in Jewish mysticism. The Hebrew word "gilgal" for reincarnation is from the root meaning circle. Then I studied "traditional astrology" with a London School, followed by two years' study with The Huber School. Although it is not recommended by the Huber School, the following interpretation is a mixture of all schools, and in particular, I have taken much of the spiritual interpretations from a book by Myrna Loftus. I have chosen this way of interpretation because it is based on the premise of reincarnation and the belief that each individual chooses the parents who will fulfil his or her life lessons. This seemed relevant to the present analysis.

My own bias in the interpretation of a birth chart is psychological, normally utilizing it as a tool for the person's understanding of their strengths and weaknesses so that they can work towards being who they are meant to be. I do not believe that our lives are totally governed or controlled by what is out there, only our reaction to the prevailing influences is what matters. Therefore a birth chart should not be used as a cop-out for not changing behaviour. However in this particular instance more emphasis has been given to the spiritual approach because the client wished to know where she might be going in this life.

The birth chart is a map like any other map, but the map is not the territory. The position of the Sun, Moon and planets at birth, symbolically represent character and basic ways of responding to the external world. The planetary positions of each day, month and year tell us what is going on externally, which in turn may influence moods, they do not cause things to happen. Those external events and conditions of our lives are what we attract to ourselves through our inner conflicts, needs and attitudes, whether they are conscious or unconscious.

According to Gregory Szanto, it is a psychological rule that when any inner situation is not brought to consciousness, it tends to happen outside as what we call fate. This is because in reality there is no difference between inner and outer. The chart is helpful in getting a better perspective of one's individuality and potential, which will help a person to work towards a more positive expression of self. The chart cannot be blamed if you take what you see as a wrong turning on the map, or decide not to take the best route to reach your destination. Because my client is now interested in past lives I have also provided a Karmic interpretation, but reserve judgement on any speculation. I have little experience of harmonic charts so my interpretation is fairly basic.

Natal Chart for Jan born 9th April 1943

The general shape of the chart as interpreted by my training with the Huber School is that of a good organizer, yet one whose real learning would begin somewhat later in life than school or college, possibly around the age of 36 years. Until that time there may have been much doubt and ambivalence about self-worth and what she was capable of doing. There is talent showing receptiveness, empathy and understanding in a practical way when working with people, and she can deal with a variety of tasks. Her learning will have carried on until her late 50s and early 60s by which time Jan will really know where she is meant to be and what she needs to be doing.

With Sun in Aries and its conjunction to Mercury, sextile Moon and square to Jupiter gives Jan many positive attributes such as courage, enthusiasm, independence, inspiration and originality when she can allow all these planets to work together in harmony. She can be friendly and sociable, tolerant and considerate, particularly in her dealings with other people at work because she will have a strong sense of responsibility towards her profession and personal achievement. On the negative side she will have had to deal with impatience, impulsiveness and even headstrong aggressiveness at times when courage turns to recklessness and initiative to impetuosity. Conflict lies between the urge for action and the desire for inner peace. She has always been in the process of becoming and building a new personality. She will enjoy work, which requires enterprise and initiative and where she can be a pioneer, but this like everything else may not have arrived until later in her life. She can assume authority and responsibility with a group because there is a joyousness in her manner and she can be an inspiration to others with ideas and projects that flow in an unending stream once she has found her energy source. She will have a gift of waking up her environment and she will not sit quietly waiting for things to happen, so she would make an excellent teacher. She will be attracted to some kind of community work as a career. Witty and entertaining she will enjoy relationships with people who are articulate and clever.

She will like business and marriage partners, to be quick witted and keen, so that she can communicate through ideas and thoughts. She may however, be argumentative at times, quick tempered, because she will not like delays or opposition. She has a versatile and receptive mind with a constant desire for knowledge. Her difficulty may have come through relationships where she has had to work for others because she needs to be the leader. Yet with Libra on her Ascendant and Venus in Taurus, she will hate hassle, inharmonious surroundings and arguments. She will be affectionate and demonstrative, when she loves someone, and she will be loyal to her friends. She will seek physical comfort in her domestic life and she herself can provide a harmonious home given the right partner. Unfortunately Jan may have to contend with an ambivalent attitude to her partners where perhaps there is a love/hate feeling and much anger when there are differences of opinion. (Venus square Mars and Sun/Mercury trine North Node) Yet she needs companionship, she is not a loner and hostility might be released in verbal or even physical fights which in turn will lead to internal distress and anger towards marriage partners in particular. She can be indecisive and unable to make up her mind between two courses of action, and tolerance can revert to lack of discrimination. Unfortunately she can see both sides of a question with equal clarity and it will be a hard job to reach a logical decision between two alternatives. It will be best if she follows her intuition. Her desire for association with others will have brought her into contact with many people but it will be particularly important for her to find the right partner who will give her what she needs. Because of her sensitive nature she may well have found herself in situations of disharmony and strife from which there seemed no escape and she must constantly adjust in her attempt to create peace and harmony.

As a child she will have needed firm but loving discipline, but instead she may have listened to limiting messages from her mother and continued to give them to herself long after they were valid. She may have been shy, doubting her abilities and suffering from depression because of her need for constant reassurance and distress about what other people thought about her. This may have inhibited her in revealing her true personality to her children as well as intimate partners.

My critics will no doubt say that I have gleaned all these conclusions from the close contact with Jan. However the same interpretation would have been given had I never met my client, and I would invite anyone else to interpret her chart even by another method to reach similar conclusions.

On a Karmic level, according to the "channelled" readings, her challenge in this life is to develop self-confidence, but not to become egotistical. There will be restlessness until she seeks to know herself through some life philosophy. However, in the same way as in past lives, she has begun the work of balancing her emotions and desires. This is so that these energies can now, be used in creative and constructive ideas. On her spiritual path now she will have the opportunity to eliminate her negative traits using all the positive traits of her Aries Sun. The only aspect, a trine between Uranus and Neptune is seen as a Karmic one suggesting that in other lifetimes Jan has learned to be independent and tolerant of other people's viewpoints so she has a great capacity to withstand crises. This strength comes from the deeper levels of her mind, which she has tapped in other times. This knowledge has given her a profound interest in the mysteries of life and the ability to solve seemingly unsolvable problems.

Her travels and communication with foreigners will help her to know herself and find a philosophy of life (Moon conjunct Saturn, Uranus in the 9th house) and if she wishes she can develop her clairvoyant abilities. She must not use her talents for self, or ego gratification. She needs to elevate her goals and seek ideas that will be for the good of group endeavours, and her service must be of a universal nature. Her way of spiritual integration in this life is to learn the "oneness of humanity". However the choice is hers.

An interpretation of the Nodes in Jan's chart also gives a Karmic reading in the terms of Spiritual Astrology.

Jan's North Node is in Leo in the 11th House, placing her South Node in the 5th House of Aquarius. The Nodes tell us where we need to do some work in this life. The North Node is the path of spiritual growth and the South Node leads to personal growth, if and when the North Node house affairs are developed. In past lives it is said that we have neglected the affairs of the North Node house so must now turn our attention to them. The North Node is the point where the Moon on its way to the earth's Northern hemisphere intercepts the orbit of the earth as it revolves round the Sun. The South Node is always opposite the north Node so the reverse is evident as the South Node on its way to the Southern hemisphere intercepts the earth's orbit around the Sun.

The signs are important because they indicate the qualities that must be cultivated. North Node qualities are the positive ones that must be cultivated in order to reverse the negative qualities previously developed. So Jan needs to develop the positive qualities of Leo in being more generous, giving, and creative. She should endeavour to develop her teaching skills and lead in the service of others. In the 11th house she needs to elevate her goals and seek ideas for the common good of the group. Her creative talents in the past have been used for self and ego glorification and she has been rebellious and detached. The way to spiritual integration is to learn the "oneness of humanity" which cannot be learned unless she establishes contact with those outside the home.

The Birth Chart is based upon a Huber chart using the Koch house system for an overview of age progression. The interpretation, has been taken in part from *A Spiritual Approach to Astrology*, by Myrna Lofthus. It is an old book first published in 1935. In her preface to the book she says that her study of Astrology was inspired after reading the works of Edgar Cayce. Cayce who consistently emphasized that souls select their time to re-incarnate in order that the planetary vibrations of that time would help them to complete karmic debts and promote soul growth.

In her book *A Search for Truth* (1996/97) Ruth Montgomery writes about a healer, known only to her as Mr A a psychic diagnostician who brought about some quite miraculous cures. Mr A would listen to a person's heart without a stethoscope maintaining that there were 36 different frequencies altogether, but each individual would operate on three frequencies which could make numerous combinations of magnetic field control. He said that as soon as he met a person he knew instinctively on which three rays that person operated on. When asked to explain what "rays" were, Mr A explained that solar rays give us life, but the position of the planets at the time of birth make us the individuals that we are. Like any psychologist, he said that certain aspects of character and potential personality are established at conception. However as a psychic healer and obviously an astrologer, he maintained that individuality was established at birth. This he held to be governed by their fixed sign which establishes a person's magnetic field. This means that a person thereafter, according to this view, is influenced by all the planets in the universe of which we are a part.

Pluto and Neptune in Jan's chart are both what an astrologer would ascertain as retrograde, and this fact is taken by some astrologers to be the most important indication of what the individual is here to learn in this life. Pluto is un-aspected, and the only aspect of Neptune is with Uranus. Poorly aspected retrograde planets are thought to indicate that the individual will have to work hard to challenge the negative character traits that have been brought forward into this life. The retrograde planets should be the focal point of the chart for development in this lifetime. In particular Pluto which, like the North Node is in the 11th house.

A further précis of an interpretation of Jan's chart in a Karmic mode taken from *The Astrology of Karma* pp. 220, 227, 228.

This states that Jan will probably be drawn towards groups who have altruistic goals, empathic ideals and spiritual goals, and she will find friendships here, but she may be overly concerned with the suffering produced by inequality which leads to a compulsive need to serve. In the opposite way she may well be disappointed in the social conditions that prevail and friends who fail to live up to the high expectations that she has of them. Because Pluto has no aspects, the general karma is concerned with meeting the outcome of past life patterns, which will manifest as a strong will and urge to bring about positive change in her world. This she will achieve through planning and working with divine direction rather than personal gain. She will have an aptitude for diagnosis and the ability to restore well-being in her clients by identifying the negative patterns which underlie distress. She will gain particular advantage from working in the field of healing and becoming a transmitter of divine energy which will help to bring about change that is beneficial to the whole. Working in these fields will bring about change in her by removing her fear of change, and the deep sense of insecurity which has dogged her life resulting in the negative defensive behaviour patterns of the past.

A further reading of retrograde Neptune and Pluto follows, from photocopies given to me some 30 years ago when my interest in Astrology was just beginning. I do not know which book they came from and my apologies go to the author.

Neptune on an esoteric level represents extreme spirituality. It is the ruler of Pisces which in turn represents the final major initiation that each individual, in this case Jan, has to take to free herself from the wheel of Karma and reincarnation. A retrograde Neptune shows that in the past she did not develop spiritually or neglected or misused or had a passive attitude towards it. In a positive mode it represents sensitivity and understanding, in its negative mode, fraud and deceit. Retrograde Neptune in Jan's 12th house is one of the most important locations shows that the cycle of necessity is completed. Neptune is the spiritual pace-maker and states that this individual has actually incarnated 12 times within a given period of 2500 years and has completed the cycle through each one of the Zodiacal signs. This does not mean that the cycle has been completed in a positive way, retrograde here says that still something needs to be done to put things right. The 12th house brings in Cosmic Consciousness and Cosmic Mind. The individual with this position has previously attained a state of At-one-ment and then let it go, it was placed before her but she failed to accept it. So service to mankind is now implied in the placement opposite the 6th house. Now the lesson to be learned is to completely integrate the inner and the outer and develop it to such a point where spirituality is reflected in her and used to influence others in this way.

Retrograde Pluto represents individual Karma and in its house position brings the lesson to be learned. Pluto is the Guardian of the soul associated with occult powers which revolve around enlightenment and compassion and will enable Jan to attain spiritual knowledge. In the 10th house it shows misused authority in the past, or she was anti-authority, too strong a need for recognition, and how everything had to enhance her own prestige. Everything was done for self, even at the expense of others. The lesson to be learned is wise use of power and authority. Career must be for the good of mankind, success must be attained, but is dependent upon proper attitudes, proper values and motives, never at the expense of others.

As a scientist I can find no evidence on which to base these interpretations, but Jan maintains that as far as she is concerned they are accurate. All of the Karmic interpretations have been drawn from diverse sources but are uncannily similar.

After much serious research into Astrology for a dissertation many years ago, I came to the conclusion that it gave a more accurate description of personality than a conventional personality profile. It appears that the position of the Sun, Moon and planets relative to the time and place of birth do play a part in revealing the aspects of character and personality of an individual. Like the rest of our surmising about human nature, character and personality, the psyche and the cosmos, we can still only theorize as to how and why.

CHAPTER 12

NATAL ASTROLOGY & REALITY

"That which we name Destiny, ... is the force by which all events are brought to pass; for all events are bound together in a never broken chain by the bonds of Necessity ..."

Asclepius 111 pp. 361–365 (cited in *Hermetic Astrology*)

In the past there have been two major languages used to classify reality. One is the language of quantity, mathematics, and this can be used to describe anything that can be counted or measured. The other, the experiential or existential, has only ever been expressed symbolically and qualitatively. Both have their limitations and a combination of both may present a clearer picture.

The limitations of the statistical approach to describe reality, is that it deals only with generalizations, groups and averages, it can tell us nothing about the individual psyche. Statistical analysis utilized in consideration of "Season of Birth" by research at Manchester University can point to certain personalities showing a preference for particular careers, or the frequency of psychiatric hospital admissions that correlate with geomagnetic field activity. However, Dr Robert Becker reported in the scientific weekly *Nature* that cycles of biological and mental-emotional activity were closely linked to geometric force-field patterns. The probability of this occurring by chance was less than 1 in 10,000 after studying 28,000 admissions. He believed that human behaviour was influenced through the direct current of the brain and central nervous system by the terrestrial magnetic field, and the solar and planetary conditions (cited in Arroyo, 1975).

The limitations of the qualitative approach are the number of perspectives from which it can be approached. There are so many theories of personality and so many questions about the Self, that the whole area has been a minefield of contradictions. One answer to these questions, has been to use the astrological approach, which is a symbolic language that explains human experience and the uniqueness of the individual within the larger whole.

According to David Hamblin, astrologers work from a different vision of reality which goes beyond Einstein, beyond Jung and even beyond Darwin, because they are all concerned with a different dimension of reality which has for the moment no one acceptable model. In spite of the fact that some astrologers work on the network or linkages model, and some work on the cycle model or the wave model, whatever the model, most base their work upon the assumption that the energy field of man is related to the larger energy field of his cosmic environment. Research today in physics, medicine and psychology are also concerned with the "energy" aspect of life.

This is not new, Indian Yogic systems have referred for millennia to "kundalini" which is libido comprising physical, psychic and potential spiritual energy. They have also worked on the "chakras" the centres of whirling energy in human beings.

Acupuncturists in China, for thousands of years, have claimed that factors in the environment, including the Sun and Moon, have profound effects on the fields of energy. They believe that the vital energy in the body links man with the cosmos. Therefore, any change in the universe changes the resonance of the vital energy, which in turn affects the physical body.

It was established as far back as 1935 by Dr Harold Burr that all living matter is surrounded and controlled by electro-dynamic fields, which in turn he states, are affected by the Sun and Moon. Burr together with his colleague Dr Leonard Ravitz, have a theory that human beings are like "steady state electrical systems".

Then in 1967 Dr Lloyd Graham, who was using magnetism in the treatment of illness and injury, wrote that the human body was an orderly arrangement of electromagnetic light wave, vibration patterns, all in gravitational motion (cited in Arroyo).

Dr Gustaf Stromberg an American astronomer was one of the first to put forward the idea that the structure of living organisms including human beings is determined by pulsing electromagnetic fields or wave systems. He talked of rhythms and frequencies and the fact that this matrix which results from these fields, gives living matter its form and shape. He further suggested that we can compare the living fields with melodies – a time sequence of frequencies. (cited in Arroyo)

Any study of music, astronomy or mathematics can show the vital role that number plays in the universe. Number is not only the pattern, it is the means of differentiation, and in DNA it is this, which creates the pattern of all living things. It is the principle that separates one physical reality from another and some will claim that it accounts for the different levels of spirit and matter. At the lowest level is the physical body with the least freedom, at the intermediate level is the astral plane of the occultist which exists with more freedom. As frequency increases we reach the spiritual level where there is total freedom. It is then, energy, frequency and number that create the pattern of everything animate and inanimate. The only difference between one kind of matter and another, whether it is a human being, a stone or a tree, a chemical element or colour is number. This theory of number holds true, whether matter is regarded as a wave or a particle. Even electrons in an atom have orbits fixed by units of whole numbers. Probability theory tells us that it is also number that creates the pattern out of chaos when the number is right for the change to take place. Then it is the rate of vibration or frequency, which confirms one manifestation or another. If the rate changes so does the substance. **So number is the pattern behind reality.**

Astrology according to Dennis Elwell, (1987) states that the human personality or character is merely the expression of those laws, principles and functions, which operate throughout the animate and inanimate realms of existence. He believes that the same forces that shape the universe are similarly condensed in us human beings. Astrology is the science of potential and the birth chart describes that potential, but it does not maintain that any potential will become an actuality. According to the astrological theory of harmonics, the planets as they move around the Sun generate waves of changing density and strengths as their orbits interconnect in forever changing but consistent patterns.

The birth chart is purported to be the graph through which we can understand how the larger energies operate within the individual. It is a mathematical computation of relationships based on number and harmonics. Birth charts are interpreted according to the aspects between planets. The circle of the birth chart is 360 absolute longitudinal degrees of the Zodiac, so the number of the harmonic is the number of times the aspect degree divides into the circle. The conjunction is the 1st fundamental harmonic and is the joining together of two bodies (planets) in harmony or conflict according to which planets are involved. The opposition is the 2nd harmonic and implies strain, two opposing forces pulling against each other, although from what we have learned earlier, polar opposites are normal and necessary for changes to take place. The trine or 3rd harmonic is the division of the circle by three, an easy aspect where the bodies can co-operate with each other. The square is the 4th harmonic and seen as one of the most difficult aspects to handle. The bodies in square aspect have little in common with each other and may have a problem working together. The last most commonly used aspect is the sextile, the 6th harmonic and usually interpreted as beneficial.

There is also more than just the amplitude of the wave, there is its power, the phase at which it peaks is important. Then its intensity where its influence fades out must be taken into account. These properties are measured by what we call the "orb", the distance of applying or receding force. According to David Hamblin (1983) the harmonic chart, which is different from other charts, provides a new insight into astrology, although harmonics has always been the foundation of much western astrology.

However if we look at the miscellany of the various theories we can once again find different ways of seeing, perceiving and thinking.

There is the "Causal Approach" in which it has been suggested that the human nervous system responds to the changes in the cosmic environment, that is called "Cosmic Conditioning". This has been hypothesized as a chain of causality through electro-magnetic waves, from planetary positions to birth quickening of a child sensitive to particular planetary positions. This birth quickening refers to an idea proposed earlier, that at the time of birth, the baby

73

is at the peak of his or her metabolic cycle and by releasing adrenalin into the mother's blood stream a child causes its own birth at the appropriate time. This assumes an underlying theory of reincarnation in which entry into this life is to learn new lessons on the way to "At-one-ment" with the universal principle.

There is the "Symbolic Approach" which considers the planets and signs to be representations of cosmic processes and universal principles, but what these symbols refer to, remains a mystery. Rudhyar along with other authors think that the symbols are the representations of qualities, which relate to wholes, whereas numbers and categories relate to the parts. According to Cayce though, the symbology of the planets will not make us this way or that, but they may reflect the purpose of our coming life. He further maintains that astrology is quite meaningless without an acceptance of reincarnation.

The "Holistic Approach" makes the assumption that the entire universe is one whole system and that within the great whole there are smaller wholes whose functions, structures, and patterns correspond to those greater wholes. This can be seen as "the principle of correspondences" and assumes that by the study of these correspondences we can learn about the cycles and patterns within individuals themselves.

The "Energy Approach" is yet another way, which deals with energy and energy patterns, which are symbolized by the planets and signs of the horoscope. Then more recently "Humanistic Astrology" with its emphasis on Humanistic Psychology which in turn places its trust in wholeness and the potential for growth of each individual person. Again, Rudhyar says the point of this, is to be able to see where everything that happens at any one time fits into the total pattern or structure of existence. He maintains that each time anything is separated from the whole and becomes individuated, it becomes itself a little whole, but it still remains a part of the whole.

David Bohm sees that these parts are in immediate connection but that their dynamic relationship depends on the state of the whole system, extending ultimately to the entire universe itself in unbroken wholeness. This holographic theory tends to fall down, if only because it is based upon determinism, and therefore implies a sense of flawless structure, which, in the terms of quantum physics it most certainly is not.

All these different perspectives have their problems of definition and explanation in terms of classical physics, but in terms of quantum physics miracles can happen. Einstein maintained that communication, which exceeded the speed of light was impossible, but on the quantum level the speed of light is reached and is exceeded.

Back to the wave and the particle and two perspectives of the same thing.

If we look at the particles and the photons, which make up the waves we see them travelling at 186,000 miles per second, but if we look at the waves as a whole, we no longer see any movement at all. Each way of seeing is as real as the other, and each is contained in the other, both ways are valid ways of experiencing reality. Eventually we may have to see ourselves as quantum beings in a quantum universe where uncertainty is a fact and we have to find stability within change. In this model, like many other models now, the separation of what is "out there" and those who observe is no longer a valid concept, indeed observers are observers no longer, but are an integral part – as participants. What we experience internally cannot be external reality *per se* but our interaction with it. So in a sense we are constantly constructing our universe from within ourselves by the very act of observing it. In this situation we cannot even begin to know absolutes, because we cannot be sure that those divisions that we make from this undivided whole, in which we are an embedded part, are the only ones available to us.

In general, Astrology has always been concerned with the meaning of Time, and the first astrologers must have looked at the world in which they lived and were a part, in order to find some kind of meaning to explain why they were here at all. The theory of astrology therefore, is that Astrology is a systems approach. It is the science of cycles, which tells us that the behaviour of any system is linked to other systems in its environment, and that everything goes on in interlocking systems. The notion of cycles is inherent in nature, day and night, the tides, together with the phases of the moon, the seasons, life and death. Man's own daily rhythms, monthly bio-rhythms, all point to the fact that we as human beings cannot escape that periodicity.

Cycles of time are merely the measurement of change. If, however, biological evolution and social change all reflect that bodies and brains and therefore minds all take place on a revolving planet in a solar system: then the central nervous system must always have been in close contact with "what is out there". Our brains and bodies must have always been capable of monitoring unconsciously even the most subtle changes in the environment in order to survive. Then through continuous interaction with the environment, brains must have evolved in such a way that they are pre-programmed to respond appropriately through many changes of consciousness.

Scientists have found in recent years many more interconnections of celestial and terrestrial cycles which go beyond the obvious ones of tides and seasons, all the laws of vibration such as harmonics, resonance, dissonance and interference to name but a few. These apply to astrology as well as to the physics of electromagnetic radiation, and what we see that appears to be solid matter, really consists of concentrated points of energy arranged in a variety of geometrical patterns.

Atoms, molecules and physical matter. including us human beings, are composed only of vibrant energy.

It has been said that Einstein's objective in a broad sense, many years ago, was to show that all forms of nature from the stars to the tiny particles inside the atom, all obeyed the same universal laws.

So basically, a central hypothesis of astrology is that the energy systems of the earth and its inhabitants all resonate to the changing patterns of the solar system. It would seem reasonable to assume then, that it never has been the planets themselves nor the signs that they are in, which influence individuals. It has to be explained by the monitoring of the Central Nervous System of the constant bombardment from space of the changing magnetic fields. Then we must take into consideration the varying pulsating waves and the interference of those waves by the inter-reactions of the movement of the planets around the centre of our solar system.

No wonder the Central Nervous System is such a miracle of complexity, but there to serve the preservation and survival of the organism.

Astrology is essentially related to Psychology according to Ruhdyar, but if we want to understand the living essence of astrology we must forget the type of medieval astrology from which modern day astrology is derived and look at it from a historical perspective. He says that the history of astrology is the history of successive transformations of man's attitude to nature as he perceives them.

If we trace this history from the animistic stage, through what he calls the vitalistic stage, and through all the many changes that occurred during the sixth century BC, in every case we see a change of level, a change of interpretation of consciousness. The intellect as it evolved and adapted through the ages became an instrument, which enabled man to raise his individual consciousness, from the physiological to the psycho-mental level. According to Rudyhar we can distinguish three epochs in the search for understanding the workings of the world: animistic, mechanical and mathematical.

Astrology eventually became known as the algebra of life in so far as it measures relationships between symbols, and the cyclically changing patterns of that relationship, whose very stability is entirely a matter of convention. A cyclic universe of cause and effect, was the basic concept of earlier thinkers, as well as Eastern thought today. Therefore according to this view, the belief in reincarnation was justified as man's progress towards knowing who he is as part of a divine plan, a cell within a greater whole – the Greater or Planetary Individual. This means the Whole of which the spiritually perfected human personality becomes a part. Whether this holds true in the light of the new physics and brain research remains a pertinent question but I see no conflict in this perspective.

One of the more fascinating instances of the application of relationship inherent in the trinity of the individual, the creative and the collective is to be found in the new physics. This is where the dualism of wave and particle is the essence of light and gravity as well as matter i.e. photons and electrons. If everything in the universe can be described in terms of particles why not brains and bodies?

CHAPTER 13

STILL MORE LIVES

SESSION 6, 14th December 2001

This session was different, a happy life, that Jan found comforting to relive. Transcript:

Wood keeps coming up ... image of being old and dying in a bed ... stones are powerful ... candles in scones ... Tower of London ... sick ... house along a river ... down the river from London ... summertime ... flat-bottomed boat ... moving quickly ... I'm in a room wooden all the way round ... panels ... ceiling in scrolls ... I love this room ... it's mine ... I'm in my late 50s, grey hair ... relaxing ... I have servants but they are not around ... I have sets of clothes that I would wear ... I wear black velvet ... formal clothes ... no jewellery ... no rings ... happy with myself ... I don't overdress ... plump and homely ... because I'm a widow ... my husband was a tradesman ... something strange, I've got the wrong shoes on ... his slippers ... material with a bow on top ... they are lovely ... comfort ... is beautiful ... reminds me of the time we have shared and how important I was to him ... even though ... I was valued ... the only person for him ... he'd have liked me to do that ... I've lived here ... he's done the work with materials ... only visited his place of work ... didn't like it in London ... life was ... hearty ... baking bread ... country person ... clean linen ... wholesome ... not striving ... solid and good ... not caught up in fripperies.

Much research into reincarnation points to the fact that lives alternate between happy and sad, good and bad, from persecuted to persecutor, male to female, as progressive learning experiences.

Although most research into past lives reveals that a soul returns to many places, at different times, other research points to the fact that soul-mates reincarnate to find each other. Some research points to reincarnation within the same family, even some to the same town or village. Dick Sutphen, a past life regression therapist in America, puts foreword a bizarre claim that he is one of 25,000 people who made a pact in Mexico in AD 681–582 to be reborn every 700 years. This is, according to him, to ensure that a belief in reincarnation survives, together with other metaphysical concepts, which must not be lost to the human race.

Much of Jan's past life regressions at this time appear to be solidly placed in and around the Tower of London. Perhaps in this particular happy life her husband worked as a craftsman in the Tower as many people did in order to provide the necessary things for all within the Tower walls. Strong gates had to be made and maintained, furniture would be made and mended and the church pews would all need attention. Even the scaffolding would need constant repair.

SESSION 7, 4th January 2002

Jan says that she needs protection, freedom from bondage. She keeps seeing a particular image of a stone vault, a river, a tower and a flame burning, but does not want to go into this now. So we do the breathing a rainbow light and a pyramid full of light to breathe in. Jan begins to speak:

Blending light, a nugget of gold ... valuable ... iridescent ... goes out ... in ... out ... infinite ... a bit that I own ... essence is so precious ... a grain of sand thing ... each individual ... but part of the whole ... if you come out ... you want to go back ... white ... blue ... violently bright ... beyond life ... enfolds ... encloses ... this piece of something ... absolutely brilliant ... its life ... in there ... to there ... to there ... like   volcanic ... river stuff ... never ending ... when the dark comes ... I actually died ... sticks ... liquid black ... river of black ... I've become black because I was evil ... I crawl ... no pity for myself ...

Once more this is part between lives and part memory of a past life. The remainder of this session was taken up with psychotherapy and healing because Jan was not ready for more past-life experiences. Jan continues to be anxious about what is happening but pursues the experiences week after week as an obsession.

Jan appears to be experiencing death and rebirth and even periods in between. She repeats over and again how life is continuous and she is part of a whole. She talks of circles, cycles and a stream of consciousness.

SESSION 8, 11th January 2002

We began again with a Visual Squash today, that previously used Neuro-Linguistic conflict resolution therapy to establish how Jan sees herself now and how she would like to be:

NOW was dark, hooded, bent down, grey, black, no contact, closed body in the mud.

FUTURE was smiling, happy, luminous, nice clothes, good feeling, young, innocent, but unrealistic, incomplete. When I asked what advice would the future part give to the present part she said:

Stand up, open eyes and ears, heart and body. Bring back more balance, things can be changed, good is very powerful, can take care, teach, nothing is taken away, can be a warmth from the stronger one. When integrating the two, different, stronger, able to see the world, not so dark, pallor not so great. Now she was ready to go into the vault.

Transcript:
Standing on pebbles ... river pebbles ... River Thames ... under an arch of a bridge ... leaning against it ... underneath a flame to light the part ... notorious for cut throats ... full of self-loathing ... never been worse than this ... Richard ... dressed in black ... my trade ... outcast ... work in the tower ... responsible for killing many ... young 20 years ... cover my face ... I don' t want to be ... I murdered someone in the name of justice ... a man ... a woman ... I did it, I'm going from it ... I can't do this ... damp and dark ... I know they want me ... I hope they find me ... kill me ... punished for what I did ... I have a sister ... I have a mother ... I can't live with this ... I'm going to stay here ... I can hear the sounds of mother in the kitchen, sister is younger than I am ... clean and fresh ... could still die ... I used to like looking out ... all these people ... the shame of this is knowing secrets ... always secrets ... I love my mother ... I love my sister ... I'm big and ugly ... had to happen fair and just ... The life I led was wicked ... what happens next ... above myself ... looking at the huddle ... something different about me now ... elevated raised ... looking at myself ... looking at myself ... I can see how different I am ... as different as I can possibly be ... face is open ... my hair is curly ... shortish now it's free ... I'm looking ... I'm looking ...

Jan stopped here, her signal that she had done what she had to do. I brought her back to her present age in this life and put her back in the pyramid of light to rest and recover.

The Tower of London has always presented an image of power, bringing emotions of pride and at the same time a certain foreboding. It has been a fortress, a royal palace and a state prison for most eminent people. Those people considered dangerous to the state and others accused of treason, as well as those individuals whose political views did not agree with the ruling dynasty, or merely those who had offended the king in some way. The Tower can be an awesome sight even today as the tide laps the wharf outside Traitors Gate and the river is shrouded in a cold damp mist. For those not of high birth or royalty one can imagine the condemned man or woman accompanied by their priest walking slowly from the Tower towards the green where the wooden platform would be waiting. The block always placed centre stage for all to see and the executioner dressed ready for work in shirtsleeves and black hood over his head. Hoods and masks were not necessarily to add terror to the scene, but for the protection of the executioner. Doing what was considered his duty could be construed as being a traitor and he could be maimed or killed by the deceased family or friends. Jan does not understand the reasons why she is involved in these "past life" sessions. She is still scared at this point in time and wonders what is going on for her. He talks of being "out of body" looking down on what used to be his earthly body, not a near death experience, but an actual dying with spirit or soul looking down.

A real past life memory? Imagination? Or merely a quirk of the brain? Or a combination?

CHAPTER 14

BRAINS AND MINDS – THE MYSTERY

Until recently the dualistic theory of relationship between mind and body has been prevalent. To be fair, those who have subscribed to this view, also held that there was a causal interaction between mental and physical events. Exactly what constitutes a mental event however has never been easy to define but examples such as sensation, perception, imagination, thoughts and feelings have been seen as sufficient evidence.

Sir John Eccles, a prominent scientist, supported the dualist–interactionist theory that sees subjective experience as separate from, but interacting with, the material world. This interaction he sees as taking place within specialized areas of the cerebral cortex. In other words, thinking produces the neural activity in the brain.

According to John R. Searle cited in Blakemore & Greenfield, specific mental states are in simple terms "higher-level features of the brain". Consciousness then, for him would be an emergent property of the brain in the sense that liquidity is a property of systems of molecules.

One of the pertinent questions however, is HOW can the mind in some way reach into the physical world of atoms and electrons, in order to create electrical forces that can act on matter. Sperry (cited in Davies (1983)) believes that mental forces or properties exert a regulatory control in brain physiology as a collective pattern of neural activity and that mind somehow produces forces that act on matter but he does not say how! Rolf Alexander MD (1989) wrote that, "action is but a demonstration of energy" based on the fact that matter is also energy. He also defined intelligence as "the purposeful direction of energy" believing that behind an individual mind was the concept of a Universal Mind.

Michael S. Gazzaniga, one of the world's foremost cognitive neuroscientists, was one of the first scientists to maintain that 98% of what the brain does is "unconscious". This means that, by the time the mind knows a conscious thought or feeling, the brain has already computed and processed the fast incoming information. This, he maintains is because the cerebral cortex is thought to be as packed with unconscious processes as our old brains. The brain he states is the most complex thing in the universe, with 100 billion nerve cells, axons, grey and white matter, working in specialized ways to convert sensation into sights, smells, sounds, taste and touch through multi-level processes.

He explains how the mind interprets data that the brain has already processed, he also shows how what we see is more illusion than reality and points psychologists towards the greatest mystery of evolution – how we become who we are. Alexander sees the mind of man today as having evolved through what he describes a slow, painful process from the steaming slime of a very young world to the scientist of today. He believes that the climb was made possible by this specialized intelligence that resides inside each of us. Intelligence that has, through successive hostile environments learnt to adapt and change, within a framework of natural law for a twofold purpose. First to give human beings a glimpse of the universe of which they are a part, and secondly to ultimately show us that always through all this time, that we have guided our own physical, mental and spiritual development.

All psychologists know that even at this time of our evolution, it takes time for the mind to process information through selective attention and gather information subliminally in passing. It takes time and repetition in order to store that information in long-term memory to be retrieved at a later date, and in order that understanding can take place and meaning be given to that information. So if a reconstruction of events starts with sensation, then perception, and proceeds from there to reasoning, then Gazzaniga is right – the mind is the last to know what is going on. He maintains that brains accrue those specialized systems of adaptation through natural selection and mutation, which are of value to survival, and provide ways of enhancing successful reproduction. No-one really knows how this is effected, and even this may not be the whole story.

Roger Penrose (1994, 1995) also thought that not very much of the brain was involved in the conscious state. According to him, at the time of his writing, the cerebellum seemed to act entirely unconsciously governing the precise control of our actions. He suggested that many more scientists might gain further knowledge from a study of how the way in which this "unconscious" cerebellar control, is learnt from a conscious cerebral one. This for many would push further the boundaries of the early work of Piaget and fill the gap left by Piaget as to HOW we move from not knowing to knowing and understanding. If however we return to Young and his learning theory we have an answer. Penrose also queried the unexplained oddity of cerebral organisation, again a fact that all psychologists know, whereby most of the sensory nerves cross over, the left side of the cerebrum being largely concerned with the right side of the body, and vice versa. For example, the eyes at the front of the head and the visual cortex at the back, and the part of the brain which is concerned with control of the hands and feet at the top of the head and the feet are at the bottom of the body. Penrose felt that this arrangement was not accidental, but perhaps that consciousness benefits in some way from the nerve signal having to take this long route. Because of the complexities still to be unravelled about the brain, he thought that whatever process is responsible for consciousness must depend on a physics that was beyond our reach for the present time.

This is not necessarily true, even from our present knowledge, if information is delivered to the brain at such speed and all at once, the mind must have TIME to sort and categorize and match with previous learning in order to make sense of the information. The brain and central nervous system is probably the mechanism that affords the time and needs no other explanation. The Central Nervous System of human beings is a miracle of complex information processing and feedback mechanisms. Robert Crookall, a scientist and para-psychologist drew his research from many sources and found that the body, whilst we are in it, acts as a kind of "damper". Without that buffer he says we would become distraught with distraction under the incessant impressions, (cited in Elwell). Many healers would agree that this is true and possibly is part of the cosmic scheme in the creation of souls.

All psychologists know that neurons make contact with billions of other neurons in sophisticated information processing. They take in an enormous amount of signals from other neurons at their dendritic synapses and pass this on chemically to other neurons. It has been assumed that because neurons, which like everything else in the world appear to behave in predictable patterns, that there is a causal factor between brain and behaviour. However, Edward De Bono (2003) challenges this concept of cause and effect, he states that because B follows A it does not mean that A caused B because in terms of quantum physics, there may be a higher probability in one direction than another. Recent brain research suggests that this "indeterminancy" is built-in to the dendritic synapses through the particular chemicals that pass across from one to another.

The firing of neurons is a complicated process. An accumulation of neurons can cause another neuron to "fire" and become active, but when neurons become active they also contribute to the "inhibition" of other neurons. Neurons get tired and stop firing, inhibition dies down and another set of neurons that have been ready to fire now become active. In the end event however, it is not just clusters of neurons that matter but what he calls the "the neural state", that includes all the elements and all the factors involved in that state.

Consciousness, it seems, is merely an ordinary and normal biological feature of living organisms with human brains and minds being of a higher order, because neurons work through excitation and inhibition, an "on/off" switch, with consciousness a variable register of information that produces different degrees of consciousness.

Gerald Edleman rejects any suggestion of dualism or any form of idealism in the research into brains and minds. For him the mind arises from the developing brain and body, and consciousness arose as a result of the evolutionary innovations in the morphology of the brain and body. I personally, have been for many years an ardent follower of Gerald Edleman *et al.* (1993) and his evolutionary theory of brain development, which maintains that neurons from the outset are always in the process of change through learning. Just as the laws of change are inherent in all things, so it is with the human brain and mind. If Edleman is right, then the brain generates and re-generates as neurons fire in response to incoming sensory information, and changes with each new "bit" of information. According to what we are interested in, some parts will grow and expand through learning, other parts will be inhibited and die. (shown in TV programme)

An MRI (Magnetic Resonance Imaging) study published in 2000 by scientist at University College London revealed that whilst learning to become taxi drivers, engaged in their year-long memory training, the rear part of their hippocampus became enlarged. Because at the same time the front part became smaller, this pointed to the fact that in the effort to learn specific memory skills, the brain had recruited from other areas. Another case reported, of learning to juggle – involving visual and motor activity – showed an increase of grey matter in both areas. Again when practice ceased the regions shrank back. Growth apparently can be reversed when the person stops learning back to its former state (*National Geographic* magazine, March 2005).

Edleman worked for many years with simple robots which "learn" to discriminate between what they like and what they do not like to back his theory that brains start with simple connections and become more complex through learning which builds value into the process. From such simple beginnings, brain behaviour – including thought – becomes more complex and abstract. The brain recognizes metaphor, develops "schemas" and finds ways of dealing with internal and external events that we call strategies.

This theory once more seems to be underpinned by both Piaget and Young's theory of learning in humans where learning begins with a spontaneous act, followed by reaction, observation and eventually control. However, where Piaget appeared to stop, and Penrose queries, Young identified the difference between an operator controlling a machine and a child's learning about the world. He maintained that the order of learning must be reversed at the end of a sequence in order to move forward. He states that "the self makes use of what it has learned to extricate itself by mastering the laws of matter" (p. 158) In stating that it turns round and goes the other way, he is saying that each one of the stages involves a process of development.

None of these theories deny that each newborn is already armed with circuits that already compute information enabling the baby to survive and function in the environment into which he or she is born, thus marrying genetics or nature with nurture and the evolution of consciousness through learning. One psychologist in Chester to whom I have often referred clients, has for many long years worked on the principle that physical exercise as well as mental exercise can stimulate brain changes in people with learning difficulties. He believed that crawling before walking in babies played an important part in physical brain development. The early research of people like Rosenberg *et al.* was published in the 1960s in *Scientific American,* in an article entitled *The Nature & Nurture of Behaviour.* Rosenberg found that the level of acetylcholinesterase was altered by problem-solving tests. He found that other dramatic physical brain changes occurred with learning, such as extra protein layers in the cell nucleus, and thicker myelin sheathing surrounding the axons amongst others. He also found that an enriched environment resulted in a greater weight of, and thickness of, the cerebral cortex.

Other psychologists in that era found that mild stress was a positive factor in growth and well-being, whilst of course too much or dis-stress caused slow growth and often despair and depression.

Neuroscience today tells us that four weeks after conception an embryo produces half a million neurons every minute. Then the next several weeks see these neurons finding their way to the brain to specific destinations, determined by genetic cues and interactions. These processes continue through the pregnancy, with neurons reaching tentacles out to each other and establishing points of contact called synapses. This is done at the astounding rate of 2 million per second. The foetus at this stage however, has far more brain cells than he or she will ever need even as an adult, so the miracle of pregnancy continues with a reverse trend towards the end of the nine months. This is where groups of neurons compete with one another to expand circuits with specific functions, and some are lost in this pruning process. The circuits that survive are already fine tuned to the world outside, to recognize the sound of mother's voice and dialect over those of strangers with other languages. Scientists also think now that the amygdala, which stores emotions with memories, is functional at birth (*National Geographic* magazine, March 2005).

Research many years ago by Rosenberg *et al.* again told us that there was another spurt of brain growth at puberty when brain cells changed and the myelin sheathing around the axons became thicker. This was thought to enhance mental capacity and provide the change necessary for what Piaget called "formal operations", whereby adolescents now could manage to learn more complicated mathematical and other relationships.

Even more recent research also tells of a spurt of grey matter just before puberty which also thins later in redundancy. (Institute of Mental Health Maryland). All these complex processes are involved in the maturing of the adult brain, which scientists say does not occur fully until around the age of 25 years. Gray matter maturity does not end the ability to learn and change. The brain keeps its plasticity and its ability to reorganize and reshape itself through adulthood, and it is constantly revising itself throughout life.

As the brain becomes more complex and sophisticated over the long period of childhood and continues to evolve through life, the unique pattern of connections between brain cells, creates what we call "mind". The memories that are absorbed by the amygdala may not be accessible to the conscious mind because of the age in which they were laid down, but they may influence the way in which a person feels and acts beneath awareness. These memories may be accessible in later life through engaging with the sub-conscious or unconscious mind.

I personally make a distinction between conscious, pre-conscious, sub-conscious and unconscious mind. Pre-conscious is that which is known but is temporarily out of recall. Sub-conscious is that which is registered beneath awareness whilst concentrating on particular aspects of the environment. In a training session to demonstrate this sub-conscious awareness I would ask my students to look around the room and notice all the things that were green. So that they thought I was going to ask them how many they could remember. However, what I did ask them was to tell me the things that they had noticed which were red or blue. It was always surprising how many things they could remember that were different to those that they had been instructed to concentrate on.

Brains then will "wire up" differently, and minds inevitably will follow suit with different sensations, perceptions, thoughts and values. By learning to discriminate and categorize through our senses we build value into brains and minds. Kant was right, in that we do have to experience the world through our five senses and I wonder if he realized that it was also this limitation which appears to prevent us "seeing" the whole?

Our five senses are apparently serving a purpose whilst we are in a human body and without them we would never cope with all the incoming information.

In his later researches Edleman together with Tononi (2000) concludes that there is no need to search for anything mystical about brains and minds, when we can construct a scientific theory of consciousness. He states that consciousness arises from particular arrangements in the material order of the physical brain, and denies that the word material cannot deal with mind, spirit and pure thought. Conscious thought for these scientists is a process, a set of relations with meaning that goes beyond energy and matter, consciousness does however, need to involve both. The mind, for Edleman and Tononi is completely based in, and dependent upon, those physical processes that occur in its own workings, but they maintain that there are no separate places for matter and mind, therefore no grounds for dualistic thinking to explain them.

Many psychologists define consciousness in terms like an individual's current awareness of external and internal stimuli, such as events in the environment and bodily sensations, memories and thoughts. Others think of consciousness as involving monitoring ourselves, and our environment. Some define it as controlling ourselves and our environment, so that we are able to initiate and terminate behavioural and cognitive activities.

Edleman combines all these in his definition of consciousness as a "dynamic property of morphology … which meshes with the brain's thalamo-cortical system as it interacts with the environment". **In layman's terms he**

sees our knowledge of a real world where physical objects do exist, as a result of physical, psychological and social interaction of minds and bodies with that external world.

There are psychologists who have tried to persuade us that the mind is like a computer and this is partly true. Edleman bases his theory on the premise that after the brain arose through evolution by natural selection, which includes a built-in value system, each brain then operates by a **process of somatic selection** rather than the rules of logic. So all of the brain is not like a computer, only some parts. We need logic because of the power of logical operations, but it is selection, natural and somatic that gave rise to language and thinking in metaphorical terms.

If minds develop as brains develop, then from this point of view, emotion is the basis of consciousness and knowing. As we learn through experience and configure our personalized brain connections, we begin to access and use memory, cultural values and a unique way of seeing the world, which is our individual consciousness. In the end we integrate all the theories of psychologists like Freud, Jung, Adler and the Behaviourist's like Watson, Hull and Skinner, and return to Einstein. Einstein said that "Experience is knowledge, everything else is just information …"

Both Edleman (1993) and Gazzaniga (1985) maintained that brains were more social than psychological in their construction because learning constantly changes the adapting structure itself. So because the qualitative differences between brains probably reflect genetic, intra-uterine and environmental factors, there will be differences in the way in which individuals construct their worlds. Add this to the way in which memory functions, with age-related differences, these qualitative differences can lead to big discrepancies such as our capacity for reconstructing events.

One of Ramachandran's patients would illustrate the enormous part that emotion plays in conscious recognition and knowing. A patient suffering from Capgras' Syndrome after a car accident and subsequent brain damage, thought his parents were imposters when he saw them because the visual pathway was damaged. He did however recognize his father on the telephone because the auditory pathway was not.

V. S. Ramachandran over the past few years has made many new inroads into brain exploration to show that there are many more pathways in the brain than was previously thought. He demonstrated in a series of television programmes, that there are old pathways and new pathways, which take different routes through the brain. The old pathway from the eyes seems to act as an orienting response, a kind of early warning system which Dr Larry Weiskrantz calls "blindsight" (cited in Ramachandran p.76) but in normal visual processing, information through the new pathway goes through the optic nerve and crosses over at the optic chiasma to the visual cortex. There are also different pathways in the brain for how, where and what in recognition. The How pathway for navigation goes to the top of the brain, whilst the What goes to the memory files of classification in the temporal lobes. Mounting research is also evident to show that emotion and knowing are essentially linked in recognition as part of emotional information processing.

Differences in brain formation can also lead to differences in ability and aptitude, even what we describe as "genius". According to a TV documentary, Einstein's brain was kept after post-mortem in order to see if there were any differences between his brain and "normal" brains to account for his brilliant mind. Two parts of his brain were found to be overlapping between the areas of mental and spatial ability and that he had more glial cells in the Parietal cortex than would normally be expected. We know that glial cells as well as grey matter increase with activity. It was thought that perhaps the degree of concentration which is essential in genius, could point to the fact that he was slightly autistic. Michael Merzinich a neuroscientist, says that the chaos in the brain that results in autism often occurs from an abnormally rapid brain growth in the first year of life (maybe with no built-in redundancy). This he thinks is to do with an over-production of cells that carry nerve impulses in the brain's white matter, as well as a possible predisposition through genetics. (*National Geographic* magazine, March 2005) Michael Merzinich studied an adolescent autistic boy who wrote his auto-biological reflections of what happened between the ages of 8 and 11 years in a book called *The Mind Tree*. The boy, named Tito, wrote about his two distinct "selves", a thinking self and an acting self both of whom stayed isolated from each other. Some research into autism suggests that certain damage can occur as early as neural tube formation. A gene known as Hoxal might play a central role in the development of the brain stem when the first neurons are forming. This apparently causes a shortening of the brain stem and a lack of the superior olive and smaller than usual facial nucleus (*Scientific American,* February 2000).

Obviously we still have along way to go in unravelling the mysteries of the brain, mind, and consciousness.

Evidence again suggests that there does exist, self-organizing processes in every branch of science, from fluid turbulence to neural networks. If this is true, then this unfolding of complexity is "built in" to all aspects of the universe, including brains. Then if this points to the implication of predestination towards a final goal, but with choice and chance inherent in the indeterminacy; then a new paradigm must recognize the progressive, innovative character of physical processes where spontaneous change is inevitable.

When critics say that recollections of past lives is nonsense we can reiterate that most people do not recall much of their childhood years, so it is not surprising that past lives must inevitably escape most of us. Yet these may be lost years that can be recovered, because hour by hour thoughts and feelings have been added to our experiences and made their contribution to mind and soul. Evolutionary processes are painstaking in their work, and if minds and brains are found to be different, then they will have a different destiny.

According to Plato, many centuries ago, our present knowledge is only a re-collection of what was learned or known by the soul in previous states as well as what we have learned in this life, but no-one knows much about souls.

It seems that the brain is a complex system, where evolution, learning, and history have all played an important role. In many ways Edleman agrees with Freud in that the unconscious influences the conscious mind, but he also maintains that the conscious mind is in constant interaction with the unconscious. He suggests that although these mechanisms have psychological significance, he also thinks that they are far from present neurological understanding. So it seems that the laying down of unconscious knowing from previous conscious repetitive activity is no different from the suggestion that we bury unacceptable memories or those too horrendous to contemplate.

I would agree that the conscious mind and the unconscious mind are in continuous interaction but would take the theory further to suggest that the mind is in continuous interaction with the physical body and the external environment as well.

Rossi however, takes all the past researches further into the far reaches of modern neuroscience. For many years he has wanted to know HOW we facilitate the daily work of synthesizing the organic structure of the brain, in order to optimize the relationship with ourselves and others to keep a harmony with the "evolutionary informational dynamics of consciousness" and the cosmos. Rossi's books expounding his work are not always easy to read, but the man is a genius in his field. His "Deep Psychobiology of Psychotherapy" can be defined as the exploration of mind-body experience, communication, and healing at every level from the cellular-genetic-molecular and the quantum to the psychosocial and cultural. Research is continually being updated by biologists, physicists, psychologists, neuroscientists and even mathematics: but Rossi's integrative approach greatly expands the phenomenological, analytical and cognitive-behavioural approaches. He brings new insights into creativity, but also tells us HOW we can make use of creative moments, from utilising the 90-minute ultradian rhythm cycle to rest and recharge the system, to his four-stage creative process in his psycho-biologically orientated psychotherapy.

Unless, however, research can show us how parts of our nervous system are open to non-physical influences, brain science will continually de-bunk all discussion of human beings as spiritual beings. This will further the materialistic view of human nature and deny the concept of a soul, thus taking all meaning away from life on earth.

If, however, in the end of all our enquiries, we find that we are quantum beings in a quantum universe and the human brain is a part of the unified field, according to Cayce the soul cannot die because the body is an atomic structure. And within that mind/body/brain, a Self, pre-programmed through evolution to realize the truth of who we are and where we came from at some point in our lives. Pre-programmed does not mean inevitably, not even probably, it means that possibly we will recognize who we are, where we came from and where we are going. However, because of the built-in indeterminancy of the brain, we have the choice of free will to take up the challenge.

Now in terms of quantum physics there is a growing theory that perhaps the mind can be subject to the same scrutiny as atoms and molecules. The problem with this is that the chief difference between the two models is not the kind of entity that they try to explain, but the evidence to which we have to refer in order to check the rightness or wrongness of the model. Neither is made up of solid material but each is an assembly of phenomena. The checkpoint of the atom to which the model can be compared is the hydrogen spectrum with its inherent mathematical properties but the mind is something less easily qualified or quantified, it has merely the whole spectrum of human behaviour for comparison. The mind just like the atom and the universe is a hypothesis, so the data that we can obtain are always going to be indirect and incomplete.

However, if the continuity of the Self is because of memory, then far memories of a self, might be brought from the past to the present to become aware of another time and another place.

Jenny Cockell, who told of a past life as an Irish housewife Mary Sutton, (cited in Stemman) believes that she has also seen her future lives. She believes that a human mind can retrieve memories of a future life, as well as past lives, because it is as if the mind exists simultaneously at two different points in TIME.

CHAPTER 15

LIFE BETWEEN LIVES AND NDEs

Millions who have reported near death experiences (NDEs) describe in vivid detail the efforts of rescuers to resuscitate them. Dr Raymond Moody a psychiatrist from Georgia published a book in 1975 called *Life after Life*. He had collected evidence since 1965 from people who described seeing their life pass before them in review, seeing relatives and beings of light and he called these experiences "near death experiences". Moody was studying philosophy in Virginia at the time. He tells one story reported by a psychiatrist of when he was a soldier and almost died of pneumonia in the army. This young soldier left his body when doctors declared him dead and travelled across the whole of the country. Then he returned to hospital and searched for his body, only recognizing it by a ring on his finger. Moody's book tells stories from more than 150 people, and although they differed in some respects, he found common elements in each story. These were, a sense of being dead, peace and painlessness, a tunnel experience, seeing people of light, having a life review, feeling a reluctance to return, and having a personality transformation.

However! "out of body" experiences can now be shown to be a quirk of the brain as some people describe it, rather than anything to do with the paranormal. A neurologist treating a patient for epilepsy in Geneva found that using electrodes on a spot called the angular gyrus in the right cortex repeatedly produced an out of body experience. The purpose of the angular gyrus is not yet fully understood, but it is suggested that it plays a part in matching up visual information with the brain's touch and balance representation of the body. (Newspaper article by James Chapman reporting on an article published in the scientific journal *Nature*.)

My explanation is that the brain might be pre-programmed to have this ability.

One of the most astonishing true stories is that of a man called Dannion Brinkley who went to listen to one of Raymond Moody's lectures, and was subsequently interviewed by him. Later, and to this day, Dannion worked with Raymond Moody extending his work on NDEs. Dannion Brinkley published his own book with Paul Perry in 1994 called *Saved by the Light*. Dannion was struck by lightning whilst talking on the telephone and was so badly burned that no-one expected him to live, including him. At the time that the lightning struck, he described it as if every cell in his body was bathed in battery acid and he had no sense of what could have caused such severe pain. Then he went into another world of immense peace and tranquillity, bathed in glorious calmness. He saw below him his body from mid-air it seemed, his own wife looking at him. The telephone was melted in his hand and his shoes were smoking and as she began pushing on his chest he thought he must be dead. He felt sorry for his wife but he himself was not concerned.

He recounts that the CPR must have worked because he found himself back in his physical body full of pain. A medical team arrived and said that they would do what they could as he once more went out of body, watching the technician giving him an injection but telling his wife that he was dead. Then came the tunnel of light – the tunnel came to him and he began to move towards the light. The light became brighter and brighter until it overtook him, and he saw a being of light approaching. As this being approached he felt a deep sense of love that intensified as the being engulfed him. Next he began to experience his whole life, feeling and seeing everything as every memory stored in his brain flowed out. It was not, he said, a pleasant experience as he saw his whole life, as a receiver of the hurt that he had inflicted on others. The depth of the emotion that he felt was astonishing, but as the being of light moved away he felt all his guilt being removed. He had felt pain and anguish in reflection but had gained knowledge from this intense experience. He was told that human beings are powerful spiritual beings meant to create good on earth, and at this point he realized that he was dead and began to wonder what would happen now. He began to move upwards with the light to another level where he began to vibrate at a greater speed and he could see energy fields that looked like prisms of light.

Then, he said that he was presented with, what he describes as boxes full of future predictions of mass destruction, and natural disasters. He was told that all these things could come to pass, but that the flow of human events could be changed because nothing was set in stone. He was also told that because human beings were great powerful spiritual beings, all they needed to do was to realize that they must treat others in the way that they would themselves wish to be treated. He was told that he must return to earth and begin his life's work In the end event he had to blow on the sheet which covered him in the mortuary to let his friend know that he was still alive. Then came his greatest struggle to return to living, with years of blackout spells and considerable weakness and pain. However from then on he had nightly visions from his spiritual teachers. In the beginning he felt very sorry for himself battling to live again, unable to see properly and wearing eye protection to block out light. After meeting with Raymond Moody his attitude changed and he went on to try and build the centres that he had been instructed to build. He realized eventually that he now had psychic powers, mind-reading the thoughts of others even when they spoke in a foreign language.

By 1978 he was walking again but in poor shape physically, his heart pumped insufficiently which caused his blackouts. However he started three businesses all dealing with electronics because he believed that by learning about our electrical and biological selves we can make ourselves into higher beings who can work with the spiritual side of life. Through all his visions he thought that when a person reaches the point where they can control their energy, it can be transformed into a powerful force, and that they have found that part of themselves that they can call GOD. Human beings are essentially, electrical and chemical beings, with each of the five senses being transformed by electrical and chemical processes in the brain! **Is this what meditation and healing is all about? And is this how we can transform our world?**

Some channelled messages tell us that we are here on the planet earth to learn how to balance the spiritual with the physical. (Cited in the Introduction to *The Only Planet of Choice*.) We are also told that we hold the key within ourselves to bring about change, it is our responsibility, but also our free will, our choice. In other words the planet earth is the "test bed" for free will.

Carol Ritberger is a theologian with a PhD in religious philosophy in her book *Your Personality, Your Health* she tells the story of how a near death experience in 1981 changed her life. Whilst having a meal in a restaurant she developed a food allergy which was so severe that she nearly choked. She reports that for 18 hours she did not know where she was. She watched from above her body, people trying to get her to breathe. As she floated she saw what appeared to be bright lights moving towards her, as they came closer she made out shapes within them. She felt safe in their presence and at one point she asked if she was dead and they said yes, but that she could still make a choice. She liked where she was because she felt free and light and had many questions to ask her new friends. She says she felt the presence of God and the purity of unconditional love. She was told that she made life too complicated and should begin to see each day like a child, everything new, when she had to come back and do what she had chosen to do. Suddenly she was jolted back to reality and the sound of her daughter's voice, but when she opened her eyes all she could see was blinding light. The whole experience had altered her vision so that she could "see" the aura around a person and eventually the chakras and colours inside a person. She spent time seeing psychologists, opthalmologists and optometrists, trying to find some answers to what she felt, was a great problem for her. Her sight however did not return to normal. She was suffering from terrible headaches and the blinding lights around people never turned off. It took many years to accept that she had to follow a new path and become a medical intuitive and bio-energetic diagnostician. We might question where these "messages" come from? Are they just part of the ancient "inborn faith" of all mankind? Rolf Alexander maintains that since before the dawn of intelligence we have instinctively known about the vital activating principle of the universe and given "it" many names, Tao, Jehovah, God and others. He feels that these names narrow the enormous concept of this power and chooses to speak about the "Absolute".

Dr Bucke, cited in Cade and Coxhead, also lists some characteristics of what some might call "the supreme experience" of dying. These include, awareness of intense light, being bathed in joy, triumph and a feeling of salvation. There is an awareness of the meaning of the universe itself, in what might be described as a lightning flash. These feelings are accompanied by a sense of immortality, no fear of death as a sense of sin disappears.

Many eminent people describe such happenings, Dante in Il Paradiso of the Divine Comedy. Walt Whitman called it "ineffable light". Thoughts abound from the earliest of times from eminent thinkers, that men and women have within them some dormant, un-manifested, divine power, which once awakened could transform them from common clay into a compassionate saint and master of wisdom.

This gradual transformation into higher states of awareness normally takes long and diligent continuous effort, but maybe NOT, when a spontaneous Past Life Experience can achieve it almost immediately. Carol Ritberger writes that she has worked with people with past life concepts now, and although initially she did not believe in past lives and reincarnation she says that it cannot be dismissed. She says that she has watched people reacting to past life information so that it provides answers to questions that have been haunting them for years.

The discovery of the electrical activity of the brain in 1875 was attributed to Richard Caton who was investigating the voltages produced by the brains of monkeys. It was not until 1924 that the same technique was used on human beings, but from then on, scientific research has advanced to provide us with visual biofeedback machines to enhance control of internal cues. The foundation of the biofeedback principle was introduced in the 1950s by one Dr Joe Kamiya a psycho-physiologist. Kamiya based his assumption and basic premises on the fact that if a bodily event can be associated with a recognizable mental state then it could be possible to control that state.

Biofeedback is a way of learning to listen and watch how internal cues can be controlled and even healed. Through electronic monitoring bodily changes can be recorded and measured and at the same time a person can observe the biological happenings of which one is not normally aware. I learned to monitor and control my own breathing rate when training at the Bristol Cancer Centre, just as heart patients can monitor and control their own blood pressure and heart beat. If we can learn to control the electrical qualities of our brains for internal problems, perhaps we can move on from there to control those properties for internal and external healing.

We know from experience that treatment in similar cases of ill health is often more effective in one person rather than another. The same drug can have a vastly different effect on two people. The answer has to be within the person, the body can repair damaged or worn out tissue, it defends against germs and viruses all the time. We are the one responsible, our souls, our spirits, our minds and our bodies, are in charge of everything that happens inside – so why not what happens outside?

The Mormon Church has long collected many experiences of NDEs and *The Journal of Discourse*, a commentary on Morman beliefs, suggests that upon the death of the physical body, the spirit retains the five senses of sight, feeling, taste, hearing and smell. They believe that when we die, this leaves a person free of illness and disability, with a spirit that can move at great speed and has the ability to see in many directions at the same time and communicate in ways other than speech. They define death as a change from one status or sphere of experience to another.

Walt Whitman wrote that death is a process of expansion, a release from the earthly dominance of substance. He said that the stages of dying are the stages of moving from solidarity to spaciousness, with each successive step one of greater and greater expansiveness. He goes on to describe the internal experience as one of floating, of more and more space, moving from the separate to the universal, from the limited to the unlimited. Whitman uses metaphor to describe the process of dying. He describes an ice cube, being solid and having form in its original state, melting in a warm room until it becomes a puddle of water. This is where the solid element becomes fluid, then the quality of the heat element changes and the fluid evaporates. His description of this process, is one of going from the water element to the air element. Clearly he states, the essence is still the same, only its forms have altered. One of his most extraordinary insights is where he claims that in all the stories of NDEs where people have left their bodies and gone to meet the great light, is the fact that few have recognized that the light was their own true nature. He says that when Jesus said, "I am the Light" he meant the "IAM" of pure being, the LIGHT ITSELF. For Walt Whitman "death is just a change in lifestyles" (cited in *Guided Meditations, Explorations and Healings* by Stephen Levine).

People under anaesthetic who are supposed to be "unconscious" have reported vivid details of conversations and medical procedures. Some report hovering over operating tables, crash sights, out of body, but aware. Does this point to the fact that consciousness, memory and other cognitive functions might be part of some extra-neurological system? One research reports a child of 16 months with his head in spasm pinned to his shoulder. In tracking pre-natal events the therapist found that the child had, as an eight-month-old pre-born, had undergone amniocentesis and the needle had nicked his neck on the left hand side. Certainly, this can be taken as evidence of pre-birth memory which will exclude many of the computer-system-only theories, but what of past life memories?

Only spontaneous past life recall seems to affirm the belief in reincarnation, but belief itself can only be based on experience. Evidence may be necessary but it may not be sufficient to prove a point. NDEs appear to be sufficient evidence that death is not the end of existence, just life as we know it and perhaps life between life. Any Psychologist, Psychiatrist or Neuro-scientist today will have plausible explanations for all of these happenings, from logical brain/mind functions to deal with trauma to vivid fantasy imagination. I personally have recorded through my years of practising psychotherapy, that not only can these things happen quite by accident, but can be learned. Children can learn to "flip" out of body to avoid abuse and pain. They learn to become part of a wall or invisible or just be "not me". Whatever they do they appear to open up channels of communication that other people do not have. Many of these individuals grow up to be mediums, healers and psychics because of this learned ability. Obviously then, some people are born with psychic ability, others gain it by accident and others can learn by whatever means. My personal belief is that there are more things in heaven and earth, and in the brain, that are as yet inexplicable, and we should keep an open mind.

CHAPTER 16

MOVING ON

SESSION 9, 18th January 2002

Jan reports that the bad dreams are fewer and there are more pleasant images. She can now dissociate from the childhood images, put them in a box (a psychotherapeutic practice that we teach). Her breathing is easier, freer and her perspective is beginning to change. She believes that unexplained images from childhood led to some of the fear, but not all of it. The feelings of dread are still an anathema and she needs to integrate a "splitness" between the I and the Me as observer.

In the trance state she speaks of parts, the good bit and the bad bit with the observer pulling her towards total-ness:

... it is a search for self ... one part feels shame and guilt and prohibition is still there somewhere ... Catholic religion brings on the sickening feeling ... not knowing ... being unsure ... still worthy no matter what ... pure part could move ahead ... but no-one to take me forward ... self assurance and self value ... innocence ... no justice ... two experiences of death ... two very different sets of happenings ... if I could only forgive myself ... leaving life into solace ...

SESSION 10, 25th January 2002

Nightmare dreams are less frequent now, they have changed in context, and are of a different nature.

Back in trance state ... Jan has gone back to a time in this life when she had been reading a book and come across a picture of a girl with her head on the guillotine. She had asked her mother what was happening and her mother dismissively said that the girl was going to have her head cut off. Jan was very young at the time and was extremely upset, though she did not know why. This was obviously a significant happening in this life, so I asked Jan to go back as a mother to her child and take away the feelings as we had done on previous occasions. This she did and sat beside her, shared looking at a different book, now she has taken the blanket away from her face, looking at more colourful pictures:

... I want her to be a child who is happy, feel joy ... pick her up on lap and put arms around her ... feels held and relaxed ... feels trust ... stay there ... feels complete ... I can take it.

I asked Jan to thank the child and tell her that she would always be with her now. When Jan was back in her present we discussed what had happened there. Jan told me that she now remembered the incident of looking at the book in this life, and seeing the picture and asking her mother about the picture, what it meant. She thinks that the picture was a trigger of past memories, a past life, part of a higher consciousness without a body which obviously resurrected the memory of a feeling of fear and dread. This could of course be a case of a picture creating imagined fantasy and horror and even be responsible for the ensuing dreams.

However, from someone who dismissed all theories of past life experiences not so long ago, Jan was beginning to be quite sure that all the things she was experiencing in trance had actually happened. She did not think that this was a case of shock and then buried terror from this life when the child was presented with material in a harsh way, nor did she believe that it was a fantasy imagination. She maintained that it was definitely something more.

SESSION 11, 8th February 2002

Jan would still arrive in my therapy room to discuss all the happenings of the previous week. Then without any invitation from me her head would go down and she was away.

Transcript:
At certain ages I have been damaged ... a child in Cheapside ... Richard Watkins in 1450 ... now I'm back under the bridge ... enormous struggle ... there is intense anger ... fury ... then trust and protection ... now talking about that life ... has images that move on ... sometimes slow ... sometimes fast ... at different times it opens in front of me ... .malignant pull ... by the powerful figures ... terrified ... holding me back ... another group come in ... I was the victim of tussle ... know where I wanted to go ... what is it that holds me back from where I want to go ... felt heat come into my hands ... couldn't touch anything ... black things pulling me ... because that was strange and scary ... ended up with a pile of black grey garb ... me with consciousness ... elevated person ... welcoming me ... I was enveloped in these amazing brown feathers ... cocooned in exquisiteness ... but I don't stay ... I go back ... something sticks there ... my fight for me ... me hating ... self loathing ... because of what I had done ... repentant and then not repentant ... wanted to have salvation ... this is the true you ... intertwining ... celestial blue and whiteness ... slime and muddy ... monks chanting ... ecclesiastical ... no

barrier between evil and wickedness ... constant reminder of darkness ... age old struggle that's been around for ever and a day ... fighting a battle ... with no ending ... heat in hands ... touched face ... so comforting ... but not my hands ... taking it away ... anchoring ... breathing ... relaxing ... calm ... still puzzled by people around me ... in France ... monks are kind and encouraging ... big shift of emphasis ... in belief system ... hands hot ... put out hands to touch ...

I intervene because of hand movement, I ask Jan to stay with movement and feeling of heat

That's good ... back under the bridge in the clothes ... I look like a ragged beggar ... I'm dirty ... I can see this group ... and I want them to go away ... I want to go where I can go to salvation ... I must turn my back away so that I cannot see them ... I must say my prayer ... loud enough to shut out the noise ... concentrate on the light ... I see the light ... I see the light ... I see the light ... feel the warmth of it ... a warm wind from the South ... I'm nearer to it but I can't take it ...

What will you have to do before you can take it?

Before I can go into that light I must make pliance ... I must be clean enough to go forward ... but I must make penances ... I must spend time in the outer chambers until I can be clean enough to go forward ... there's no other way ... I must remember prayers from my youth ... say my beads ... until I feel acceptable... I must be penitent ... stay in this place ... I feel the warmth ... the comfort here ... the breath touches my face ... .caresses my skin until the time is right ... I see that there is light ahead ... but I must stay until the time is right ... I will know when the time is right ... I know my guide is there to help me ... but I cannot go with him yet ... this is the place of peace and tranquillity ... I still feel that I have got earthly garb ... envelops me until I know I can move on in grace ... I remember when I was small ... a service priest ... in red and gold ... he is here ... not music I can hear ... chanting is uplifting feelings going through me ... a place of infinite peace ... (Jan sighs and rests) ... the music of the stars is incredibly beautiful ... more beautiful than anything I have ever heard before ... I feel like I'm moving ... I'm moving don't know how I got here ... hands floating ... sky is full of stars and other things ... speed ... I'm being pulled through this blue ... too fast for me ... things come whirling ... flying past me ... have I gone mad ... can't see anything for miles ... just this ... I must stop at this place ... this point ... I feel like I'm suffocated by the power ... it is so great ... I don't know where I'm going ... I know I'm leaving it all behind ... I don't know where I'm going ... but this is nice ... it belongs to me ... I'm changing ...

Jan sighs, and I intervene to tell her that I am there when she is ready to come back to her present age in this life at this time. She is still flipping from a past life in London to a past life in France and then to between lives.

If Jan is correct at the beginning of the session with the date, London in the 15th century was a harsh and difficult life. In the time of Henry VI's reign there were many complaints about corruption, public bad behaviour, law and order were in a state of collapse. Western Europe had regarded itself as united in the Catholic Church and held together by a belief in a divinely ordered universe but within the English Church there were stark contrasts. Lollards listening to the teachings of John Wycliffe were attacking the church, which was sermonizing and piously moralizing. They were even questioning its authority in spiritual matters. In 1450, a date that Jan mentions, there was Cade's rebellion that challenged the Royal Government, and the Archbishop of Canterbury took refuge in the Tower. Ruthless rebels made a fruitless attempt on the Tower, but the treasurer, Lord Say, was surrendered to, and murdered by, the rebels in Cheapside. If Jan did experience a life in this time it would have been fraught with uncertainty, apprehension and fear no matter what social standing she might have enjoyed.

This may be Jan's brain and mind working through problems in the four-stage creative process described by Rossi. On the other hand it could be a symbolic representation of those problems, perhaps childhood conditioning by the church, or even evidence of life between lives. Or it could be her working through as an individual, like the rest of mankind towards a higher consciousness in perpetual transition and change, it could even be a combination of all these factors.

Dr Brian Weiss, in his book *Same Soul, Many Bodies*, at the end of his sessions with his client Catherine, was convinced that it was part of the process that each one of us has to go through towards gaining a higher consciousness. Catherine experienced many more "lives" than I have witnessed. The Masters using Catherine as a channel told that individuals must experience life on earth many times in order to learn the lessons that have been neglected in prior lives. We must experience poverty and riches, pain and joy, good health and disability before we can return to the ONE. We must balance our Karma, pay what we owe because that is the only way that we progress. Karma is memory, but memory they say is not enough we must do it and most of all FEEL it. **People who experience near death episodes do report having to feel the pain that they have inflicted upon others. So that limbic system in the brain may not be just a sufficient part of being human, it could be a necessary cause wrapped up in the evolution of consciousness.**

CHAPTER 17

BACK TO VERSAILLES

SESSION 12, 5th March 2002

Jan is not having bad dreams now, but is not sleeping well. She wrote after the last session in trance state at home:

I'm here ... but in Versailles ... talking ... got a scar ... healing myself with the help of light ... carry scars ... part of you ... essence is never damaged ... handsome clothes ... blue sparks that I change into healing self ... can be done by redeeming power of God. The scar is totally around my neck. I saw myself after death with a red healed mark right around my neck. I touched it, felt it and knew that I had gone beyond death into the mercy of GOD. The feeling was one of infinite peace, complete, I have never known that feeling in life.

I ask that when images come what is it that triggers the trance state? We explore the things that might do this, seeing is important, so is sound. Feet always shift, then an image comes, followed by sound but Jan is not sure, sometimes just sound:

... looking down at shoes and I'm somewhere else at the same time ... I know that I'm at Versailles ... all true ... it belongs to me ... I remember the apartments and hearing the clock ticking ... surrounded by gilt everywhere ... polished ... beautiful ... Marie Antoinette lived here with Louis the sixteenth ... his clocks were in every room ...

If this is a real memory, then Alexander Dumas more than a century ago wrote about the large hall of the palace of Versailles. He told the story of a room called the Saloon of Timepieces, he described how a young man waited. The young man appeared to be about seventeen and no one could mistake the family of this young man from his profile. He was Louis Auguste, Duke de Berry, Dauphin of France (later Louis XVI) he had the Bourbon nose even longer and more aquiline than his predecessors. Dumas goes on to write how this young man stopped before a large clock which marked the days of the month, the years, phases of the moon, the course of the planets as well as the time of day. He watched for a time the second hand, which glided rapidly on, when all at once it stopped. Surprised by this sudden happening occurring before his eyes the Dauphin forgot why he had come and how long he had been waiting. He opened the glass door of the crystal pagoda and put his head inside to examine the timepiece. He thought that the person in charge of the timepieces had perhaps forgotten to wind the clock, so he took down the key, but it would only turn three times – this was proof for the young man that something was wrong with the mechanism. He began to unscrew the many parts, laying them all in order on a console beside him, searching into the clock's most hidden and mysterious recesses. Then suddenly uttering a cry of joy he discovered that the screw, which acted upon the springs had become loose, and thus impeded the motive wheel. He began to put this right, and was busy at his work when the door opened and a voice announced "the King". The Dauphin with his head in the clock heard nothing until the King tapped him on the shoulder. "What the devil are you doing there," he asked?

"Sire – your majesty sees I was amusing myself until you came." "Yes – destroying my clock, a very pretty amusement."

"Oh no sire! I was mending it."

"But you will blind yourself looking into that thing". The young man told the king that he understood all about it, because he took to pieces, cleaned and put together again, the beautiful watch that the King had given him for his 14th birthday. (Paragraph précis taken from Chapter XXV *The Saloon of Timepieces Memoirs of a Physician* by Alexander Dumas, Vol. 1, original edition circa 1800s.)

Another reference to Louis XVI comes from a novel by Eileen Townsend. An old man is telling stories to his grandson about the child's great grandfather and the invitation to attend the declaration of the new German Reich in January 1871. He described the mirrored splendour of the magnificent Palace of Versailles with its white and gold hall and clocks all over the palace all striking noon at the same time … Is this evidence or something Jan had read and forgotten?

In an earlier session Jan had mentioned running through corridors with her brother and sister – and the "mirrors". It is on good authority that we know there is indeed a hall of mirrors in the Palace of Versailles.

We used to run through the corridors me and my brother … I grew up here … that is a memory … running in my mind's eye … but from another side … I remember the day I sat outside … and the world was changing … felt like impending doom … we were innocent and nothing was more important … the more I saw that day I'll never forget … people … filthy in rags … taking down our house … they took the queen and the king … and they took me … what happened after that I don't know … the images that come now are too … I was young … no idea … I shouted … screamed … and they pummelled and pushed … they were trash to me … we were trash to them … it was late afternoon … when we got to the terrible place I'd never seen before … it was dark … we didn't know what was happening … around us … I had no idea … I'm watching … thinking how I was huddled in a corner … some other young girls were with me ... we were there for days ... getting dirtier and dirtier ... they cut my hair ... they cut my hair ... I can't ever forget that ... the image keeps coming ... but the fear and the panic ... the pains in my throat ... I wanted someone to kill me before they did ... I saw sights I can't speak of ... but I know I died ... and it's black ... black ... from the filthy and hateful people around ... and it's black ... then I see it ... the light comes like the colour of fire and it calls to me ... with no voice ... and I'm walking towards it ... I know I'm in my mind ... I don't know about the rest of me ... but I know I'm in my mind ... I'm being taken forward ... I don't have a will ... I'm being taken forward and the light spreads and it's around me ... I can somehow see me ... my mind and body assembled and I'm seeing me in my clothes like someone has arranged me out in clothes I should be wearing and I'm looking at me ... there's a recognition ... and we are smiling at each other ... how can that be ... and I pick up my skirts and walk forward into a place where there is wood around and candles and I know that I've been here before and I hold a book that I've held before and I know that I must wait until someone comes for me ... is this the place where I must stay ... this is the place of peace and tranquillity ... where I must stay ... this place is about the peace and tranquillity of the love that is above understanding ... it's the key ... it's the place that puts everything else in its place ... it has value beyond any value ... I could not have known about it unless I had experienced it ... it's the place that shows me the way I lived my life ... I was as nothing and now that I know ... I can never be anything else in this life or in any other ... it's impossible for me to describe it ... it has a depth that I've never reached before ...

Does this place take away the fears about the scar?

Yes it does ... it's the place that puts everything else in its place ...

And now that you know this place ... and know that you have been there many times before, what can you do now?

Just to be in it and know that it's there bathed in a knowledge that there is more than I have ever known ... to praise it is a greater gift than anything to do with money ... there is just a void ... then something comes and takes me out ... more powerful than me ... no end ... a new beginning ...

The situation in France at the time of Louis XVI and Marie Antoinette was having a grave negative influence on the people. The climate was seething and ready for the Revolution. France was in debt and at the mercy of poor decision making, Louis XVI was said to be a weak and incapable king. He had married Marie Antoinette, the youngest daughter of the Archduchess Maria Theresa of Austria in 1770, and she was thought to have influenced him to attend to the interests in Austria rather than the financial crises in France.

Her lavish spending and the fact that she was a foreigner made her unpopular with the people. The Government was bankrupt, but rather than paying back the debts Louis increased taxes. This increased the tensions between the nobility and the peasants, who were stepped upon from all sides. They endured poor living conditions, they had no rights whatever and they struggled to survive. They ate inferior food, wore clothing made of cheaper material if they had any at all. They were reported to have spent half their earnings on bread and the other half on taxes, that is, if they had work. Unemployment was rife and lagged behind the basic needs of the poor, they either worked very hard or not at all. The result was death, homelessness and begging, despair and eventually revenge and criminal behaviour. Eventually, history tells us that the French Revolution mob did burst into the Tuilleries to insult the King and Marie Antoinette and drag out all the people in the palace, servants and royalty alike – all privileged and thought to be wealthy. If Jan did live in this time, it would have been once more a life filled with uncertainty and fear.

CHAPTER 18

MORE TRAUMA

SESSION 13, 15th March 2002

Jan is still troubled with images, which come unbidden during the day and at night, but she seems to be more in control and can send them away if she wishes.

Transcript:
A figure ... bastard looking at me ... not there in a physical way ... but a presence ... in a green or dark grey place ... hands on hips ... mocking me ... I hate his guts ... get out of my flaming head ... just looking ... then smiling ... changed over time ... becoming familiar so can get rid of him ... I am standing there in a mirror image ... now see me in his place ... image of a room ... first there was no-one in ... there is now ... a young girl ... brick coloured hair has changed ... ochre colour but no idea of the vista ... I don't know what I am doing here ... don't want to go there ... it was not too bad just looking ... but then he put his hands out to touch ... he wasn't dangerous ... not come to get me ... come to acknowledge me ... mocking smile has become a smile of greeting ... frozen by it ... there but not in it ... something about the struggle between remaining decent and succumbing to him ... the executioner can't make head nor tail of it ... only allowing it to be flashes ... I'm scared ... sick to my stomach ... pick up something familiar ... look and focus on the here and now ... brings me back ... look down at my feet ... I go ... I will walk away into another world and can detach myself ... swing between wanting to go with it ... when I can see the scenes ... but it's not me ... bastard has had a life but not a good life ... all linked ... different sex ... different outlook ... in today's life ... he represents a shadow side of life ... today that I don't want ... all appeared without logical conscious effort ... good ... evil ... when taken out from under the bridge ... white energy pushed me ... couldn't take the help ... something hovering ... white ... wanted to take the salvation that was offered ... I would have slipped into the black pool ... powerful being ... no reading ... can't explain ... whilst in therapy no reading ... so as to experience it is as it happened ... if the theory is to work and re-work 1450 ... looking at myself looking at myself ... I can see how different I am ... as different as I can possibly be ... face is open... my hair is curly ... shortish ... now its free ... I'm looking ... I'm looking ...

Back in this life now, I put Jan into her pyramid of light to rest then she goes again ...

Vault ... underneath a flame to light the part notorious for cut throats ... stone ... standing on pebbles ... river pebbles Thames ... sound of water ... leaning against the bridge ... full of self loathing ... Richard ... dressed in black ... my trade ... outcast ... work in the tower ... responsible for killing ... maiming ... young ... 20 years ... by covering my face ... I don't want to know ... I murdered someone in the name of justice ... a man ... I murdered a woman ... I did it ... I am going from it ... I can't do this ... damp and dark ... I know they know me ... I hope they find me ... kill me ... punished for what I did ... I have a sister ... a mother ... Happy times ... I can't live with this ... I'm going to stay here ... I can hear the sounds of mother in the kitchen ... sister is younger than I am ... .clean and fresh ... I want to protect ... could still die ... I used to like looking out ... all these people about ... the shame of this is knowing secrets ... always secrets ... to see what I want to see ... I carry my axe as I have done ... because I am good with it ... It is part of me ... I hear the noises of people ... shouting and yelling ... but I will not look ... I am in position ... I raise the axe ... and I have done it ... that's the end of me ... I hear the sound ... I see the blood ... around my feet ... and the bile rises in my throat ... and I am sick ... I see skirts ... I have killed a woman ... I take off my hood ... and I know I am done for in this life ... I am down the stairs ... .and I am so clearly disgusted that I can only make amends with my own life ... the people who knew her know me now and they will kill me ... and that is how it should be ... I cannot live knowing what I have done ... I love my mother and I love my sister ... I'm big and ugly ... I'm fine ... had to happen ... fair and just ... point of death ... only me ... the life I led was wicked ... what happens next ... above myself ... looking at the huddle ... elevated ... raised ... something different about me now ...

Death by decapitation was the method of execution in this era for the nobility because it was considered the most honourable way to die. This was supposedly a privilege to die in this way by an edged weapon as if in battle. However the weapon used, known as the heading axe, was more often than not little better than an unwieldy chopper, crude and lacking in balance in its design. Being an instrument of punishment any attempt to improve either design or accuracy were probably thought to be quite unnecessary.

Why beheading? According to the historian and retired Yeoman of The Tower of London, Geoffrey Abbott, it was because the head of a person is what we recognize as that person. The head was for them the powerhouse, the control centre where we think and emotional responses take place. As a psychologist I agree with this symbolic interpretation but there is more than this.

What if a person's face is so disfigured that they are unrecognizable, the only way that we could be sure that a friend was our friend, would be by his memories that we might share. Only this would convince us that the person we knew was still the same self.

CHAPTER 19

MEMORIES ARE MADE OF THIS

Memory we know is fallible, so critics and scientists tell us. It is not like a video tape, it can be shown to be altered by the passage of time and subject to error and distortion even in the normal course of events. Some of the latest research suggests that our memories are always dynamic, and even from the moment we experience any event, perceptions are broken down into fragments that are stored all over the brain and therefore recreated every time the person thinks about it. So if memory is a constructive and reconstructive process that is subject to forgetting by intervening events then memories can be accurate, inaccurate, fabricated or a mixture of all these. Therefore there is no easy way of distinguishing between true and false memories or indeed between actual experience and fantasy.

The core debate initially is about the nature of memory, then, whether or not there is a difference between memories laid down in an altered state of awareness such as a hypnotic trance state or during a traumatic experience which basically is similar to the trance state.

Morris Netherton (cited in Woolger) who has collected much data on prenatal memory, maintains that, unlike the conscious mind, the unconscious memory of a child "in utero" is like a tape recorder because it is yet free of the ego discrimination filter. So if we are born with an unconscious memory that belongs to the whole of humanity it may be like a tape recorder.

Rossi and many other psychologists now maintain that memories are always laid down together with the emotions and sensations that accompany the event. In other words, memory is "state dependent". So if memory is contained within a stream of consciousness which arises through the unconscious, then traumatic feelings of fear and dread will resonate. The accuracy of the memory is also affected by which hemisphere is used. The brain's two halves are separated by the Corpus Callosum and experiments with "split brain" patients show how the left hemisphere has a seemingly "built in" interpreter and the right hemisphere has not. So new-born babies, with their limited neural wiring would be registering only with the right brain.

According to Gazzaniga this interpreter attempts to keep our personal stories together through establishing a running narrative of all our actions, emotions, thoughts and dreams and provides the glue that unifies our existence and creates a sense of wholeness in our being.

False memories, some critics suggest, are more often than not facilitated by the therapeutic process, classical hypnosis being the most criticized, which makes memory more confident and less reliable, and in the process of recall the influence of the therapist may alter completely the nature of the memories produced. This may also facilitate the theory of crypto-amnesia, where clients remember stories read or films seen and long forgotten. However, other research suggests that under most circumstances people can distinguish between events that happened from events that were imagined.

So! Where does this leave us in the memory debate?

If we remember the days before we had at our disposal the artificial memory of books, computers, calculators, cameras and television, our ancestors had to remember everything. According to Ostrander and Schroeder, natural memory is what you are born with and shifts with different cultures and is shaped by the attitudes, beliefs and values of the times.

Both Aristotle and Plato believed that memory was a gift from GOD, but Plato also thought that memory was the medium that could lead an individual back to the realisation of our own divinity, back to wholeness. For Plato memory was a ladder to be climbed, back to enlightenment and unity with the divine source. This implies that descending to earth has led to forgetting who we are, and what we are here to do. It would seem however that psychic wisdom and ancient memories are available in varying degrees to all those who will "stand still" and listen to an inner knowing.

Giordano Bruno many years ago, once tried to spread the idea of a universal hermetic religion wrapped in a memory system. He created the Book of Seals whereby students were to work their way through the seals, so that eventually, they would be open to cosmic energy and the highest knowing. He conceived of memory as the inner act, which preceded outer expression, the drive to organize the psyche so that it could realize its divine heritage. Mnemosyne, the mother of the arts seems to be making a comeback in the new thinking.

According to homeopathic theory all disease is memory, that is why vaccination and immunisation work so successfully. The immune system has such a tremendous memory that it can recognize a virus that it has not seen for thirty years. The body makes conscious that which it already knows. So perhaps it is a fact that memory never dies and is passed on through generations.

As well as many theories about past lives, there have been numerous explanations about how reincarnation might appear to be a fact.

One such theory is genetic memory whose hypothesis is that the personal memories of people who lived in the past are genetically stored and inherited. Konrad Lorenz did show through his experiments, that animal memory exists pre-natally. A chick can recognize sounds and voices that were heard whilst it was still in the egg, and that it learns the language of its kind while the hen is sitting. Based on these findings other scientists extrapolate and suggest that what used to be called instinct may be due to hereditary memory transmitted to the nervous system by memory chromosomes. Some go so far as to think that there the design for each species includes an initial hereditary memory developed primarily in the chromosomes.

When cells divide and transfer copies of genes to daughter cells, recent research suggest that chromatin, the portion of the cell nucleus that contains DNA, provides support for the delicate ordeal of holding firm whilst the cell divides. Cell division is largely considered a "black box" where we know that cells go in and duplicate chromosomes come out, but not much is known about the process (internet source: University of Illinois). Everyone however, is controlled by the overall plan of the cells, which are the programmers of any species, so we may say that the design for each species includes initial hereditary memory developed primarily in the chromosomes. Because the exact chemical process by which memory is recorded is still unknown, we may yet be in for some surprises. Memory transmitted through chromosomes may be through some sort of energy like electricity, which could explain why someone sees a place and remembers it (internet source: University of Arkansas for Medical Sciences).

If memory is recorded in DNA perhaps part of other bodies and souls are not annihilated but may persist in time through their descendants. When these memories are triggered in some way in this life they are real far memories, albeit hereditary memories, so these people have lived before and we need no other explanation of reincarnation.

Sylvia Browne believes that each one of our billions of living, breathing, thinking cells contain our spirit, subconscious mind and memories. She further believes that these spirit minds remember everything we have experienced in this life and in past lives. She also maintains that "morphic resonance" can explain the feelings of déjà vu, of having known some place or someone before. She works with releasing cell memories in past life regression with a large measure of success.

Robert Charroux writes that there are many examples that support hereditary transmission through memory chromosomes. He tells the story of a farm where there was a stream channelled along several ditches. A dog on the farm always drank from the same ditch and refused to have her food in anything but a blue bowl. She died giving birth to puppies several of whom lived, to exhibit the very same behaviour. These hypotheses according to research on memory, have no plausibility yet in fact, as no genetic memory inheritance has been established, nor is it likely to come from the contents of regressions. Yet almost all past-life memories include vivid recollections of death, and research into memory is still in its early stages and based solely on the computerized versions of storage.

Many more scientists now believe that memory does exist pre-natally. A French medical researcher, Dr Alfred Tomatis (cited in Ostrander & Schroeder), has devoted his lifetime of research to exploring what he calls "ancient memory". He utilizes his findings by summoning the ancient memory to help people back to renewed health, well-being and creativity. He thinks, that a lot of intense learning and remembering must go on in "pre-birth" life that is essential to the functioning in adult life. His first experiments involved song birds, and he found that if unhatched baby birds did not hear the repertoire of the mother bird's song, they never learned them after hatching. He concluded from this that the unborn child's primary sense mode was hearing. In further experiments involving how a mother's voice would sound to an unborn baby, that is filtered through water, he worked with a four year old autistic child, who had until then been uncommunicative. The child responded to the sounds, which were initially like high pitched squeaks, and Tomatis gradually altered the sound until it resembled sound through air rather than sound through water. Tomatis and his colleagues have since worked with both autistic and dyslexic children, producing some astounding results. He believes that the mother's voice filtered through water recalls this ancient memory and awakens a sense of mother and child as one and **"touches base" with a oneness of the universe**.

Sound may be very important to the human individual, when he or she wishes "to touch base". The power of vibration as sound is perhaps beyond our understanding, but what we do know is that it can shatter a glass, and soldiers always break their regulated step to cross a bridge. "In the beginning was the word …" The sacred word or vibration is thought to have been a primary force in the pattern of creation. Sound, resonance and vibration are intimately connected and astrologers maintain that each of us responds to those vibrations present at the time of birth. The most famous mantra is the AUM which the Hindus take to be the most sacred of all sounds. "This simple sound enshrines an entire philosophy," according to Naomi Humphry (1987). The three letters refer to three states of being which the soul can experience, daily consciousness, dreaming sleep and dreamless sleep, which represents pure consciousness when self-realisation is a reality.

During a time called "The Harmonic Convergence" in the 1980s when all the major planets were aligned, computer scientists screened out all the possible sounds around the earth. When this was done, they were left with a sound like AUM, which they claimed to be the sound of the earth travelling round the Sun and known as the Schumann Resonance. So once again it seems that we are in some measure programmed to respond to external sound, resonance and vibration, in order to be at one with the universe. Whether this manifests as conscious response or unconscious response remains a debatable point.

If we only assume that being human with a brain and central nervous system is the limiting factor in our understanding of the universe, because the brain functions on a linear basis of cause and effect we may reach a dead end of questioning. Whereas, on the other hand if we ask the question HOW does the brain enable the mind whilst we are here on earth as conscious beings and what benefits does it serve, we might just expand our knowledge of human creativity.

If the recall of past lives is not possible because such memories cannot be stored in the physical body then recalling past lives might be regarded as paranormal ability. Esoteric or Gnostic clairvoyants mention three possible sources of reincarnation memories:

1. The continually re-incarnating soul.
2. A kind of general memory store the "akashic records".
3. Personalities of the past lives.

Hundreds of Edgar Cayce's sleeping sessions, which operated midway between spiritualism and hypnotic regression, illustrate the concept of reincarnation and individual cases would sometimes be checked and verified. In the final analysis, belief in reincarnation, or anything else for that matter, is based upon experiences, reflections and arguments that convince people of its plausibility.

It seems today, that those things which were once seen as mysterious, psychic happenings, talking with GOD, out of body experiences, and near death experiences can be explained scientifically as the work of some part of the brain. Then again, it is also possible from the evidence presented to date that brains are somehow pre-programmed through a variety of mechanisms to know all there is to know about life, the universe and everything!

CHAPTER 20

MEMORIES OF MY FATHER

Saturday 16th March - Jan writes at home:

My first mental image – he's here again – why – why – 6 a.m. on my own. He smiles at me – beckons me, he holds out his hand and I take it, it is warm, I shudder and release it with a feeling of revulsion and disgust. I feel physically sick I hate, loath and detest this bastard. When he put out his hands to touch I can remember this was a point of terror, he was THEN and I was NOW . Then I did not know this man, he disgusted me and I recoiled, but now I know. I can hear the creak of the leather stuff he wears like the sound of saddles and bridles, he was my father. When I was alone before it was him that was responsible for what I did and why I was rightly wired off the face of this earth. He got me into it, I want to cry and that he hold me as his son."

Sunday 17 March - Jan writes at home:

When I wake he's there ... he looks at me and I look at him ... he is appealing to me ... to trust him ... I just stare ... there is another figure behind him ... it's a woman ... she looks old ... white cap ... grey hair ... solemn expression ... she leans her chin on his left shoulder and puts her arms around this terrible man ... they are cheek to cheek and they are my parents ... he puts out those stubby hands that have been covered in blood to touch me ... to comfort me now that I am alive no longer ... in a way he never was with me in life ... I blink my eyes into today ... and I am shocked, puzzled ... odd ... I am a son to him ... them ... but I live now ... he visits me throughout the day and I feel a presence ... that offers me a crude attempt at comfort ... "come on son" ... and a touch on the shoulder that is meant to be gentle but is like that of an ox ... I tell him to go and he disappears ... I am becoming used to him ...he somehow belongs to me ... I don't understand any of this ...

Jan writes at home:

I am in the chapel, come in to take communion. I panic and I leave – what is going on for me – my stomach turns over. I am only seeing the floor. I get outside and breathe – I look at the flower beds, I see the colours and I am in today. In my mind's eye I know I looked around before I crashed down those steps. I saw what I had done. I cannot even write it – it belongs in the realms of the devil and his works. In the filth of the gutter in rags and muck. I am closing the circle, but the pieces have not yet come to me. There has to be something symbolic and correct to put this spirit to rest. It will come as all the rest came. The old boy weeps beside me – he did love me then. I want to cry today – and I do – I have never shared any of this before. I might be considered mad, borderline or worse unfit to work. My work is actually better than it has ever been – who does this deep, deep shame belong to? Why this incredible fear of retribution, where does it come from – why this character? It makes no sense – or it makes every sense ... down through the times – why me?

Jan's stories reveal the source of deep fear and dread, of waiting in deep anxiety for what she knew not what. The feelings first of injustice, then guilt and shame, then abhorrence at a way of life that she hated. **Surely not an easy way through therapy, and not one that she would purposely choose.**

20th March 2002 - Jan writes more at home:

I'm sitting in Chelmsford Cathedral. I hear the sound of footsteps and they ring clang on the flagstones. The candles are burning, I'm alone in the side chapel. He's here with me, he won't stay because I bid him gone, but he stands behind me and pats my shoulder in a crude attempt to placate me in my sorrow. He seems to mistake me for his son in an earlier life and in my today life. I can feel the link and I am comforted by him. He does not see me as I am now, but as I was then. This is completely without explanation for me – but saying that, it still feels right, and I do take heart from this man whom I hate and loathe and detest for what ended in my death. I now see that he must be dead, he can comfort me down through the ages. He could not do that in life. As a son of an executioner I was to have no time for church, books and learning, or the feminine ways my beloved mother taught me. I loved her and my sister with devotion, and I was a good son and brother to both of them. I was in awe of my swaggering father who thought nothing of death, his own or anyone else's. People were a profession to him and as his son I was expected to follow him, and indeed I did. I hung around the Tower for years as a young boy. I managed to avoid everything unpleasant – I learned to stuff my ears with material so I could not hear. I put a stupid smile on my face and took to the river whenever I could. I was not a simpleton but I behaved like one. I dressed in the required black and grey and sat with my father in taverns and I drank to forget what I was expected at some time to do.
I am feeling sick.
I want to vomit ... I must stop ...

Jan writes at home:

Child protect me from what I saw and what I became. The dreams are coming now in this life. Joyce I can't credit this stuff, I'm trenching my childhood loss, that which I don't speak of, my Dad was there but I never think he was enamoured by me, quite the reverse, I grew up without male influence. Is this my black missing torment? Is this why I can't be free of the presence because I haven't completed a circle?

What does she mean by "I haven't completed a circle?"

Because Jan was experiencing so many images and tending to slip into them when she was alone and quite scared, we did a session on what a therapist would call "anchoring" and "grounding". This was to enable Jan to have some control about when and where she would access the images for therapeutic reasons. This included images of rainbow light surrounding the body for protection and "roots" growing down from her feet into the ground for security. Suggestions of peace and calm, serenity and safety were given and put onto tape so that Jan could have these whenever she needed them.

SESSION 14, 22nd March 2002

Jan appears again somewhat troubled today, she closes her eyes with her glasses still on, hunches forward.

Transcript:
I want to remember it as it was ... when it was a family ... I'm much younger ... about twelve or thirteen ... I play here ... .arches and cobblestones ... lots of grass ... it's a good day ... sunny ... I'm hanging about ... never much to do ... Dad's around somewhere ... I won't call him Dad ... he's my father ... 'cos I'm younger, he's younger ... seems quite tall ... menacing ... others are flaming terrified of him ... he's with my mother ... she's got a white head thing ... pulled down ... she's so clean ... a happy woman ... she's all so clean ... and look at him ... look at them both ... stands there like he always does ... laughs at the world ... I'd like to be like that ... not give a damn ... but I'm not like that ... I'm like her ... there are other people there ... someone comes and stands beside them ... she's got a pale blue apron ... something green ... unusual ... because its colourful ... she smiles at me ... just talking ... father just knocks me flying ... he laughs because I whimper ... I get up and he does it again ... I hate it there ... I hear noises ... I know what goes on ... if I wasn't such a wimp I'd leave ... get on a boat ... then my mother looks at me and I don't go ... I wish I was a girl ... then I could stay with her in the kitchen where she cooks food ... I like it there ... it's safe and warm there ... we stand together the four of us ... I'm scared to live there ... I'm always scared ... I'm going to bother him ... it's not the sort of thing I should be

115

wearing ... I'll play the fool ... I strut around like my father ... half the size ... hands small ... sometimes he'll turn around and I'll hide ... that might last for about half a minute then I can't bear this place ...it's black hearted ... some home ... people stand about laughing ... but I know the place is full of death ... I know that one day I must leave here ... feel like a child who has never been a child ... known about horror since I've been old enough ... I've grown up being slapped on the back ... listening to the tales ... bits of this bits of that ... king of the castle for only half a day ... sometime I go and find safety ... where I can find some semblance of God ... spend hours praying about nothing ... for hours I feel safe ... but he'll come and haul me out ... he knows where to find me ... then I'll get a cuff ... that's not a plaything
I'm scrawny ... got no muscles ... not like the other boys ... they make sick jokes about what they say they see ... bad things go on there ...

Jan stops. (I do a relaxation, grounding, warmth of love spreading to every part) then another image comes:

Saw another figure ... didn't like it ... was more menacing ... same figure at different stages of life ... smaller ... younger ... more vulnerable ... I have a scar ... I don't know where that comes from ... need to talk about the scar.

Jan writes at home - no date. Interprets her own session:

I'm in a safe place, a place to pray, in a cathedral. I know now that my deep shame can only be salved by writing it down and in some way offering it to someone more powerful than I am. I suppose I mean GOD – not the powerful destroyer but the benign gentle, kind and merciful being that can take away all the sins of the world, and you Joyce who can hold it with me. The day came, my father had pushed and threatened me into this life, a murderous "right" doing. I had to be his son, a man who could kill and maim, no conscience, only the work of the king. Don't ask questions, do it, or else he would kill me, and I knew he would, I had no doubt about that. I had no practice with the axe, I chopped wood, swede, anything, I got used to the action. I would have been a woodman without equal. I'm feeling sick here, my legs are weak and my muscles freeze. I want my mother, I long to see my sister alive and running about yelling as she does, holding my hands – but I've got him, I'm at the tower. There is a scaffold on the green. That's where I must go and murder someone, they don't tell you who. I've been in the tavern and I'm full of ale, it's as much as I can do to get up, but he's there reminding me of his bloody pride and honour. He drags me to that dark room the guards meet in. On goes the black garb and he shows me out to the scaffold and the bottom step appears before me. I am hooded and only choose to see what I want to see. I carry my axe as I have done because I am good with it, it's part of me. I hear all the noises of people shouting and yelling but I will not look.

116

I'm in position, I raise the axe and I have done it. That's the end of me, I hear the sound, I see the blood around my feet and the bile rises in my throat and I am sick. I see skirts, I have killed a woman. I take off my hood and I know that I am done for in this life. I am down the stairs and I am so deeply disgusted that I can only make amends within my own life. The people who knew her, know me now and they will kill me and that's how it should be ... I cannot live knowing what I have done.

This is reminiscent of a time when boys had to follow in the footsteps of their father's work, and the work of the executioner traditionally went to the son at the time of his retirement or death, whichever came first. Only this boy hated what he had to do, unfortunately, because he was more like his mother, gentle and kind. Has Jan brought forward all those memories of feelings from her past lives? And now, in this life they are all mixed up? Feelings of being first an innocent victim of violence, then to being a perpetrator of violence?

When executions were held in public the crowds were told in vivid detail about the behaviour of the victims but little was said about the executioner. They were the objects of scorn neither liked nor likeable. Jan's description belied the fact that they did not care about what they did, but it was duty that some were unfortunate enough to inherit. They were individuals like anyone else and they had a life apart from the work that they did, and whilst there was a death penalty someone had to do it. Some would gloat with the power and some no doubt like Jan would weep. It is easy to assume that from reading books today that the blade descended, the victim died and the crowd roared with delight and justice was done. We assume that executioner just swung the axe and that it was done, Jan tells that it was not so easy she/he had to practice and practice to become even competent. No executioner was so accurate because the instruments were crude to say the least, yet death by decapitation was that of the nobility, the common criminals were hanged, drowned or burned.

SESSION 14, 19th April 2002

Transcript:
How does this happen? Here is my story book, if I don't look down at my shoes I can watch, see the picture ... .hustle and bustle ... awake in the scene ... look down to see if the shoes are right ... .anything that is relevant ... helping with problem ... learning about me in other lives ... can go on to different lives ... don't have to go back ... open a book half way through it ... beginning is known can go back ... forward fear is very relevant ... certain noises ... inside now ... is too deep to be relevant to this life ... too big to ignore ... buried feelings never die ... phobic fear cannot be explained ... huge amount of understanding has helped to control fears in this life ... breathing has helped with blood pressure stress management marvel at what

it's given me ... effect of atmosphere around ... mind blowing ... entranced me ... quite something ... sensitive to atmosphere ... need to know ... two therapists together ... journey of discovery ... acceptance ... if this is all there is ... it's been powerful ... scooped up ... moved on ... I've found a space ... massive energy source ... drama of life and death ... death is nothing at all ... particular attitude ... hear people who have gone ... feeling in head ... massive moves from then to now ... unstuck ... moved on ... not solved ...

Jan came back now – breathing relaxation and "Journey to the Self" script. This is a healing meditational script that I used frequently in hypnosis sessions, because it is about love, healing and wisdom for the self.

Jan appears to have reached some resolution to her problems, and because I had planned to be away for 3 months, Jan had decided to visit Versailles with her husband.

July 2002 Jan writes at home:

I actually felt very excited about Versailles, about going back there, although on the day that we went there it was quite overcast. There was cloud and that in a way was important, because when I had gone there it was a sunny day, then it had changed into what was impending doom. The place was teeming with people, and there were barriers to where I wanted to go in a way I hadn't experienced it before, and the gardens had been shut off and there were guards all over the place. It didn't feel right then, and this was a replication of when it didn't feel right now. I felt very sad to be walking with my husband who knew nothing about what had happened. It was like walking beside myself, and although I was in today's clothes, in my mind's eye, looking now through different eyes, there were the same noises, I'm hearing children playing and there was a lot of fun where we all used to go. I hadn't been there long because I was 19 or 20 when what happened, happened. I had been taken there by my mother whilst my father was still away, I was there not as a servant but as a young companion of the queen and the aristocracy. I was a silly young girl doing silly things, frivolous, playing with animals, the place was set up as a farm, so the noises in my head were of a past time, nostalgically quite pleasant, but when I walked back towards the house the feelings I had were invasive, feelings that I recognize, debilitating me, immobilising me, and it was like that in this life, and I left the place feeling pained by what I had felt. Because I couldn't get to the fountain area, I wanted to get to where I could hear the music, but it was the wrong music, it didn't belong to the time. I felt that I had done this and I needed to do it again because it hadn't worked for me. I went into what I know now to be the village I walked over the cobbles, I'd walked there before in different shoes. I was acutely aware of this, there was a void which I didn't like and added to that, I had to leave there because of how I felt, and I'm sitting here holding my head because that's what I feel like and I don't know how to put a label on that, it's like a story half told. In Paris I went to the entrance of the place where I was taken, I'd finally arrived after I'd been pushed, shoved, dragged, where I was reviled, humiliated, hair pulled, they hated us trash with passion, I was white and clean, they were dirty, hungry, I was well dressed, beribboned, and well fed. I could not go through the door, and I have to say, I stood in the concierge in a trance state, I just stood and I said that I just wanted to stand there for a while, so my husband walked away round the corner and said let's go sit over there. But the sense of doom, the greyness and blackness that swept over me was not what I expected because I'd hoped to do something very different there and I don't know where this puts me because the fear is something I don't want to touch now, even though I know that I have known death and life in this life I couldn't do that unless there had been some way of talking it through and if I had gone there on my own. Sometimes it feels like there is a fine line between me today and then, I can't explain that because I don't understand it, so it left me quite distressed, partly because I had wanted to do that, I don't know how to describe the feelings or the state I was in when I first went to Versailles and then when I went to the concierge, my going was to have a practice run at things. I had hoped that I could close the circle, if that is possible, but if I close that door I am actually shutting off some episode some connection, because these thoughts don't go away they stay with me. If I say it's against my will, maybe that's the issue, and if it's against my will I cannot close those circles because they are not ready to close and maybe they never will be, and I've never known this. It's coming to me as I'm sitting here talking about it, and it makes no sense but it does, it's patterns that are new to me, although I have been doing this for some time now every step I take brings a new understanding an occurrence that takes me down my road. I can shut the box on those other selves, close it off, my unconscious stuff. In my conscious state I wanted to be able to close it down, to stop the images coming, the unconscious would not let me do it, so when I relax those thoughts come unbidden as do the scenes in my head, and they are as real as going to the kitchen to make myself a cup of tea. So the hope of closing the circle is not possible. This other life can't be shut off because its part of me.

We have a discussion here and I explain that therapists who deal with past-life regression attempt to close off a life at the point of death, in order to finish any business that has been left undone.

Jan goes on to say that she doesn't know what therapists normally do but :

I can only speak for myself, but to close a life, doesn't work for me, it would feel like closing off a chunk of myself. Moving on from work we have done before, to have opened it means to know it, can't be unknown. If I know I have been these people, then I've been these people. I don't know because I have not spoken to anyone who has done this work but past lives have explained how I am today, each piece has led me on to something different and seeing things in a different way I think that I have to learn to embrace that fear and look upon it face on, because it's part of me my process and makes other things possible I think it's tied into my ability to actually feel a range of feelings so its all part of the total ME. The deep seated fear, when I feel it, actually tells me when I'm "out of step with myself", and I think It's about some of the things that I have run through to avoid. It's about justice and injustice and I don't know what I'm saying here, I believe it serves a purpose, not the whole purpose, I still don't understand it. When I think about fear what I see is black rocks, black sea, dank, dark, dangerous and I really don't know what's caught up in here, it's like the "holding place", I really can't explain what it feels like. There's a residue left of enormous terror from the past and it does seem to be associated with the lives I've spoken about, here and there, feels like a memory, deeply embedded in me, may not have a purpose, maybe it's just a memory, memories it certainly is. In the beginning it was feeling without a memory, now the memories go with it, with the depth of feeling that's for sure, that much is clear.

I had told Jan to phone a colleague of mine a fellow therapist if she needed to talk when she got back from Versailles.

CHAPTER 21

RETURN TO ENGLAND

Jan and I meet once more face to face:

I phoned Anne when I got back from Versailles not knowing how to cope with all the feelings. I told her about the figure that I have been aware of, the figure of my father when I was a young man working in the Tower, patting my shoulder and he's still here it's good and beneficial when he pats my shoulder, a very peculiar kind of anchoring. When he pats my shoulder I feel better ...

(Jan pats her own shoulder to show me how it is)

... as if he's saying "that's not for you my son," it's enough. Anne said something about guardian angels, that was a phrase that she used. I feel quite strange about saying that, because before I started this I wouldn't have given credit to a guardian angel. I'd only had a couple of things in the past with Nan and Dad about three days after he had died came and said it's OK, which is about as much as he would have given me. He wouldn't have given me that sort of comfort that this old sod has given me and I have to think differently now. Where does this leave me now – in a better place I think. I think that these thoughts, sights, visions and feelings are going to stay with me now in this life, bad as it's been it's of value, I can't put a price on this emotional quota, because it's beyond what I have experienced in the past and I've wanted to go with it.

I asked if the images still come?

They still come at night when I am at a low ebb, not always, they can come in the middle of the day, any place, any time. Now I can actually shove them away and say "not now", then I think very powerfully about something today. At other times there is a familiarity because of the other facets of the lives with it, there was a pleasant side and I like that. it was the fear before the deaths but afterwards I've had these wonderful sights, sounds and experiences that have shifted me on beyond that into a place I could not have articulated about if I had not experienced in the past, so it's been gaining such an extra experience that it probably alters the way in which I see myself getting older and endings and actually talking about it to people. I don't have the same sense of doom and gloom – I am careful who I'm talking to. I ask them what they think, it is as it is. I make no attempt to reason, I've suspended reason I don't say I've gone through horrible deaths, scarred but come out the other side joyful. In my intellectual self I would have wanted a beginning, a middle and a conclusion. I think that this has sat with me for years and now only in my 59th year have I been able to speak about this, because you have been able to manage it. It might now enable other people to talk to me. I have had such trouble saying to someone that I think there is something in my past. I experienced death in the most fearful and disgusting way on more than one occasion which leaves me feeling as I am today. they would have had me down to the nearest psychiatrist. The fine line between then and now is a real fear and if my mind thinks things – everything else responds "as if I am". This is how therapy works, if I believe that these past lives existed, are my history and I believe that things must follow through, it's part of my unconscious feeling. I've been talking to people now and they begin to say something and it's obvious that I recognize it now, I don't dismiss anything that people say and if they are having a series of long dreams, I say would you like to talk about them, I handle it in a far more compassionate way because of my experiences, and I can share that.

Jan believes that her own therapy is beginning to show changes in the way that she works with clients. Perhaps we have achieved what "own therapy" is all about, that she can now deal with her own clients, as well as her "self", from a different place. She has faced her different "selves" in different places at different times and faced the same fear and dealt with it.

Jan writes at home:

To Joyce,
When I started the work with you, I had no idea where it would lead. I was in a situation that I could not resolve on my own. My husband had gone to work in another area and I only saw him once a month. I was in deep pain that I could not seem to do anything about. The dreams had increased until I was too scared to close my eyes. I did not feel that I could share the content of those dreams, they were too dreadful, the location of the fear was in the back of my neck.

It often happens during massage or reflexology that clients have visualizations, or they burst into tears. Many psychologists and therapists believe that pain and suffering is locked into the body as tissue memory like an armour.

It all seemed unrelated to what was actually happening to me. It was by chance that one visualization of a place I wanted to be turned into something beyond my comprehension. I was in Versailles sitting on the edge of one of the fountains. It was me. I looked down, and my shoes had changed, so had my skirts, my hair, my age, it was me. There was a wind in the trees and a sense of impending doom. The atmosphere changed, and I felt fear in my heart. The noise that then occurred was a howling mob who were filthy and foul smelling. I was terrified and stayed that way until my death on the guillotine two years later. I was so young and innocent of any crime other than being who I was and where I was. I was at the start of an unravelling that, which has no equal in my experience. I cannot explain the images or the places I have seen.

Although crypto-amnesia can never be totally ruled out Jan still refutes this theory.

I have never read anything of this nature. What has come to me has come to me. I had no special insight, it has never happened before. I have had dreams since I was small, but they have never linked or been so much part of my waking days. The people who I AM or HAVE BEEN are in a stream of consciousness that makes no sense, yet makes every sense.

CHAPTER 22

MOVING ON

Bad as it was, blades, axes, what I have come up with is a completely new view of trauma and come out the other side with no bits missing ... in particular my head.

SESSION 14, 13th July 2002

Jan relates how life has changed since beginning therapy:

This space in this therapy has allowed me to have different choices in my mind. When I first came here, what I thought I was bringing was a huge amount of fear in my life. It was greater than I felt I could manage. I had no idea where it was about to go, so you were offering me different tools to explore with, to work with, and what happened, happened which is the relevance of it, because nothing else had touched it before. Therefore I'm saying that this gave me the a choice, a chance to work with my fears about death, pain and destruction in a completely different way and I'm choosing to stay with the fear and move through it into a completely different state which was completely unlike anything I had envisaged or experienced before. It was work that was pertinent to me and me alone as part of my historical memory somehow. Although I'm walking around today I've walked around before. So the choices you gave me, were to go and experience, and some of it was very uncomfortable and some of it was bloody hard to do, but I had the choice to do it and its as if in this life I have a real choice to go beyond my fear and because in a past life, I've been able to go beyond the fear into a different state I can do it now in this life, and that feels very real and very appropriate. What I have come up with, is a completely different view of how it can be to go through trauma and come out at the other side in one piece, actually with no bits missing, very relevantly in my head. That's been a revelation, I would say so. My aims are very different now, that's to say I am far more available now, I would say that this has added a different dimension to my work. I hesitate to say spiritual, but it's certainly added a different feel around me, it has strengthened my ability to speak out when I think that clients are not being particularly well treated.

(Jan is a trainer and supervisor.)

Hasn't made me terribly popular but it has sharpened things up a lot, it really has.

*I've put my job on the line, really I'm looking at things in a different way. It's always been there, but I don't think I have quite had the courage to speak about it – too scared of losing my job, my popularity, losing my sanity or thinking what do I know? But I'm thinking now after seventeen years – maybe I might just know something about people, about practice, about quality of work and to say NO to certain things I have been asked to do with clients because it's not in their best interests, and ended up in a confrontational situation with my manager. But I'm convinced that I am right so I'm sticking with it and if I'm found to be wrong then it's not the place I want to work, because I do believe the practice and code of ethics might as well be thrown out. I've slowed down, I think more, I know that I have changed because of what we have done here. My duty of care is even greater than it has been, and because I've got all these trainees, I'm passing this on, the way I want them to be with my clients. They don't always agree with me, but that's fine, but there's a dialogue there now – what do you think? What did you see? What did you visualize? And it's changed my life completely, it's like the whole counselling scene – I know that the lives that I touch – I'm a good couples counsellor, I get all sorts happening but I think individual work I might do a lot more of it because I'm in a better place. It's obvious that there is something there and I've begun to recognize it now and it's possible that they recognize it in me. I don't dismiss anything now, I suppose before in a way I would have been very scared of being labelled crackers, mad, bizarre, odd – because I'm not, I think that I am in very good company really, people are too scared to speak about anything that moves outside of what is comfortable – because **this is not reality but it is – and it is reality to me.** I'm looking forward to my next year being very different to the last one. But individual work – the depth of it has changed, and ethically I'm aware I can't offer in depth until I have more time. But what I have done has been beneficial, but it does mean that I'm looking from a different perspective – if it happened I would deal with it. It's brilliant and I think and feel that I would like to learn more. Images still come at night when I am at a low ebb, not always, can be in the middle of the day, any place, anywhere. Now, I can actually shove them away, think not now, think very powerfully about something today. At other times there was a pleasant side. It was the fear before deaths, but afterwards I've had these wonderful experiences. So I have seen the fear in a different way. As it is, is as it is, no attempt to reason, I've suspended reason, intellectual self, start, middle and conclusion. The fine line between the then and the now is a real fear, the mind has got to be the most amazing thing. If my mind thinks things, everything else responds "as if I am". This is how therapy works. If I believe that those past lives existed, my history, I believe things must follow through, part of my unconscious feeling. When I first came the fear was greater than I could cope with, so the relevance that therapy* *gave to me was CHOICE to work with it or not, to work with my fears about death, horror, pain, some of it was blindingly hard to do. My choice was to stay with it, which was completely different, the work belonged to me. Choice is to go beyond fear, into a new state of being and I can do it in this life too. Bad as it was, blades, axes, what I have come up with is a completely new view of trauma and come out the other side with no bits missing ... in particular my head. Therapy has added a different feel around me, strengthened my ability, and determination to speak out.*

Jan says that "this is not reality, yet it is!" It is her reality.

So! What is reality?

Realism as a philosophical term refers to the doctrine that objects exist independently of sensory experience, however, others will continue to argue that nothing exists until it is observed.

It is a well-documented fact that for ordinary people we do need to verify what we see, hear and touch is REAL. We ask others if they see what we see, or hear what we hear. We also know from psychological experiments throughout the years that some individuals can be persuaded that what they see is not a fact, if enough people tell them that it is not. What seems real to each of us is very important to our sense of comfort and security, we would not want to be thought mad at worst, stupid and lacking at best. A psychologist named Soloman Asch many years ago designed experiments where groups of people were shown a simple card with three lines on it and asked subjects to choose the shortest or longest line of the three. This was easy when people were asked as individuals. However, when in league with the psychologist, everyone in the group would choose the wrong line even though it could be seen to be wrong, almost every person who knew perfectly well the right answer, would agree with the group. We obviously need to conform to what the group says is right, REAL or true. This was confirmed later in the Milgram experiments, which showed that people are more likely to conform to someone who is an authority figure, and they would give electric shocks to other subjects because they were told to by a psychologist. Even against their own better judgement, knowing it was wrong, knowing it was painful, they would do as they were told. Most people then, conform to what we come to define as "group norms", and even more so, to those in authority as to what is real and what is not? So it is true that therapists can if they wish distort reality for a client. A reliable therapist however will not do that, they may ask the client if they can imagine another reality – but that is not the same as putting thoughts into their head.

In the first quarter of the twentieth century, two mind-stretching theories were proposed, the theory of relativity and quantum theory. From these came most of twentieth-century physics, which revealed more far-reaching conclusions than just a better model of the physical world. However, physicists realized that their discoveries now demanded a radical reformulation of the fundamental aspects of reality. They had to learn new approaches to their subject matter in totally novel and unexpected ways, which seemed to turn common sense on its head and find that what was real was more akin to mysticism than materialism.

Now, today, after all the surmising and theorizing, many scientists are shifting their stance towards what is real, and embracing such theories as the relationship between internal vibrations, oscillating membranes, and the external waves of sound and light. Each object or element in nature apparently has a particular rate of vibration and the art is to tune in through the correct sound through meditation or prayer to align with the cosmic force.

Eastern philosophy has always assumed this to be true, even before the research into quantum physics, and astrologers have always thought that each individual resonates to his or her particular pattern of harmonics, established at the moment of birth with the universe.

So nothing is new! Scientists today are perhaps only just finding out what philosophers, eastern mystics, and astrologers instinctively always knew and understood. Paul Davies, in his book *God and the New Physics*, states that scientists just like philosophers are interested in the deep questions of existence, they want to find meaning in life, the nature of life and consciousness. He claims that physicists theorize about the self-creating universe and a cosmos that erupts spontaneously like a sub-nuclear particle which pops up from nowhere in certain high energy processes. He wonders if modern physics has abolished God when we can conceive a scientific explanation for all of creation. I think not! It may rule out the idea of God as Creator, but it does not rule out a universal intelligent mind existing as part of the unique physical universe.

Teilhard de Chardin, many years ago, proposed that evolution is directed according to a pre-existing plan, shaped to converge on a yet to be achieved superior final stage which he called the Omega point – communion with GOD. Hermetic Astrology proposes a similar theory as does the theory of Reincarnation. Danah Zohar (1990/91) argues against any parallels between quantum physics and eastern mysticism, but I disagree. I believe that any parallels found can be just one more example of different perspectives, two different descriptions of the same reality and both contribute to the "whole" picture.

IF there is a grand plan, and a universal consciousness does make its slow progress over thousands of years, I would argue that, it is BECAUSE of the interaction with individual consciousness. The new physics has given the observer an integral role in the nature of physical reality and physicists have over many years now been faced with compelling experimental evidence towards this view. This principle begs a complete and fundamental re-appraisal of the nature of reality and the relationship of the part and the whole. Perhaps it means that the concept of life is only meaningful in the context of the entire biosphere. People as living organisms are active matter, and life itself is characterized by a whole host of unusual properties such as complexity which is organized and harmonized by a network of feedback mechanisms and controls at every level and between levels, which propel us to decide to pursue a purpose.

Scientists now know that life began much earlier than we thought and can survive and adapt in the most extreme environments. One theory states that at the beginning of time, in the primeval phase of the universe, there began a cascade of self-organizing processes triggered by gravity, that led eventually to us, these conscious individuals with brains and minds who search the universe with our telescopes and planetary probes. Not only do we search to understand the physical universe, we contemplate the cosmos and wonder who we are, where we came from and where we are going to.

What I think is important is what is REAL and meaningful to the INDIVIDUAL. Emmanuel Kant appeared in his day to take the pessimistic pole of reality research that we can never know reality, which is of no concern to the ordinary man and woman. The optimistic researchers however, maintain that as human beings are part of nature, nothing prevents us from experiencing or conceptualizing reality itself.

But HOW do we do this? It seems that from the evidence presented, that in the end event we are pre-programmed to know more than we do at the present moment in time, and it is only the limitations of the human brain and central nervous system in its present state that holds us back. In exceptional circumstances, such as life threatening trauma, electric shock or injury to the brain, some of the limitations are removed and extra-sensory perception and psychic ability appear. If the main purpose of science is to go beyond fact to the reality underneath, then, like any other human enterprise the practice of science requires a constantly shifting balance as ever new evidence comes to light. There is evidence now to show that brains normally respond only to duality and contrast, that is how we learn to discriminate between one thing and another. Unfortunately classification and discrimination has a negative side which leads to prejudice and exclusion.

If reality, like beauty, is in the eye of the beholder, it is the individual's own unique reality. It does then of necessity acquire the characteristics and learning of the person, which means that its greatest asset is that it can change over time.

I have obviously become more philosophical as well as sociological and psychological in my attempt to create a synthesis of Neuroscience, Neuro-Linguistic Programming, Ericksonian Hypnosis, Eastern Philosophy, Astrology and Quantum Physics. **All this in order to suggest that spontaneous Past-Life experiences like Jan's, might be a soul experience and could be part of a human consciousness that interacts with a universal consciousness by a quantum leap rather than by the slow progress of meditation or induced trance.**

There are many books about past-life experiences, mainly descriptive, and many books about reincarnation, some descriptive, and others, which offer some kind of research evidence, but which still contain many contradictions. A quantum leap, to show a continuous series of lives where matter only changes form, and birth and death are a cyclic process is a different concept altogether.

From both first-hand experience and first-hand witness I have come to the conclusion that a spontaneous past-life experience is not the same as, or even similar to, visualization in what we call a "trance state". It is different in depth and subjective involvement, you are not watching, you are there, it is "a quantum leap" of MEMORY into a different body, in different clothes, in a different time, but it is still the essence of the self that you know and recognize. When something is only the object of our thinking and seeing, it is outside the self, whereas direct involvement seems to create a very different interaction. When someone experiences a spontaneous past life, enlightenment can come in a flash, it is a quantum leap that changes sensation and perception. The caterpillar becomes the butterfly in an instant and transformation can be instantaneous. Some people search for years for what happens in one session of a past life experience, and I have come to see them like the Moebius strip where Past and Present are one.

CHAPTER 23

REFLECTIONS

Jan writes near the end of therapy :

It's four o'clock in the morning and I wake to know that my life today is free because of the experiences I have had the privilege and pain to work with. I could not have held those on my own and I would never have known the sure and certain hope of life after death without your ability to keep me safe when I felt I was at such risk. I constantly see myself sitting in the chair, bathed in the golden light with that dreadful scar around my neck, whole, complete, and redeemed. That life ended before it had run its course, unfair, unjust. I know my name now Gianetta, I can identify now that for me what happens is not about fine details, and only a few facts feel certain. It's about a compelling intensity that was magnificent but deeply disturbing at the start as it was so far away from when I first entered therapy.

From my own experiences in Psychology and Psychotherapy, it might be thought somewhat strange that religious experiences can come through the stimulation of the temporal lobes and that "truth" may be revealed through the limbic emotional centres, rather than the rational logical thinking part. Ramachandran wonders if repeated and frequent electrical bursts such as those that come from seizures, or from external situations, can somehow permanently facilitate certain pathways or even open new channels by a process called "kindling" to enrich a person's emotional life (see the kindling hypothesis in Phantoms of the Brain).

Jan is still bewildered by the memories flooding in, both inside and outside the therapy room, she is scared, yet fully aware of what is happening. She is experiencing two selves and yet she is conscious of being a complete "self" in three very different times. Another patient of Ramachandran described "flashbacks" after experiencing a seizure, when he could recall every small detail of a book read years before. He could remember every line, every page, every word. Perhaps when Jan began to have her flashbacks this is what happened, she remembered word for word some previous thought patterns, behaviours and events, not brought about by a seizure, but the stimulation of the brain through visualization and hearing. We have always learned about "normal" functioning in the central nervous system through work on abnormal patterns of behaviour and "split brain" patients, such as is elicited through trauma or accident. So if the stimulation of electrical circuits in the brain can result in certain patterns of visualization, audition and feeling, can we be pre-programmed to know the purpose of life on earth, but have not yet recognized or acknowledged it?

Once more Zohar maintains that on a quantum view of the self there can be no distinction between one's own past and that of another with whom one has been intimate. She says that there are always elements of others present, after closeness has been a part of our being. Once more she draws again on the basis of the wave/particle duality to explain her theory that the quantum self is both a self in its own right, with all its sub-selves, but also as a self with others through what a psychotherapist terms "empathy". Everything is energy and dynamics and can be understood in terms of the physics of the self. Zohar suggests that the unusual orderly quality of our human attention through our five senses considerably limits a choice of physical explanations because of its rarity in other dynamic systems. It does exist, however in some materials, which exist in "condensed phases". She makes the comparison with a number of electromagnets lying on a table in a shielded room, and because the room is shielded the magnets all swing randomly in any direction when the table is jiggled. However, when the electromagnetic energy in each compass is increased, the needles exert a "pull" on each other and slowly line up in an orderly pattern. She would then explain this phenomenon by saying that the needles have gone into a condensed phase. It might then be possible she feels, that a "pumped system", first described by a Professor Herbert Frolich (cited in Zohar pp. 65–67), and known to exist in biological tissue could take place in human brains. Frolich in his experiments demonstrated that beyond a certain threshold, any additional energy pumped into a system causes molecules to vibrate in unison. Then if they do this increasingly, eventually they can pull themselves into the most ordered form of condensed phase possible, a Bose–Einstein condensate.

I believe that it might be possible that the brain works in this way to take all the random input of sensory material, and when it reaches a particular threshold the random input becomes a "whole" of creative thoughts and ideas. Could the Bose–Einstein condensate explain how the state of consciousness arises in individuals and then, how eventually through learning, the other computer-like manifestations of the brain, thoughts, become orderly, logical and rational? This may go some way to explain consciousness in this life, but can it explain how consciousness is re-incarnated as memories of past lives?

SESSION 15, 19th July 2002

Jan sits down and begins to pat her shoulder as she tells me that there is more to be confronted today. I ask her to keep patting her shoulder and see what happens.

Transcript:
It leads me into to a place where I was very upset ...

131

I ask her to stay with it until it changes, be sensitive and aware of the changes.
Jan shudders, sighs deeply
That's good, just have the courage to stay there, Jan sighs loudly,
Stay with the feeling until it changes

I think it's a feeling that goes back a very long way ... and I'm confused as to where it comes from ... but when that happens it's like I'm jettisoned back to that first person that I thought was me ... and the fear that was there at that time ... I don't know how this can be ... and my father's there doing all this to me and saying "there, there ... there, there" ... he's saying, "you'll be all right it's not for you" ... dying ... it goes back to the fear of having my head chopped off ... that's where it all comes from ... I don't understand it ... I don't understand it ... it starts here to here (Jan points to her stomach and shoulder) *like something is churning in my guts and then somehow it gets to here* (shoulder) *and ... it's like calm down ... calm down ... calm down ...*

So the shoulder tapping is a calm down?

Yes!

And when you stay with the tapping how do the feelings change?

I wanted to breathe something out ... to get rid of something ... pushing fear out of me ... (Jan demonstrated) ... like something I can push out ... push that out of me ... is like relief ... yes ... yes ... because it feels different ... but I have to do something ritualistic ... do something that acknowledges that I'm terrified ... out of my wits ... that I can somehow breathe to get rid of it ...

And can you?

It seems that I can ...

So when you breathe you calm down and feel better?

It's like taking in life ... it felt like taking in life ... .breathe because I want life ... I don't want death ... I want life ...

How can you do that? How can you get life?

When I'm fearful into death ... this is where I am ... like this ... when I breathe something else happens and I can open my eyes ...

What happens that you can open your eyes?

There's a feeling that comes over me that I'm not alone ... I'm not alone ... the memory of it is powerful ... the comforting is powerful ... that strengthens me ... like any soothing can take comfort from it ... like any soothing ...

And the feeling tells you that you are not alone?

The connection tells me that I am not alone. It's my hand but the memory is of him.

Your father?

Yes ... it's been the same ever since we did this.

Not just your father in this life?

No not this one ... not this one at all ...

So the father in France or London?

The father when I was a boy in the Tower ... the father ... the dad in France was away a lot ... it was the father in London ... it's very powerful ... very powerful ... but it doesn't belong to today ... it's unfair but it's here now and it's a heavy-handed thing (Jan slaps herself) *like it's reliable ... somehow.*

Like an anchor?

Yes it has felt like that ... well I suppose that sometimes I'm aware I feel like saying well here you are again ... like I'm still here and he's still here ...

He's still with you?

My dad's still with me since we have been doing this work and I can call on it and use it ... and that's the feeling that carves me to the soul ... not just to the stomach ... it's the other part of me ... that's how it feels ...

How long in this life have you been doing it?

I did it to my kids ... I haven't done it to me before ... but I do it to my children ... always have ...

When did it start?

When they were tiny.

When did it start that you did it to yourself?

Since I've been doing this work ... since I have been working here ... I felt nothing before ... this is to do with what has opened up ... and for me he was there it's tied into dreams from a very long time ago ... but it's never been as clear as it has been since I have been talking here ... because before in mind's eye ... I used to see the family group ... but this goes back years and it was always the Tower... .on the green in the sunshine ... most bizarre family who were normal in an un-normal place ... and my dreams processed that and I never encouraged it then ... at all because I hated them ... but they have been there for years ... but this other figure has just come it's almost as if one day he just walked up to me and at the time that it happened I was absolutely terrified ... he came to me and I thought Christ ... I'm finished here ... I remember it very clearly because of the garb ... and then it was slap ... slap ... there you are my son ... and I just knew that he wasn't bad for me ... a wicked man in some terms but ... a good father to me ... maybe just doing a job he had to do ... doesn't make him wicked ... no ... no ... because I think the kindness he showed to me although it was very clumsy and rough ... it was undeniably there ... my mother was around ... but it wasn't her ... it was him ... and I do find it very strange when I'm talking about it ... it's just like somebody has been calling to me from way back in time ... and here it is today and I see him as clear as day ... he's a lovely old sod ... short and very strong ... very solid somehow in a way that I wasn't I was skinny and pale ... not at all you would think out of the same ... that's what it was and I was about to say ... more like a girl to him ... rather than a boy ... but I was a boy and I followed in his trade ... I did his bidding ... because I wanted him to think well of me ... because he was kind and he did care ... and in the end ... what happened ... happened because of my conscience ... but this is like heavy ... warm ... reliable and it touches me far beyond a touch ... I think it touches me in a way that no other touch can ...

So you are not alone?

No it seems not ...

There is someone there who believes and comforts you?

Absolutely ... but I'm sitting here thinking ... crackers ... because this is a way beyond an imaginary friend ...

Perhaps there are more things in heaven and earth than we know about.

I think so ... I think so ... and I've got to believe it.

And there is something remarkable about that life where you were a boy but more like a girl and in this life where you come as a girl and a boy was wanted.

That's right ... bizarre ... and although my mother was there ... but not there ... yet at that time he was there for me ...

So that takes away the feeling of fear?

Yes ... it's obvious that if I can do this it will ...

It's what we call an anchor, it is an anchor isn't it?

Yes it is.

It changes a feeling?

It certainly does ... interesting that ... .and I think I need to use it more than I have allowed myself to do ... actually ... well he obviously stands as some kind of guardian in my mind ... either in this century or the last ... whatever ... he is there maybe forever ...

Maybe wherever you are or wherever you go he can be there for you.

He's never failed me so far

So you don't need any other anchor do you?

I think it will stand me in good stead ...

And it's not a manufactured anchor, it's one that came spontaneously.

It belongs to me ... it absolutely does and I can call it up now very quickly ... all of it has happened very quickly and as soon as I do that all this stuff comes rushing in ...

Really, then when you do it again and something else happens ...

Yes ... it's been a surprising journey hasn't it? Well it has to me ...

So what are your conclusions about this bizarre journey that we have travelled?

I think it's been like rolling back the times ... I'm sitting here thinking it's like all these waves of time ... waves and waves of time ... have just gone rolling back ... so accessible ... it seems ...

But when you first came and said I don't believe in past lives, so is it metaphor? Or the brain sorting out problems, what do you think it is?

I actually think it's more ... but with an element of metaphor ... in it ... and there has got to be something about the storyline ... in it ... I can't have any other view except that it's got to have been there ... I don't think it could have happened as it did if it had not been there.

So what are you saying now, that you are not using metaphors?

It doesn't feel like it ... I could have found an easier way ... it doesn't feel like I'm using metaphor.

The other explanation was the brain sorting things out.

Could have found a simpler way – I do believe in them ... yes I believe in them.

So believing that have you changed your mind?

Yes ... and it changes my life in that I know that this life is not the only life ... and I know that when I go beyond this ... it's not the end of anything ... this is just a temporary stop here ... I've had a few temporary stops and this will be just another one ... I think it's taught me about the fear I've felt before through this life ... I come back and know that I can go beyond the fear ... and it's really been that more than anything I think that I've gone through here.

And what do you think now in the therapeutic situation, about taking something that someone does, feels or says, and asking them to stay with it until the feeling changes?

I think it's spot on ... I think it's accurately right ...

The feeling does change?

Yes it does no doubt about it ... no ... no ... and if I ever got to that I would be encouraging people to stay with the feelings and gestures ... because they are obviously unconsciously and intrinsically linked to whatever is in there ...

because it's without guile it's without thought ... it accesses things that other methods don't touch.

Here I explained the theory behind both Ernest Rossi's work and Roger Woolger's way of working.

I know that I have sat here and felt it change ... I know that when I wake in the middle of the night and I've got all this ... that I can do this ... (Jan taps her shoulder) I will overcome it ... and I can say that I have done it ...

You will find a resolution?

Yes ... and it's the most reliable anchor I could have hoped for ... really because that will stay with me now for the rest of my life ... mmmm ...

We discussed how what Jan had unconsciously done to comfort her own children, she had pulled from her memory something that she had found comforting.

I think that's a revelation ... it feels like a very significant piece of work ...

Jan may still be using some metaphor because metaphors communicate indirectly. Simple metaphors make simple comparisons like white as a sheet, black as night, but complex metaphors can be stories with many levels of meaning. Metaphors are inner world process information and the plot will match the person's psychological experience. They are also what we call reframing devices e.g., It could mean this or that! Which is where Jan began these sessions.

Neuro-Linguistic Programming (NLP) is a mixture of Art and Science. It is an art because it has to be tailored to a unique personality and it is a science because it is a method and process for discovering patterns. In NLP terms an anchor is any stimulus which is linked to and can trigger a particular physiological state. An anchor is anything that accesses an emotional state, it can be visual, auditory or kinaesthetic, and either negative or positive. It appears that Jan has been responding to negative states through what she sees and hears whilst dreaming and in the trance state whereby she accesses the past-life experiences. Jan has conjured up many images that appear to be anchors from the past. The kinaesthetic anchor that she has now discovered for herself in patting her shoulder elicits a feeling of "there, there, it's all right, relax". It takes away the fear, calms her down and puts her back in control. Our minds naturally link experiences, that is the way we give meaning to what we do. A red light means STOP if we are drivers. The word POISON on a bottle of liquid stops us from drinking it. Words and pictures have a pervasive influence on our thinking and behaviour and they are always linked to our emotions because our emotions or "gut" feelings tell us what seems right and what seems wrong.

CHAPTER 24

REINCARNATION – THE PROGRESS OF A SOUL

For many years the subjects of reality and consciousness in eastern philosophy has started from quite a different perspective to western thought, for them incarnations, and therefore conscious individuals, are for God to know himself and reincarnation is a vehicle for the evolution of the spirit. Hinduism believes that all matter is a manifestation of spiritual reality. Consciousness for them is immanent within form! Hindu's believe that reincarnation is the prison of eternal return from which wise men seek deliverance, but that the moment of enlightenment may come at any point in the endless circle. (Jan talks about completing the circle.) Although Carl Gustaf Jung was very wary during his lifetime of any mention of reincarnation, he did apparently remark at one time "I could imagine that I have lived in other centuries". Yet he certainly worked along the lines of Hermetic thought as he advocated "as above so below".

Roger Woolger (1987) was to suggest that we could build on Jung's concepts of the complex and archetypes. A complex is defined as being a collection of associated ideas or beliefs. Archetypes consist of individual predispositions towards special talents, personality traits and even predispositions to certain diseases. Jung calls them archetypes because according to him they have been moulding all life on the planet since the beginning of time.

What Jung calls archetypes, astrologers call zodiacal signs because of the way in which they manifest in personality types. Because of this belief, Jungian psychology has been the basis of some modern-day astrology and personality testing. As well as individual dispositions, Jung believed that all human beings share a common set of motivational and behavioural patterns carried over from generation to generation, and these are part of our evolutionary heritage. He further believed that these could sometimes be detected in dreams from the collective unconscious. Roger Woolger, even though refuting reincarnation as a fact, still proposed that there might even be a third term, "the past life complex", or "samskara" as adapted from Hindu psychology. Samskara is a Sanskrit term for the dispositions, propensities or tendencies to act according to certain patterns established in the past, repeating those patterns again and again.

In Yoga theory, a samskara can carry over from lifetime to lifetime and therefore can be regarded as a past-life complex, whereby a disposition can be equated with a memory. Edgar Cayce states that reincarnation is not a theory, but a practical code of ethics which directly affects human morality. From his readings where he categorically states that reincarnation is a fact, he insists that Karma is memory, and that positive and negative conduct in earlier lives actively affects behaviour patterns in the present.

If Cayce is right it follows that the underlying theory is one of mankind moving towards perfection and the "at-one-ment" (atonement) with God in the fullness of time. Karma is defined as the moral law of cause and effect in some religions, but it is man himself who creates cause and effect. Karma is the universal law of harmony, which unerringly restores all disturbance to equilibrium, applied to man, in one life he sows, in another he reaps. According to some researchers Karma is a beneficent merciful law relentlessly just – not favour, but impartial justice. The Buddha explained that "Karma is the heart of love, the end of which is peace and consummation sweet". Reincarnation therefore, cannot be considered as equating with progress, only the opportunity for progress, we human beings have CHOICE. The idea of Karma for Hindus commits them to complete personal responsibility, which also brings about social control. For them, to locate the source of an individual's difficulties outside themselves is immature.

Edgar Cayce also maintained that the subconscious mind does remember its past-life experiences, but that there is a very good reason why the conscious mind is spared this dubious privilege. After much pain and "soul searching" as a devout and practising Christian he came to believe in reincarnation through his channelled experiences. He said that we could liken the lives of the soul to the instalments in a serialized novel, as the body dies at the end of a life, "to be continued" is added in small print to that instalment. He furthermore maintained that when you appear in the next life you pick up where you left off. This does tend to suggest that Mind is something more than Brain! And the consciousness of mind and brain is just a part of a larger whole? Hermetic research into reincarnation maintains that the angular relationship between the Sun and Saturn at birth is the same as the point of death in a previous life.

If there is such a thing as reincarnation, but we are not meant to remember past lives, then the birth process itself might provide the answer. Animal researchers maintain that when animals are given the hormone oxytocin, they develop amnesia and cannot remember tasks they had learned previously (cited in Ostrander& Shroeder). During human birth, the hormone oxytocin is produced in the mother's body to control the rate of labour contractions, so past lives, if they exist might be forgotten. If, labour contractions are not well controlled, with oxytocin in short supply, perhaps this might explain why some very young children are able to remember past lives vividly and accurately. There has been much research to suggest that some of these have been verified as true in spite of the fact that many have also been found to be untrue.

The most intensive research has been done over many years by Dr Ian Stevenson, a leading scientific investigator in this field. (cited in

Reincarnation The Phoenix Fire Mystery, 1977/1979). He records one verified account, the story of a woman who had a sister some fifteen years younger than her, this child from a very early age would tell herself fairy stories. The elder sister kept a diary of the stories, and was amazed that these stories contained specific knowledge that a baby could not possibly have absorbed in any sort of way. Everything the young child did she seemed to do from habit it was not learned in this life. She would lift her mug of milk with what she called a "roistering air" from the age of three years, and gulp it down in one fell swoop. The child's mother would reprimand the child for doing this, but the child's reply was always "I can't help it, I've always done it that way". One day in all innocence the child told her father that she had been here on earth many times sometimes as a man sometimes as a woman. Her father laughed, which made the child very angry, as she protested that it was true. She went on to tell a story about the fact that she once went to Canada and she even remembered her name. So, what was your name that you remember so well? asked her father? "It was Lishus Faber," the little girl replied, at least that's how it sounded. "I took the Gates," she pronounced triumphantly! No-one understood what the child meant by this odd phrase. The child's sister began to study the history of Canada to no avail, until she was directed to a very old manuscript by a librarian, this was a documentary of history written in old fashioned script. In it was a brief account of the taking of a little walled city by a small company of soldiers. A young lieutenant it stated named Alysuis Le Febre, with his small band of men "took the gates".

Another story was told by a British Psychiatrist, about a patient who had persistent nightmares which had occurred regularly since she was small just like Jan. She appeared to be a perfectly sane ordinary housewife. She told the psychiatrist that when she was a girl she had written the dreams down and other things that "just came into her head", things about people that she could not understand. When the papers were examined the psychiatrist found verses in medieval French – a subject that she had never heard or studied. The writings were sent to a professor at Toulouse University in France who said that they were accurate accounts of the Cathars, a group of people in the thirteenth century. The child had told of the massacre of the Cathars, and told in horrific detail of being burned at the stake. She also said that in a previous life she had been imprisoned in a certain church crypt. In 1967 in an investigation of these facts it was found that everything she had said was accurate in every detail. Some of the songs that she had written as a child were found in the archives, correct word for word. So much for cryptomania!

One more story recorded by Stevenson was about a five-year-old boy, whose mother noticed him uttering strange sounds. At that time she thought that they were just the unintelligible sounds left over from babyhood. However, as time went on and the child could speak fluently, she thought it extremely odd that he continued to utter these strange sounds. A friend asked if she could listen to the child and was convinced that he was speaking real words. The child was not in the least inhibited by listeners, so eventually the friend brought a Professor of Asiatic languages to listen to these strange conversations. He told the mother that the words were from a language and dialect used in Northern Tibet and asked if any of the child's family had ever been there? The answer was no, so the Professor asked the child himself where he had learned the words. The child said in school, but the child had never been to any school. "When I went to school before," he said. When asked to describe the school the child said it was in the mountains, but not like the mountains we went to see in the summer though. The teachers were all men but they didn't dress like Daddy, they had skirts with a sash-like rope. The Professor was so impressed that he went to Northern Tibet, found the school in the Kuenburn mountains and everything the child had said was correct, even the dress of the lamas (priests) who taught there. So much for Xenoglossy!

Many years ago my colleague and I used to run a meditation group every week and one of our group told us about his daughter then aged about three-years old. The child and her father were playing a game, when suddenly the child asked if they could play it the way in which they used to do before? When asked, "when did we play the game before?" the child replied "you know – when I was the mummy and you were my little boy!"

One story that for me does defy disbelief is that of a lady called Dorothy Eady. She knew that not many people would believe her story so she confided only in two close friends who collaborated in writing a book taken from her secret diaries *The Search for Omm Sety*. By Dr Hanny el Zeini & Jonathan Cott (cited in Stemmen).

Visitors in the 1970s to Abydos, one of Egypt's most important archaeological sites, were shown round the temple by an English woman called Dorothy Eady. This woman seemed to have an immense knowledge of both the place, and the man who built it. Thought to be something of an eccentric she offered insights into the daily lives of the Egyptians of the time that surprised not only the visitors, but even the experts in Egyptology. As a child when she was three-years old, she was declared dead, after falling down a flight of steps. Soon after this accident she began to have recurring dreams and was frequently found weeping. When her parents asked why she was crying she told them that she wanted "to go home". There was apparently nothing to explain her love of everything Egyptian, but when she was taken to the British Museum, at the age of four, she was delighted. She refused to go when it was time to leave, kicking and screaming she was carried from the museum shouting "leave me these are my people". When she was seven Dorothy saw pictures in a magazine of the Temple of Sety at Abydos, She told her father excitedly, "This is my home, this is where I lived ... but why is it all broken and where is the garden?" She was, like so many other children, scolded for telling lies, but many years later during some restoration work to the temple, workmen found her garden exactly where she had said it was.

Dorothy believed that she and Pharaoh Sety 1 had been lovers when she had been a virgin priestess of Isis. They met in private because she was temple property and no-one was supposed to touch her, not even the Pharaoh. Because this was crime punishable by public death, Bentreshyt as she was known, committed suicide rather than reveal her lover's name. In the 1950s Dorothy got a transfer to Abydos from Cairo and she became known as Omm Sety where she lived and eventually died. She is buried close to the Temple where she clamed to have died once before as Bentreshyt. Critics say that this story begs more questions than it answers, but it is an intriguing tale well worth reading in more detail.

There is evidence for the Buddhist explanation and belief, on account of the way in which the Dalai Lama is always found, and where memory plays the most important part. In Tibet, many years ago, a group of old men went to a house where a two-year-old boy was playing. The boy ran to the eldest member of the group touched his prayer beads and said, "I would like to have those". He was told that he could have the beads if he could guess who the man was. "You are the lama from Sera Monastery," the boy said., and then he was asked, "who is the master of the monastery" The boy correctly replied that it was "Losang". The men returned, again and again to question the boy and observe him, until eventually the man revealed that he was indeed the lama. The child is said to have passed all the tests to confirm that he was the fourteenth Dalai Lama. It is further claimed that the last Dalai Lama had left indications of where and when he would be re-born and to which parents. The little boy ascended the throne of Tibet in 1940 as the latest incarnation of the line of Tibetan spiritual leaders dating back to the year 1391. Cell memory perhaps?

Jan seemed to see her incarnation, if it indeed is, in this life as both punishment and a great learning experience. She kept talking about reparation and "pliance" which suggest the theory of Karma and being on this earth to learn through our past mistakes and bring balance and peace back to our souls. She sees life as a continuum and death as no "dead end", and Edgar Cayce's *On Reincarnation* cites many dozens of typical cases.

Roy Stemman in his book *Reincarnation – true stories of past lives*, also cites many cases from very well-known people such as General Patton, Air Chief Marshal Lord Dowding, amongst others. However, I did not set out to prove or disprove the theory of reincarnation.

If reincarnation is a fact, what interests me is HOW does it happen? Theories about reincarnation are merely hypotheses, and Hans Ten Dam puts forward from his research some eight hypotheses. There is materialism, which suggests that mind is merely a by-product of body and therefore rejects totally the concept of a soul which is independent of a physical body. For materialists life begins at birth and ends at death. Psychic collectivism, maintains that a mind is temporarily individualized vital energy at birth, and when it separates at death it goes back to the encompassing psychic field by re-absorbing the soul. Psychic transfer, a generic term for the concepts related to Buddhism which suggests that a mind, the psychic patterns and characteristics, goes from the dead to a new born child. Creationism is another theory, whereby a new soul is supposedly produced by GOD at birth. Traducianism which theorizes that a soul can split off from the souls of the parents which then joins around the embryo to form a new soul. Generationism where in very much the same way as Traducianism the theory conceives of a soul produced by the parents who have their own creative power to form a new soul during the sexual act. Pre-existence assumes a previous existence in a world of souls, although where this might be is controversial. Reincarnation which states that human souls incarnate in different times to learn by experience those things that have not been learned in previous lives. It is thought to be in order to fulfil past karma, on the premise of what we sow in one life we will reap in another and harmony in the universe must be balanced.

The materialist hypothesis is a reasonable hypothesis, which all the other hypotheses reject. The alternative hypotheses are all put forward on the basis of near-death experiences and reports of out-of-body experiences, evidence from spiritualist mediums, people who recall birth memories in regression and sometimes the preceding period in the womb and spontaneous past-life recalls. According to Ten Dam, there is little evidence to support the paranormal and much of the spiritualistic material is vague and contradictory.

Perhaps though, there is no need to speak of the paranormal, if brains are part of the energy system of the universe, and are capable of much more than what we call "normal" at this stage of development.

CHAPTER 25

SOME QUESTIONS AND ANSWERS

5th August 2002 last session

The dreams are not happening at the moment ... I still have images ... I don't think that is ever going to change ... but they are all linked to things that I've dreamt about ... .but they don't come at night and I'm not so terrified to shut my eyes as I was before ... and I've accepted them more now as very much a part of who I am ... and if you like what I am ... so there has been an acceptance on my part that those dreams belong to me and they are part of me and that's how I got to where I am now.

I question what she believes has happened?

I believe that there has been a clearing ... and I think it's been an extremely painful and essential clearing about pain and loss ... fear and dread ... from past trauma as well as what I've been experiencing today ... because it was excessive ... I would say it was deeper than I had known so there was a sense of plumbing the depths and then something because of all this happened and it's freed up life to a great extent at this time.

I ask about the feelings of dread and fear?

They were terrifying in their intensity ... almost as if the feelings could kill me never mind anything else.

I ask what has happened to the feelings now?

Because I know that I can handle them in a different way ... I still have the feelings occasionally ... but because of the work that we have done that the feelings belong to the past to the feeling before the death experience not the after death experience and I can see that in my mind's eye.

So you have insight now into where the feelings were coming from and they don't have the same impact on you now?

No they don't ... before I didn't know ... now I do know.

How has therapy changed your beliefs?

I would say that my belief system has changed considerably ... more than considerably ... I thought I was to blame for not being able to cope ... for being very scared at times and probably difficult to live with when I was having dream after dream ... night after night ... because the impact on me was enormous ... I would still be living the dreams the following day ... so it's altered my belief system about me ... and it's altered it about other things ... I believe now that I can understand where the pain came from I don't have to be annihilated by it ... I can actually understand it ... hold it ... embrace it and move on.

Before you came to see me how long had you been having the dreams?

Many years, I'm talking twenty to thirty years ... I'm talking years ... years and years ... if I dreamt at night it would overhang the day.

But it was the dream that would overhang?

Yes.

You wouldn't go into it like you have done here?

No ... no ... nothing like that ... absolutely not ... all I had was this thing that had gone on during the night-time ... no ... nothing ... no.

So what therapy has allowed you to do is to re-live, re-experience and, as you say, hold and embrace it?

Yes ... I've entered the dream.

Did you have any thoughts about where the dreams came from?

No I don't think I did.

So they were just terrifying experiences?

Mmmm ... nightmares ... they were the worst of nightmares ... night terrors ... in no uncertain terms ... but no idea how they came about.

Did you talk about them to anybody?

No ... no I have never told anyone before.

So would you go along with the theory that it might be the brain controlling these images.

I don't like the idea of the brain just ticking around just doing it's own thing ... I think the way it makes sense for me to be tied into this past life theory.

You said over and over again there is no end, it's cyclic?

Yes ... that's what I've come to accept and recognize because of the work that I've done ... I would not ... could not have had that idea previously.

No, because we talked about metaphor and Jungian images

Yes but it never hits the spot in quite the same way as this does ... when you say "past lives" I think ..."BINGO" it all falls into place ... .that's the "Eureka" factor that I hadn't actually got before ... because that puts the framework around it ... that's acceptable to me ... .even though I didn't come here expecting to get that ... but I have.

So brains might be just part of a wider cyclic flow – does that make sense?

Yes it would ... I would have to think to get my head round it ... but yes ... it's like everything's linked to everything else ... nothing stands alone ... whatever the nothing is it does not stand alone ... and I don't know if I'm talking about energy flow ... or what I'm talking about ... but I have to think that's how things operate.

I discuss here that I believe that consciousness in the individual is for self regulation and insight into the unconscious mind, but that it is part of a wider consciousness

Yes ... yes but the linkages are universal ... if you like ... the personal aspect is your own ethos ... .ethic something ... the notion is there ...

So there is a consciousness of self but also an intuitive consciousness of the link?

Yes everything conscious and unconscious is like this inter-swirled ... intertwined ... inter-related affair ... it's actually been an experience of being re-born ... because what I am beginning to feel now is a feeling of being freer than I have ever felt before ... .coming up to this 60 thing I think, God better late that never ... because the next few years will be very, very different ... because of this ... it's a lot about not feeling isolation ... it's about integration ... it's made an enormous difference in the way that I work ... and that's about integration ... the depth of understanding has changed ... it's like I'm on another level, increased intuition, sharpened perception. I have a feeling that as I go on I shall be more and more satisfied with the work that I do

146

because I'm there in a different way ... it's something about mundane and the word for not mundane whatever that might be (sacred perhaps?) it's like the feet of clay stuff that you are bound here by cement boots ... but you don't have to be once you tap into all this stuff ... it can be changed for you ... and because I had cement boots and now lost them and shed them I can recognize that there is a lightness that I am experiencing now that I very much hope will last ... because it's wonderful to be so different ... it's really freeing ... it's living life in a different way.

Here we begin to discuss the "today" happenings because the weekend had been a turning point in the relationship with her husband. As far as she is concerned the present situation has been a growth space for her. Jan went on to explain that she could not continue to live in the dark space that it has been for her, she will not go there any more and:

This is about where I am going to be from now on ... .moving forward not backwards so that's the way of it and I don't think that I could have got to this without having done the work ... I'm quite certain I could not have ... because what it has done ... it's given me a massive awareness of past pain that can be put to rest ... it can be ... certainly not buried ... that's not the word ... I'm looking for it ... but it can be ... something about being bathed in light and I don't know a word for that ... but that's what it feels like and it's terribly beneficial ... and I think it's because I actually saw myself dead ... if you like ... where I know I'd gone through these awful experiences ... and I saw the wound and I was able to see the light and was able to touch the wounds and feel the healing start when that happened ... the healing started I'm quite convinced of that ... and things were different after that ... I can't talk in terms of having visions or whatever ... but those were the images that I saw ... these were the pictures that I saw in my mind.

These were the images that you had lived?

Yes I did ... yes I did ... that's where they came from.

You kept saying "it's not me but it is me."

Yes ... and I look at that now and I'm seeing so clearly ... that that's as much me there as me here ... so they have somehow managed to merge.

And you said Catholic kept coming up again and again, have these images changed anything for you?

I think that when we use the word Catholic I immediately have this idea of something I've been with at some time and I think that that comes from one of

147

those images that I have never explored here because it came to me afterwards when you had gone to Spain that there was one more and the one more was ... .do you remember when I was in the Tower and I said that I had a vision an idea of me in a corner of the room and I can see it in my mind's eye there again ... I'm a very young woman ... and I'm waiting I'm in prison and I'm waiting I think it's all tied into the Tower ... and probably why I wasn't able to go back there at that time ... because this one had not really formulated as it now appears to have done because I do believe that means another occasion when I literally lost my head ... on Tower Green ... and this all kind of fits in God help me.

So you have lost your head on two or three occasions?

God only knows but I hadn't got to that one when we finished ... I knew there was something kicking around ... because I knew that it wasn't cleared ...

And is that something that still needs to be done?

I don't know ... I don't think that I can go there yet I think that it's sufficient to say that ... that girl came back to me while you were away ... because I know that I hadn't quite done with that place ... it's extraordinary ... but I know that I hadn't quite swept through there ... but there is something there about actually knowing what happened and actually recapturing what was lost ... because at the point of death ... yes you are dead for sure ... but then you are NOT then you see it like you are here ... and it's there ... and it's like leaving the mortal stuff and becoming visually calm ... spirit ... I don't know ... but that's what it's been like and when this happened although you were not here ... I knew from what I had done before ... how to deal with it.

So you dealt with it yourself?

So I dealt with it and now I'll be able to say it here and now ... to say I dealt with it is a false thing ... really ... it's not like sitting here talking to you about it.

But you allow things to happen now until the brain does resolve it?

Yes ... if you stay with it.

Do you remember staying with a pain or an action?

Yes ... I've always got this ... (Jan taps her shoulder) ... to pull me through ... I've used this quite a lot ... there have been times when I've been so desperate to get comfort ... if it has to come from me ... then you know ... here it comes

... it's then that I know about it and I can use it and of course the breathing ... the breathing starts because I remember one session we had here and I was sitting in something that felt like a pyramid and all this golden stuff came down all over me ... almost like a balm ... a radiance or something and I breathed and I could feel it choking me like I had to get up and get it out somehow ... an extraordinary feeling like taking in life and that in the end is what I've done.

Is there any need now to go to the Tower?

I don't think there is ... I don't think so ... I don't think there is at this time I think I'm still a little queasy about it to say the least ... but I think I can see a time when I will go ... and it will be different ... and I'm not sure when that's going to be ... but I'll know when it is and if you are here then I would like it to be us that went because you are the only one who knows about this stuff and I think to go and touch the walls and look through the windows would be a great thing to do and what seems like the last piece ... no ... I don't know ... it can't be the last piece of anything ... it would be I'm about to say ... therapeutic ... but it wouldn't feel therapeutic at exactly this moment ... but I think it will feel benign at some time ...

So that is what you would be looking for, that it felt benign?

Yes ... yes it would be calming which is completely the opposite of what it would have been like if I'd done it at the wrong time ... I think I've had to find the strengths in me to actually embrace what's happened in both here and in my personal life because of touching the scared dreadful part of what I've known and it's taken this to get me into the strong part of me when I can hold what was bad ... because previously I would have said that it was too terrible for me ... it was too terrible on my own ... but now it feels different.

You know when you said you had had this feeling for years and years?

Mmmm ...

Can you pinpoint it now more accurately, say from thirteen or fourteen?

No, younger than that, I started dreaming when I was about five years old ... but not the same sort ... I'd say that I have been dreaming since I was quite young ... and all this gained on me and the appalling nightmares came when I was about thirteen or fourteen.

We discussed here the theory of Roger Woolger that often the fears begin at the age a person died in a previous life and the fact that the images were of a very young girl

Yes that's true ... very true ... but there had always been this big thing about me ... I've always worn high necks a lot ... even in summer ... people laugh at me because I always wear high necks ... and I always have the cover up around my neck in bed ... and there's always been this cold thing up here something I couldn't possibly explain because I was a lot younger ... but it was always that kind of thing.

What about the cover around your neck in bed, could you not bear them?

No ... it could be a sweltering hot day and I would always have something round my neck ... from early years.

Protection?

Protection ... yes but those things continued and I mean they were really fearful around nineteen, twenty, twenty-one which was the age I saw myself in Versailles and that's very relevant to me ... they were very powerful at that time ... so it was in the very early stages I think from twelve to twenty-one, twenty-two I had a huge amount of dreams ... they would stop for a while ... but they came back and back over a long period of time ... and there was this time when they seemed to follow a programme which was very strange as if my dreams would burst through in the night somehow ... but they have always been the same sort and they have always been around the same subject and that's understandable now.

Do you listen to your relaxation tapes?

Yes I do ... they are my emergency kit if I dream ... they tip me over into sleep if I'm having trouble ... but it's nothing like it was ... these are my safety things that I know about now ... now I've got to where I am now it feels like I've everything out and the energy can come back in and I can start to do things again ... I feel freer now to do learning ... whatever ... because the last course I did was agony ... because I was so unhappy and the next piece I take on will probably feel very different.

CHAPTER 26

CONTROVERSIAL EXPLANATIONS

Many scientists would argue that some of the experiences that came up during therapy were possibly remembered images of the actual birth process, that remind the individual of being strangled, cut, and buried. Other authors such as Grof (1984) in his book "Beyond the Brain" would say it might be a dynamic constellation of memories and fantasy material representing different periods of a person's life. He would say that the common denominator of those experiences would be an emotional charge of the same or similar quality that he calls a system of condensed experience (cited in Woolger p. 120). Because both the brain and body are thought to store many unconscious and deeply buried stresses and complexes, anything from Counselling through Psychotherapy to Advanced Hypnosis, and both massage and reflexology can, and often does, initiate many images.

Jan only had to repeatedly pat her shoulder to release the memory of her father – **NOT, I hasten to add, her "this life" father**. Roger Woolger would describe the cluster of feelings as resonating symbolically in Jan's unconscious mind with something long buried (**very long-time buried in this case**). Edgar Cayce would maintain that the mind was remembering other episodes of a past life. Many years ago Freud called dreams the royal road to the unconscious and it is obvious that Jan's unconscious mind has been working towards release for the greater part of her life. Zohar would say that because of the bond with those who have lived before, that Jan has taken up aspects of those she has loved into her own being, and woven them inexorably into her own, and so re-incarnated them.

However we explain the experiences, whether they are real memories of other past lives, or symbolic images, they have radically changed Jan's life, her attitudes, her beliefs, her values, and the way she works and relates to other people.

I have no doubt that the powers-that-be that are making guidelines for training therapists do not have in mind what Jan endured through her 50 hours of therapy.

Throughout the therapeutic sessions with Jan I was not often even a facilitator, I was there in case Jan needed me. I rarely spoke during many sessions except to bring a session to a constructive close.

Jan continues to write during July and August:

*I am writing my part of the story. The "gap" has told me quite a lot about me, I've had time to think more. It's not all in my favour sometimes. It does make so much sense in terms of body memory. When I started working with you I intended to work on why I seemed to have "blocks" in my behaviour I felt that I should have been able to overcome these, but I could not. There were additional factors of feeling, I was traumatised in situations that did not merit such a strong reaction. Ever since I was small I have been susceptible to atmospheres. The Tower of London was my first introduction at about seven years old, when even then I felt I needed protection from something (this may not be so unusual). However, when I started to experience other lives the pattern seemed to become clear. I had been there before. I did know the stones, I feel I had been there as a perpetrator and as a recipient of that justice of the country that separated head from body. Again when I visited Versailles I knew what my fate was as the work progressed. The fear and terror in my memories, the sense of justice, fair play, right and wrong underpinned by the love/fear of GOD seemed to make more sense to me than I would have believed possible. The drama of my dreams and the way I learned a "lesson" and then later more would come, was the most exciting but deeply scaring journey. As I worked more the line between yesterday and today lessened and I could feel myself being drawn backwards in time until I felt I could turn a corner and be in another place and time. **My reality was not as secure** as I had considered it to be. My dreadful father from my young days as a boy in the Tower stays with me. He is my guardian and his hand comes from the past with his customary pat on my right shoulder. He nearly knocks me over, smiling his menacing smile that is meant to be kindly to me. He's a wicked sod but to him I am a precious child, even though I do not exhibit the strengths he wants. I am far too feminine for him. I always was at odds with myself then in the year fourteen hundred and something to now. My mother wanted a boy so I could never be what she wanted either. I followed what my father then wanted me to do at the cost of my life. My mother put the fear of GOD up me then and the fear of GOD was also present as I am convinced that I was Catholic and religious and knew the power of the church even though my profession was as disgusting as it was. All at odds, no peace until I knew the mercy of divine redemption and salvation after death. Somewhere in there I thought I was going mad, but if I believe in past lives and I do then it makes sense in a way it never did before.*

Dear Joyce,
At times my head is so full of questions but rarely answers. Peace would be a wonderful thing in terms of mental activity quieting down. I wonder if the last reincarnation is the one where you recognize that there have been others? I know that there was one more that I have not explored but it does make a

152

particular and especial sense and pattern, knowing what I do know now. I relish our trip to London – that's a change! The Tower lures and calls to me now. That's a shift but it cries out to something in me. This is scaring as my guardian angel pats me and says "GO ON". Can you explain to me how we are linked? I have had such strong thoughts that it is only us that can do the London part, I am not safe otherwise. I can feel the pull backwards into the past down a tunnel that has persuasion?

During my time back in England Jan and I did go to the Tower of London. It was quite a traumatic day in parts, full of fears, feelings of dread and anxiety, but Jan saw it through and we ended with a time in the chapel. She was most upset about the way in which the tour guides made almost a dramatic mockery of the beheading of the past. No doubt it was meant to lend atmosphere to the proceedings, but Jan found it provocative and disturbing.

10th August 2003 Jan writes about her experiences in the Tower:

Just steps, I'm feeling quite sick as I walk up the steps to the temporary entrance to the Tower of London. I look at my feet and I'm aware that I must not allow myself to "tread through that other time" when I was nothing more than a common butcher. The atmosphere is so heavy and I can only think of the pain and suffering that these walls have witnessed. We walk ... the gravel crunches ... the sound of voices float around me ... but I am alone. I walk past the "Traitors Gate" and the malignant push in that area makes me move well away. The loathsomeness ... the blackness makes me want to vomit. We walk up to the green but I know that I have to go into the chapel, only there can I find peace. I cannot raise my eyes to look at others, it's only through supplication that peace can come to me. The cross on the altar keeps my attention and I see the sign of the resurrection as a certainty now I know what I know. I found a place I thought I knew, the place where I was murdered for executing the woman ... as was right. It was night, the arch, the mud, the slime and filthy wet clothes. It was there by the river that the three black spirits came to me, calling and beckoning me to slide into the river to become one with the blackness of evil. It was there that the feathered guardian came to me and when I faltered, I was scooped up to a place of light in a power that was infinite and pure. It was here that I heard the music of the spheres, clashing and banging with their celestial chords in the blue of the ethos about me. It was here that I felt the pull of light so bright, up into a tunnel, a vortex, that I no longer had a body, only spirit. One and One, indivisible, purity from a higher source. A filthy sinner who repented and asked for redemption and absolution. I know what I did was outside the Tower, I remember the wall and the rounded towers, the crowds and the shouting. Vile sinners all of them, inhuman bastards, oblivious to another's fear and trepidation. The souls of the dead are in this place. Tread carefully stranger, you may be next. My wicked old dad was with me as I walked around. He always sneered at my feminine ways but it didn't matter, he's standing by me and he pushes my right shoulder down through the ages. It's a comfort to know that I'm not mad. I have asked the question time after time. Why did the dreams start so young? Why does the Tower have such a pull on me? I was rooted to the spot at one time, palpitations and nausea, I wanted to die. For days after the visit, I felt odd ... not here ... not there ... I don't belong in that time or this time. I've been to church and I have felt that I have been forgiven ... I needed to be in there to feel the age of stones around me ... I've been so sad, for no real reason. I've almost got on the train and gone back to follow through.

12th September 2003

Dear Joyce,
I am actually feeling better and stronger and I am happy. I never thought I would say that again. Sixty has proved to be an amazing age, if I am open to it. I went to a workshop with ... it was about medium-ship, but I had really just said yes I'll go.

Very odd day, I left at lunchtime ... I was taken aback by the intensity around me. I did not care for the commercial talk, but I was constantly in the company of my guardian dad from the Tower days. He obviously felt I needed him I am so glad to be free of ... he was blocking me and I was trapped in his behaviour patterns. It was all meant to be I suppose.

It's four o'clock in the morning and I wake to know that my life today is free because of the experiences I have had the privilege and pain to work with. I could not have held those on my own and I would never have known the sure and certain hope of life after death without your ability to keep me safe when I felt I was at such risk. I constantly see myself sitting in the chair, bathed in the golden light with that dreadful scar around my neck, whole, complete, and redeemed. That life ended before it had run its course, unfair, unjust. I know my name now, Gianetta, I can identify now that for me what happens is not about fine details, and only a few facts feel certain. It's about a compelling intensity that was magnificent but deeply disturbing at the start as it was so far away from when I first entered therapy.

I live in today what happened before, does that confirm that this is my last earthly return? Is it ended when you actually know some of what went before? My times have been violent, a murderer, murdered, who found redemption under the bridge, a place where mud and water lured me down into the depths of hell, beckoned by those dark figures of doom. Then an almighty energy of brown wings lifting me up into the precious light, taking me to safety to the next level. I know now about different levels beyond the place I am today. As I write I can feel the surge of feelings of heat come into my hands and lately into my feet and legs. I have no idea what to make of it but I have come to accept what comes to me. It appears to be another piece of a jigsaw, I have no illustration to follow.

154

It confirms for me that the journey is over centuries and I am an old soul as I know are others around me. There is comfort in that I sense others' depths in their company. I had no idea what a drastic way our work would affect my life. I had the weight of chains around my legs and neck ... a dream of my childhood. Shambling along in a line, male without clothing, only a cloth, dirty, unshod and abject in a place of execution. I do not know how I died but I know I walked into brilliant light that took away fear, the incredible peace of God's holy person.

CHAPTER 27

THE QUANTUM THEORY

"No language which lends itself to visualisability can describe the quantum jumps"

Max Born (cited in Herbert)

On the basis that the universe was made up quantum "stuff", quantum theory was devised in the 1920s to deal with atoms and atomic structure, and extending to the realm of elementary particles and much smaller elements. It is a method of presenting quantum "stuff" mathematically, as it seems that *a priori*, although the universe appears to be of a homogeneous nature, it is thought to be more peaceful than atoms. This is because scientists have found that there are many types of atom of unstable structure, which are buffeted about by turbulent forces. The word quantum means how much or energy packet, so defined in this way every experience, every feeling or emotion can be described as energy force. Yet quantum waves carry no energy and are sometimes called empty waves. Quantum waves are a measure of probability and during the act of measurement one quantum possibility is singled out to surface in the material world as an actual event. However, the British chemist, Humphrey Davey, cautioned that if the word atom meant anything at all it could only realistically be seen as a chemical reaction not any kind of material entity. (Cited in Herbert)

If this is so then the brain with its perceived built-in indeterminacy because of the different chemical reactions at the dendrites, might be construed as just another form of energy, force, or consciousness. In a similar way a Russian physicist Yuri Orlov (cited in Zohar) argued that any creative thinking and probability states must be playing a part in the openness of the brain to all the potentialities latent in consciousness. For example, the ability of most intelligent human beings to see many possibilities at once.

Quantum theory predicts accurately the results of measurement but it does not tell us what the unmeasured world is like. So it may be with brains and consciousness. A German chemist, Wilhelm Oswald, proposed an alternative to the hypothesis that the universe was made up of atoms, based on his theory of thermodynamics. He maintained that atoms and molecules were imaginary fictions and that the real component of the universe was energy in a variety of forms. In this electro-magnetic universe, everything that is found in it, has an energy vibration. Anything that is matter has energy vibrations, and according to Karol Kuhn Truman (1991) feelings and thoughts are energy. The important fact about this statement for therapists in particular, is that matter as taught by physics, cannot be destroyed – only changed.

Werner Heisenberg on this question, states that the world is twofold and it consists of both potential and actualities, but the two worlds are bridged by a special interaction that physicists call measurement. What for him the two realities have in common is that only phenomena are real, the world beneath phenomena is not. Do we raise a glass to Emmanual Kant? Classical physics used to account for all the variety in the world by means of two physical entities, matter and fields. The two fields were electromagnetic and gravitational, but later James Clark Maxwell found that although the two were separate fields, like the wave and the particle, they were just two different aspects of the a single electromagnetic field. So! "things" can be two aspects of the same field, one thing or the other, but not usually both at the same time. Like anxiety and relaxation, love and hate, pain and no pain in therapy, polarizations that change with focus and concentration one into the other, because change is inevitable. By dissolving these distinctions between matter and field, physicists began to realize that the world was ultimately composed of the same substance, whatever we want to call it.

A metaphorical explanation can be found in Rolf Alexander's book *The Healing Power of the Mind*. He describes the framework of creation as a "loom" upon which "the Absolute" was to weave the intricate tapestry. Such a loom, which the physicists call the "Field", is the fabric of space itself. This is not just empty nothingness as was once thought, but in reality, a large ocean of **directive intelligence** which governs the formation of all physical bodies, and directs their course. The loom or field also propagates light and other electro-magnetic phenomena such as radio waves as well as more subtle vibrations across interstellar space. Furthermore he goes on to say that it is the immaterial wave structures which organize neutrons, electrons and positrons etc. into molecules, and solid matter. He calls the Field the Universal Mind, which guides the physical development of all living things. The reason Alexander gives for the amazing POWER of the individual mind, is that the Universal Mind responds to the individual mind. His hypothesis is that the Universal Mind takes up the desires of living things, amplifies them, and answers them, by bringing about the right conditions for those desires to be fulfilled. This for him is where, prayer or meditation bring healing through the natural laws of the spiritual aspect of the universe.

Quantum physics demonstrates the underlying unity of the universe, which must change our view of "reality". Many believe that observation creates reality therefore human beings create their own reality. Conflict arises through the fact that human perceptions create a world of unique actualities that is inevitably classical, and quantum reality is not that way at all. Quantum reality consists of simultaneous possibilities which are anything but classical. We cannot take off our coloured spectacles through which we see our world, so what we experience is not external reality *per se*, but our own interaction

157

with it. We cannot distance ourselves from "what is out there" to subject it to impartial scrutiny because we are not observers, but participants.

We construct our own universe from within, changing "what is" by the very act of observing it. However, if every particle of matter connects with every other particle, the brain itself must be interconnected with the rest of the universe. Other authors think that the brain does generate its own constructions and images of reality but generates them in such a way as to resonate with what is out there. In quantum psychological terms then, the microcosm is a reflection of the macrocosm, and vice versa, just as Jung, and the astrologers of old have always told us.

There is no conflict, no mystery to be solved. Physics by implication says that the universe is an interrelated system, so nothing can arise that in some sense is not already there. So! If human beings are capable of purposeful action, they have not summoned it up from nowhere unaided out of their own resources. GOD, (The Absolute), the source, the first cause, is alive and well. Alexander says that it is impossible to speculate on the nature of The Absolute or First Cause because there is nothing to compare it with, and it is difficult to conceive of anything being "infinite" or timeless.

What intrigues me most is the theory of Vladimir Braginski, (cited in Herbert) about the two senses in which an observer creates reality when he makes a quantum measurement. He says that the first sort of reality creation occurs when an observer exercises his or her "meter option", that is selects the attribute to observe. The second created reality is when the observer "collapses" the wave function. The first person to suggest that quantum theory implies that human consciousness creates reality was John von Neumann, who takes the previous theory further, he sees human consciousness as the site where the wave function collapses. **The collapse of the wave function is also called the "quantum jump". Because the gap between the measured world and the unmeasured world is a logic gap, the quantum jump is the gap between the measured world and the unmeasured world in which "the miracle occurs".**

For me this is where the spontaneous past-life memory is born. The collapse site cannot be located by appeal to experimental methods at this time, but it might be likened to Zohar's condensed phase if the process of wave function collapse occurs whenever a system's phases become sufficiently random as to bring about a change. The trouble with theories is that as different people look at the same theory they still come up with different models of reality, but because consciousness creates reality by choosing what particular attributes of value shall materialize, makes the most sense.

The quantum world then seems to be both objective but objectless which does not seem to be logical. However, Herbert gives an example of a phenomenon which is objective but not an object (p. 162) He puts forward as an example a rainbow which has no end (shame no pot of gold to be found) because a rainbow appears in a different place for each observer. However it

158

can be photographed so it is an objective phenomenon, yet subjective for each person who sees it. It is the same for human bodies with what holistic healers call the invisible, or subtle bodies. Invisible bodies are simply refined matter, matter vibrating at a higher rate than physical visible matter, atoms vibrating at ascending rates. These so called invisible bodies, can now be photographed by Kirlian photography which previously had only been "seen" by clairvoyants. So according to quantum reality those dynamic attributes when not observed exist in a wave-wise superposition of possibilities. Yoga and Theosophy postulate as many as seven or nine bodies, which they say go "down or up" to the Divine Spark or "etched atom". The latter is according to them the essential self who holds the memory experiences, the "I" which reincarnates and persists, the seed spirit, the higher self or moral principle. It is thought that the etheric body disperses soon after death, the astral body dissolves when the seed spirit , the essential self is ready to reincarnate into a new physical body, or progress to states of being higher than astral. (Just like the melting ice cube.) It remains still however, the biggest mystery for scientists to reveal. At the moment we can only speculate that it is possible that consciousness is some kind of quantum effect, and perhaps human awareness has under certain circumstances access to the inside of the quantum world.

In his book *Feelings Buried Alive Never Die* Karol Kuhn Trueman tells of an experiment prepared to discover what takes place at the moment of transition from life to death by means of measuring the wavelengths of the brain. Trueman *et al.* had a device, which had a needle pointing to 0 in the centre of a scale, and each side of the scale was calibrated to 500 points positive and 500 points negative. Their volunteer was a woman on the point of death. They record that at the point of death the woman started to fervently pray. The prayers were full of love, praise, thanks and belief in the power of his being. Measured on the positive scale was 500 plus, and they reported that this had registered 55 times more than the power used by a 50 kilowatt broadcasting station sending a message around the world.

In another experiment at the other end of the scale, a man shrieking verbal abuse and cursing, registered 500 on the negative side of the instrument. The experiments were set up to show how positive and negative thoughts, words and feelings as vibrational frequencies, might draw a person closer or further away from their "source". The source being considered as Divine Source, GOD, Universal Intelligence, Universal Mind, Nature, First Cause, whatever.

The material world consists of relatively motionless energy whereas at the level of sub-atomic energy the material world dissolves and as we reach towards the spiritual there is pure energy. We can however, it seems, create harmony in the physical world by means of our senses and by the way we choose to think and discriminate. **We can certainly create harmony in the spiritual world by aligning our own pattern with that of nature and the universe, through prayer and meditation.**

CHAPTER 28

DISCUSSION

From the overwhelming evidence presented here, it seems that consciousness must be everywhere in this self-generating, self-initiating, self-maintaining, self-organizing universe of ours. Consciousness is pure potentiality and the field of all possibility and creativity, of which personal brains and minds are just one more part. It may be that in individual brains a specific state of organization had to be reached for consciousness to arise, but it could not have begun with man. Consciousness must necessarily have been present in primitive neural systems, and evolved as a useful product of that selective process which confers biological advantage for survival. It must also have contained our spiritual essence, because nothing arises inside unless it is already there outside.

The obvious conclusion about reality is that both Kant and Hegel were right in their own way. Bohr and Heisenberg later than Kant and Hegel, also saw a world forever divided into two types of reality, quantum reality that we can never experience and classical reality that we can. However, it seems again from the evidence presented here, that the theory of individuals being part of the whole means that we are not just observers but an integral part of the equation, so we do have access to both worlds. We are quantum beings in a quantum universe. Quantum physics demonstrates the underlying unity of the universe, which changes our view of the "nature of reality".

If reality is a seamless web, and the universe an unbroken whole in which living and non-living things are constantly unfolding, the brain/mind/ body problem takes on a whole new meaning. David Bohm (cited in Wolinsky) introduced the concept of explicate and implicate orders where all boundaries are observer created rather than being inherent, which is in agreement with Einstein's quotation about form and emptiness. Einstein maintained that everything is made of emptiness, and form is condensed emptiness.

Form creates what Bohm called the explicate order of sizes, shapes and mass, but if we could look at the world through a sub-atomic lens, all we would see would be particles and waves floating in what looks like nothing. This would not provide human beings with any kind of stability or security, so the explanation for me is that the five senses are there to filter and change what looks like nothing to something. As to the peculiar arrangement of the physical body, questioned by Penrose. If everything from the outside world in quantum terms, occurs with such lightening rapidity that they are here and gone before consciousness can register them, we need a buffer to dim down the incessant clamour of impressions. The buffer then will be served by the

Central Nervous System itself which will limit perceptions by means of the bodily sense organs of sight, hearing, taste, touch and feeling, and then for better or worse, our CONSCIOUSNESS creates our REALITY. However, reality will always be a matter of probability where an electron at one time will be a wave or a particle or both, an atom may be in this orbit or that orbit, and in brains as well as everything else, it all depends on number, frequency and density.

Minds must be able to make sense of the world, so if all information comes into the brain simultaneously we need a time delay in order to select that which is useful to survival and to understand the meaning for us as individuals.

The Central Nervous System then will allow the mind time to sort out what is relevant from what is not, by simply providing the "lag" in order to change sensation into perception by matching with prior learning the virtual bombardment of information which assaults our brains from the external environment. It is the "fine tune" instrument of co-ordination of all those known and unknown pathways in the brain to provide the parallel processing of information to give us the confidence of knowing what is right and what is wrong. It is the delicate balance of the hypothalamus that organizes our sexual, eating and drinking patterns. It is the constant monitoring of chemicals in the brain, which manages the changeover from serotonin to melatonin in our waking, sleeping behaviour. The brain enables the mind to change state through the regulation of brainwave patterns from beta through alpha to theta and delta, which may unleash unconscious knowledge from the locked recesses of the mind.

Perhaps there is no mystery! No argument! Perhaps GOD works in mysterious ways. We can use our brain, abuse our brain, find, by accident, therapeutic means or research, the miracle of how the brain enables or indeed, enhances the mind. A lightning strike or a car accident can bring about heightened perceptions and unusual powers of mind reading. A Mind Mirror can monitor and display the difference between one state and another and show how by thinking we can change those states and gain control. Our brains can enable our minds to find out by whatever means, who we are, where we are going and where we came from. If we believe that we have no soul, then we can state quite categorically that it is only our brain going through its electrical and chemical changes. Or we can say that it is only conditioned behaviour.

If we believe that we are more than brains and minds, and have the courage to admit that we are powerful spiritual beings with a soul that seeks its source, then we can change the world with our thoughts and our behaviour. Channelled information cited in Ruth Montgomery's book states that "immortality" is the one reality in an unreal world. It is only the fact that we are hampered by our senses that lends it the "unreal" note.

If we look at some of the new strategies of practitioners, who deal with the problems that individuals bring to the therapist, it may hold the answer to how to solve those earthly problems. According to Stephen Wolinsky (1993) it is TIME which is involved in most of our daily problems, and strategies which employ what Neuro-Linguistic Programming calls "time line" therapy work extremely well. Thinking about the past and what might have been, bringing with it shame and guilt, can cause depression. Worrying about the future brings anxiety and fear, which is why so many people visit clairvoyants and astrologers. In the case of Ericksonian advanced hypnosis, clients are asked to go back in time in order to change their perceptions of the past by doing things differently, or to go forward in time to "see" how they want things to be. When clients step "out of time" and stay in the NOW problems can disappear. These strategies are particularly useful in dealing with present pain, because the intensity of present pain varies with the amount of remembered pain and fear of imagined future pain

Many authors say that even TIME itself is a form of energy, and perhaps we should look to the properties of time that so that we can find the source that maintains the phenomenon of life in this our material world. Time links us immediately to all things in the universe, it has a "flow pattern" from past to future as can be shown on time-density detectors. Perhaps the question we should ask is, if the sightings of energies on a universal scope could be an all-pervasive memory field called time?

Diane Dreher (1991,1995) put forward her theory that because TAO is the essential energy of existence, consisting of both principle and process, those energies which are constantly evolving, can be compared to the quantum theory of physics. This means that sub-atomic energy patterns are the scientific equivalent of CHI, which according to eastern medicine, is the creative force beneath all existence. This energy is not quite a particle, a predictable and solid part of matter, neither is it a wave, action or process. It is both according to how it is perceived. TAO means "the way", at one and the same time, a path and an order, a single principle underlying all creation, all the laws of nature, the truth and the source of all life. TAO asks that we each take responsibility for our own lives, so that through a shift in attitude, we as individuals can begin to experience greater peace. This then can bring about the necessary changes for peace amongst social groups and eventually peace in the world.

Jan talks about how always before, she would want a beginning, middle and end, but now she feels there is a very thin line between past and present.

So! If there is no time there can be no cause and effect, and this has great implications for our common sense theories about reality as well as how it might apply to mind. If every particle of matter interconnects with every other particle, the brain itself must be interconnected with the rest of the universe.

Rossi's psychobiological approach of staying with the energy force so that eventually something will happen is good, because it allows the natural flow of an experience to run its time-bound course. With no resistance from the beginning to disappearing out of time, a client has freedom from the identification with the constraints and limitations of time-bound reality and energy force. Change is inevitable because we live in a world of opposites, and in order to have any experience there must be contrast, something different from something else. Our whole reality is constantly constructed by making those comparisons so removing a client from a time, energy or mass experience. It also moves them away from a time-locked frozen limitation.

However, change is not always continuous, sometimes there is a discontinuous leap which scientists call the quantum jump and it is this change that cannot be tracked. In one instance before the jump, a particle is occupying a given region of space, then an instant later with no intermediate state when the process is taking place, the particle is somewhere else. No duration of time separates them and no physical process connects the two physical states. "A miracle happens!"

This is how I see spontaneous past-life regressions taking place.

It seems then, that human perceptions create a world of unique actualities that is inevitably "classical" and quantum reality is not that way at all. Quantum reality consists of simultaneous possibilities which are anything but classical. We cannot take off our coloured spectacles of human perception but is it possible that consciousness, human awareness through brains and minds have access to the inside of the quantum world through therapy, meditation and spontaneous past-life experiences? I will acknowledge that there are instances of cryptomania, xenoglossy, and manufactured memories, but I would still ask if it is possible to know first-hand about the quantum world just by sitting and looking inside our heads, and experiencing those spontaneous unasked-for experiences of other possible lives?

Wolinsky and Zohar amongst many other psychologists maintain that human mental experience is of two kinds, what they calls computer consciousness, facts, memories, emotions and body states, and "raw awareness" that human quality that distinguishes us from computers. He calls raw awareness ordinary awareness, which has a direct connection with quantum reality. Edelman defines and explains this woolly concept by making the brain, mind, body connection with external cues.

We have a long way to go with our theories of brains, minds, reality and consciousness but our time will come. Human beings are part of a whole called the universe, but it is a part limited in time and space. We cannot distance ourselves from what is "out there" to subject it to impartial scrutiny, because we are not observers, but participants. What we experience is not external reality *per se*, but our own interaction with it. We construct our own universe from within, changing "what is" by the very act of observing it. Perhaps energy, force, life, spirit, soul or consciousness, are only different names for varying aspects of the same REALITY.

What can we say about reincarnation? Prenatal experiences although upholding no particular theory do suggest the possibility of pre-existence and reincarnation, or at least evidence of memory being in some sphere outside the body, or continuously available by some other means.

Jack Schwarz (cited in Ostrander & Schroeder) states, like Zohar, that it is possible that we may resonate with the past but that does not mean that it is necessarily with our own past lives. Rupert Sheldrake ventures a similar idea in that we may resonate with what he calls "morphic forms" or memory fields. These morphic forms, if the theory is plausible, are one way for memory to be carried through generations. (Cited in Szanto)

Yoga texts tell us memories of the self reside in what they call the "causal body" which carries the seeds of Karma. This may be similar to the SEED SPIRIT the ETERNAL DIVINE SPARK or the REAL SELF of the spiritual healers. The Chinese hold that "CHI" energy fields imprint the physical body with the memories of multi-incarnational events that the Self has experienced in former lives.

Healers talk about invisible bodies of different vibrations. The first of which is the ETHERIC body. This they maintain is the counterpart of the physical body. Or perhaps it should be the other way round, as the physical body is said to be moulded upon the ETHERIC body. The Etheric body is thought to be GOD's perfect and unique pattern of that particular individual. Then as the etheric body interpenetrates the physical, so the etheric interpenetrates the ASTRAL body. This is the body that can amorphize itself into any shape. It is also the body that mediums are said to communicate with during a séance. There is then the mental body and the seat of the WILL. On an even higher vibration, is what healers call, the SEED SPIRIT or higher self or the DIVINE SPARK. The SEED SPIRIT is seen by the healers as CONSCIOUSNESS, free in time and space but retaining life-memory patterns. When the etheric body leaves the physical body at the moment of death the astral remains until the seed spirit, the essential self, is ready to re-incarnate, or to progress to states of being higher than the astral, when it will dissolve. The seed spirit or divine spark is for them the indestructible and eternal spark of individual consciousness, which will eventually return to the whole, the omega point, the universe, nature or GOD.

All these ideas of tissue memory or cell memory may seem far-fetched, but as an experienced hypno-therapist of many years I have witnessed in age regression, present evidence of past life injury. One man mentioned earlier limped for hours after the spontaneous age regression where he re-lived life during the American Civil war. A previous burn may resurface as a blister during age regression, an allergy to flowers can occur, or a full blown panic attack can arise just by the mention of a bee, a wasp or bird, or even more bizarre everyday things. This shows how the reliving and re-experiencing of far memories can bring about real molecular change in the body.

Apart from these instances there is little experimental evidence to show that reincarnation is a fact of life. To Jan at the end of therapy it was the only answer that made any sense, even though she kept saying it made no sense.

June 27th 2005

Jan came to see me for a further counselling session, then afterwards we talked about past life sessions. At the end of the session I asked her to write down all things that she had told me.

It must be about three years since I did my revealing therapy sessions with Joyce. Seeing her today and hearing her ask me to put my images into sequence shook me, as I had actually avoided that part. When I started to speak it out loud I acknowledge the strangest feeling of rolling back down centuries to where for me it all began.

I was the young son of an executioner at the Tower, the acknowledged follower in my father's occupation. The dreadful day came when I had to prove myself and I took a young life, innocent and pure. My life was then taken from me. I was murdered in the mud which was as filthy as my crime. I was lifted from that at my death, with no acquiescence from me in massive wings to the bright white whirling vortex of light above. My death was violent, as had been the death I had inflicted. This was somewhere around 1450.

Following that I had the experience of dying in my own bed, later in Tudor times. I was an older woman married to a tradesman. I lived a simple but adequate life in a house by the Thames but outside of London. Angels were at my head and I thanked God for my years of joy, peace and tranquillity. I was an honest but reclusive woman, free of pretence, secure in the knowledge of life everlasting, but I gave nothing back to the world.

My next most significant episode was in France. As a young aristocratic girl, I was caught up in the hatred of the revolutionaries and spent my last days in the "Cour de Mai" at the conciergerie. I submitted to my fate but have no recollection of the actual event, but came into the place of prayer through blackness. I was kneeling on the prie-dieu and saw benign figures, as monks, robed taking me on my journey down the tunnel of light. I was young and innocent without sin. This appears to link with making reparation for another innocent life hundreds of years ago. I had become the young girl I had butchered although of a different gender. It went again towards atonement, but I gave nothing back to the world. I was selfish and vain and cared little for those less fortunate than myself.

Today I am caught up with ethics, fairness and justice with my work. For many years I have followed Counselling as my profession, and thousands of hours in a never ending quest for spirituality and understanding. At last I give back to the world. My life events have not allowed me to settle. I have felt like I am in a spiral moving upwards towards that blindingly brightness above. As an ordinary person I have been shocked at the ferocity of the images and the ongoing thread of destruction and redemption that featured in the reincarnations that I have been privileged to see. I have become a seeker of salvation, but I have not found it in the church family. I have found an awesome presence in blessed places that salves and solaces me. My path has been shown to me by others further on who hold out their hands to me in the open generosity of sharing knowledge. I have such a lot to thank Joyce for, she came at the right "time". My images of celestial spheres and the sounds in the blueness of eternity never leave me.

CONCLUSION

WHAT HAPPENS NEXT?

"And the end of all our exploring
Will be to arrive where we started
And know the place for the first time ...

T.S. Eliot, from the *Four Quartets*

It was not the same for the ancients, our refusal in these modern scientific times to take into account that which we cannot measure. They did not shut their eyes to anything beyond the purely physical. For them the universe was no less mental or spiritual than it was physical in nature. They were less well equipped to investigate the physical environment, but they were to all accounts well equipped to explore the realms of mind and spirit. They firmly believed in the great astrological years, which changed the consciousness of man.

They saw that in the age of Leo a new cycle had begun with Leonine humanity at peace and at one with itself in an age of psychic wholeness. They saw the great Sphinx of Giza as a symbol of man's alert higher faculties, and higher man in harmony with the lower. Indeed the bearing of the summer sunrise from what they called the archetypal Sphinx, the guardian of the Giza necropolis, still leads the eye from the pyramids of the three kings to the city of Bethlehem. Or at least it did until the shifts in the earth's tectonic plates aligned it differently.

By the great age of Cancer the great ice age thaw had been in full swing for millennia, old lands were being swallowed up and a new way of life was beginning. Sun worship became Moon worship and things changed. Cancer is the sign of reproduction and unbridled growth, a time to go forth and multiply. At this time, the historians tell us, man started to lose his sense of spirituality. The great age of Gemini brought a psychic split, where men had to realize that psychic duality was just unity in disguise. Man had to look into his real nature to discover his soul. The chief cult now was that of the serpent-power, which gave rise to the legend of Quetzalcoatal in Central America and in China the cult of the dragon. In India the concept of "kundalini" was born.

The great age of Taurus brought the message of the Bull. In Gemini, man had re-discovered the source of self-knowledge, now he must plant it, take care of it and allow it to grow and change form. This was the age of agriculture and the realization that by his own effort man must now plough the narrow furrow of self-salvation by way of his own sweat and toil.

Then came the great age of Aries the Ram, this was the age of great prophets, and priest- kings, who were the shepherds of the people. Moses was supposedly the manifestation of the Arian initiate, the law giver for his heavenly guide Jehovah.

At the close of the age of Aries around 150 BC, the vernal equinox moved into Pisces. The time had come now for the Piscean avatar to be born in a stable and as the cycle reached its zenith, the sixth age had begun. There are two fishes in the sign of Pisces, two directions, two possibilities. Free to rise or to descend, free to choose to rise to a new plane of existence or remain in the watery darkness. One decision will take man in the direction of cosmic evolution, the other will go against it

Ilya Prigogine described in his Nobel Prize winning theory of 1977, a theory that emphasized that we human beings are at a turning point in history. He suggested even then, that the stresses and conflicts of our time could thrust mankind into some higher order. He was stating what Thomas Kuhn the science historian and philosopher called "movement towards a paradigm shift". A paradigm shift is that of a scheme held by individuals for understanding and explaining certain aspects of reality. He saw the new paradigm as supporting an awareness of the fact that there are intrinsically dynamic processes or forms of consciousness that begin to show the new patterns and structures of our lives.

When we know for sure that personal truth can never be objective, but that it can be the inner source of knowledge, then we might become aware of the messages that all of the great spiritual teaches have revealed over the last thousands of years. If and when this time comes, we can begin to understand the transformation that we are seeking.

If we can put together all the knowledge and understanding of the philosophers, the astrologers, the mystics and the scientists, we might begin to know that we are related to a far greater consciousness that goes beyond what we call ordinary awareness.

THE MAYAN PREDICTION

If the Mayan prediction comes to pass, perhaps this will eventually fulfil the requirements for the beginning of the Age of Aquarius, together with a new consciousness that will bring together physics, metaphysics, intellect and spirit, self and nature, in a unifying pattern of resonance. What the manifestation of this galactic shock might be we do not know.

Our earth is always at the mercy of being hit by objects from outer space, and because it is approximately 750,000 years since the last reversal of the magnetic field, we are due for one any time now. It is also predicted that the Yellowstone Park volcano could be about to erupt. The Moon is said to be slowly moving away from the earth at a steady rate each year, which may add its own peculiar effect. Apparently the tidal friction, or gravitational forces between the Moon and the Earth cause the Earth to spin more slowly and so is making our "day" minimally longer by 20 seconds every million years. This may sound to be of no consequence, but earthquakes, hurricanes, ice ages and El Niño all have their overall effect. (*National Geographic* June 2005).

On the other hand it may be that the human race needs no help, they can sabotage the planet all by themselves. Every year we dump billions of metric tons of carbon into the earth's atmosphere and less than half of it remains there according to the scientists, who wonder where the rest is going. Trees, crops and phytoplankton all absorb carbon as carbon dioxide in order to grow, but we are messing up the works somehow or other. The oceans have always acted as sinks, mopping up huge amounts of carbon, of which a share is utilized by molluscs to build shells. However, what if nature withdraws its helping hand? We know that we are on track in the next century, to add more and more to the atmosphere. Added to that, we are destroying the very means of dealing with it. The smooth running of the carbon cycle depends on large quantities being taken out of the atmosphere and stored in the forests, oceans, and underground in deposits of coal, natural gas and petroleum. We humans are disrupting the natural cycles by de-forestation and the burning of fossil fuels, flooding the atmosphere with enough carbon to affect the global climate (*National Geographic*, February 2004).

Then there are the theories of climate change if the Gulf Stream stops rotating in its present cycle, and presents part of the world with a new ice age.

Whatever happens, the planet earth tends to look after itself. The latest scientific reports contain convincing evidence that life on earth in the form of one-celled microbes replicated billions of years ago in the most hostile of environments. Deep in rocks and water, in extreme heat or cold, DNA was present on this earth long before it had been thought possible. The other interesting finding is that life on earth in no matter what form, has always effected changes in the outside environment by creating the very chemicals that now support life by interaction with it (*Horizon*, BBC2 February 2005). Today, forests grow again after burning and harmony is restored in the continuous cycle of creativity, some in French Guiana with the help of tough little fruits from Cecropia trees and some beneficial bats. Worldwide, bats aid the spread of plants by simply eating their fruit and defecating the seeds as they fly. Cecropia's unusual fruit is especially useful in reforesting (*National Geographic*, April 2003).

In whatever way the universe began, whatever "stuff" it is made from, it represents matter, which is endowed with dynamic creativity and will, and apparently backed by intelligence. There have been mass extinctions before in the history of the earth. Joel Achenbach reporting in *National Geographic* (April 2003) tells us that 250 million years ago the Permian-Triassic extinction wiped out about 90% of the planet's animal population. Then 65 million years ago the Cretaceous-Tertiary extinction wiped out the dinosaurs and triggered some large-scale debates about what really happened. One important fact we might consider, is that if the dinosaurs had not been wiped out, there might never have been an age of humans like us wondering who they are and where they came from! It might be tragic that species are wiped out but those that survive will remain, to enjoy a whole new world of opportunity, through change. It is called an ecological reshuffle and re-deal and human beings are, if any survive, to say the least adaptable, innovative and creative. According to channelled material from *The Only Planet of Choice* there need be no calamities, no re-shuffles. If we can only realize that each individual holds the key for change, it is our responsibility, our free will, our choice! **The power of thought, the energy of love can make the world a representative of the Universe**.

If matter was created – it suggests a Prime Mover that we may call GOD, the Omega point, Intelligence or Creative Thought. If matter has always existed then the Prime Mover informs and is identical with it. So we then must identify GOD or thought or intelligence with the whole universe and NOT with an intelligent principle which only exists outside the universe. The Taoist concept of change may then be revealed as a tendency innate in all things, that always occurs spontaneously as action. The concept of change being a continuous dynamic interplay of opposites, where up and down, day and night, life and death, are seen as a unity.

Perhaps, the present interest in past-life therapy, eastern religious thought and the seeking of enlightenment through meditation is moving people towards this re-evolution or re-evaluation. It may be that it is through the new therapies, which allow the client to find their own way to resolution of a problem that they will begin to know who they are and where they are going. Edgar Cayce insisted that " karma is memory", if this is true, and death just a change of frequency in the memory field, then memory never dies. It could well be possible to know first hand what it is like to dwell in the quantum world just by sitting still and looking inside our heads and hearts.

The practice of meditation is to become slowly aware of who we are in relation to the whole? And for me a spontaneous past life regression is that quantum jump where the miracle happens to show us that life and death may be just part of the cycle, and another step on the way of eliciting the memory of who we are, where we are going and why?

Religion maintains that we are all brothers and sisters under the skin and recent research in genetics tells us that we are all descendants from the same woman. Now physicists agree and tell us that the very atoms of our bodies are made from "quantum stuff" which combine the wave and particle together at once in some peculiar quantum style all its own. If human beings are necessarily part of the whole that we call the universe, the feeling of being separate is just delusion or illusion. Furthermore, if motion and change are the essential properties of things, and the forces causing the motion are not outside the objects, as classical thought would have us believe. What if the forces are an intrinsic property of matter, and the image of the Divine is not that of a ruler who directs the world from on high, but as Fritjof Capra said, a principle that controls from within? Then, human beings are indeed in control of their own destiny through the tremendous power of their own minds. Now, however, those minds must give way to heart-centred thought and action. It is only through the transposition of consciousness form head to heart that will bring about the reorientation that is needed.

The search for self-knowledge is the search for the higher self, and this Christ principle must enter into a relationship with the lower self so that we can regain the spiritual reality of the cosmos. It has been said that each person must give up the illusion of duality, and with it the clinging delusion of uniqueness and separateness; then the destiny of mankind might be fulfilled and Man and the Universe become ONE.

It matters not from which perspective we seek our knowledge, Psychology, Neuro-science, Philosophy, Theology, Astrology, Archaeology or Physics, they all lead eventually to the same conclusion. Modern Psychotherapeutic methods it seems are pointing the way to aiding self knowledge, and meditation and prayer are bringing many people in touch with their higher selves and nearer spiritual awareness.

Joyce Stableford, 2005.

REFERENCES

Abbot, Geoffrey, *Lords of the Scaffold*, Eric Dobby Publishing, 1991/2001
Alexander, Rolf, *The Healing Power of Your Mind*, Healing Arts Press, Rochester, Vermont, 1989.
Arroyo, Stephen, *Astrology, Psychology and The Four Elements*, CRCS Publications 1975. *Relationships & Lifecycles*, CRCS Publications 1979
Blakemore, Colin & Greenfield, Susan ed., *Mindwaves*, Basil Blackwell Ltd, 1989.
Bohannon, Cynthia, *The North and South Nodes: The Guideposts of The Spirit*, Arthur Publications 1979
Bono, Edward de, *Why So Stupid*, Blackhall Publishing, 2003
Browne, Sylvia, *Past Lives Future Healing*, Judy Piatkus Publishers Ltd, 2001.
Bauval, Robert & Hancock, Graham, *The Keeper of Genesis*, Arrow Books 1997
Bauval, Robert, & Adrian Gilbert, *The Orion Mysteries*, Arrow Books 1988/1994
Cade, C. Maxwell, & Coxhead, Nona, *The Awakened Mind*, Element Books, 1979/1987/1989
Capra, Fritjof, *The Tao of Physics*, Flamingo Fontana Paperbacks 1975.
Charroux, Robert, *The Mysterious Unknown*, Corgi Books, 1973/4/5/6.
Dam, Hans Ten, *Exploring Reincarnation*, Rider Books, 2003.
Davies, Paul, *God and the New Physics*, J. M. Dent & Sons Ltd, London & Melbourne, 1983.
Dreher, Diane, *The Tao of Peace*, Thorsons, imprint of Harper Collins 1990 - 1995
Edelman, Gerald M. *The Remembered Presence*, OU book 2,SD206
Edelman, Gerald M & Giulio Tononi, *A Universe of Consciousness*, Basic Books 2000
Elwell, Dennis, *The Cosmic Loom*, Unwin Hyman Ltd, 1987.
Flem-Ath, Rad & Wilson, Colin, *Giza – The Truth*, Virgin Publishing Ltd, 1999.
Gazzaniga, Michael S., *The Mind's Past*, University of California Press, 1998.
Greenfield, Susan, *The Private Life of The Brain*, Penguin Books 2000
Grof, Stanislav, *Beyond The Brain, 1984* Charles University of Prague
Hamblin, David, *Harmonic Charts*, Aquarian Press, 1983.
Head, Joseph, and Cranston, S.L, *Reincarnation-The Phoenix Fire Mystery*, NYork Julian Press 1961/67/99
Herbert, Nick, *Quantum Reality*, Anchor Books, 1985/1987.
Hudson, Liam, *The Cult of the Fact*, Jonathon Cape Ltd 1972/76.
Humphrey, Naomi, *Meditation the inner way*, The Aquarian Press, 1987.

Kopp, Richard R., *Metaphor Therapy*, Brunner/Mazel, 1995.

Langley, Noel, *Edgar Cayce on Reincarnation*, edited by Hugh Lynn Cayce, Warner Books Inc, 1st edition 1989

Levine, Stephen, *Guided Meditations, Explorations and Healings*, Gateway Books, 1991.

Lawton, Ian & Ogilvie-Herald, Chris, *The Atlantis Blueprint*, Little Brown & Co. 2000

Lofthus, Myrna, *A Spiritual Approach to Astrology*, CRCS Publications 1983

Montgomery, Ruth, *A Search for Truth*, Ballantyne Books, 1996/97

O'Connor, Joseph & Seymour, John, *Introducing NLP*, Thorsons–Harper Collins, 1990.

Oliver, Lucy, *Meditation and the creative imperative*, Dryad Press Ltd London, 1987.

Ostrander, Sheila & Schroeder, Lynn, *Cosmic Memory*, Souvenir Press, 1991.

Peel, Rosemary J., *Astrology & Heredity*, Blandford, 1994.

Prenrose, Roger, *The Emperors New Mind*, 1994/1995

Powell, Robert, *Hermetic Astrology Vol 1*, Hermetica, Kinsau, West Germany, 1987.

Prabhavananda and Isherwood, *How to Know God*, Vedanta Press, 1953, 1981.

Ramachandran, V. S., & Blakeslee, Sandra, *Phantoms in the Brain*, Quill William Morrow, New York, 1998

Ritberger, Carol, *Your Personality, Your Health*, Hay House Inc. 1998

Rossi, Ernest L., *The Psychobiology of Gene Expression*, W W Norton & Co New York & London, 2002.

Rowse, A.L., *The Tower of London*, Book Club Associates, 1972.

Rudhyar, Dane, *The Galactic Dimension of Astrology*, Aurora Press 1975
Person Centred Astrology ASI Publishers Inc. 1980
Astrology and the Modern Psyche, CRCS Publications 1976

Schlemmer, Phyliss V., & Jenkins, Palden, *The Only Planet of Choice*, Gateway Books 1993.

Searle, John R., *The Rediscovery of the Mind*, MIT Press, 1992.

Stableford, Brian M., *The Mysteries of Modern Science*, Routledge & Keegan Paul, 1977.

Stemman, Roy, *Reincarnation – true stories of past lives*, BCA by arrangement with Judy Piatkus Publishers Ltd, 1997.

Szanto, Gregory, *The Marriage of Heaven and Earth*, Arkana London, Boston, Melbourne and Henley, 1985.

Truman, Karol Kuhn, *Feelings Buried Alive Never Die*, Olympus Distributing 1991.

Weiss, Brian, *Many Lives, Many Masters*, Piatkus Books Ltd, 1994.
Same Soul, Many Bodies, Piatkus Books Ltd, 2000

Woolger, Roger J., *Other Lives, Other Selves*, Crucible – Aquarian Press 1987/1990.

Wolinsky, Stephen, *Quantum Consciousness*, Bramble Books, 1993
Young, Arthur M. *The Geometry Of Meaning* Robert Briggs Associates 1976
Zohar, Danah, *The Quantum Self*, Bloomsbury, 1990, Flamingo/Harper
     Collins, 1991.

Articles:
National Geographic, April 2003 & February 2004, March 2005
The Psychobiology of Gene Expression, by Ernest L. Rossi PhD. Handout
     course material.
The Great out of body experience 'Myth', by James Chapman, Daily Mail
     Sept 19 2002
Scientific American, February 2000

Internet Sources:-
Edelman, Gerald, *Gerald Edelman's theory of Consciousness – Neural
Darwinism, re-entry and selection. www.consciousentities.com/edelman.htm*
Bauval, Robert, *Keeper of Genesis – The Message of The Sphinx
http://eclecticviewpoint.com/evbauval.htm*
Bauval,Robert, theory of the true age of the Sphinx, cited in The Sphinx from
the Oxford Journal 1998
www.geocities.com/Athens/delphi/3499/sphinx.htm?200631
The Age of the Sphinx, *www.touregypt.net/historicalessays/sphinxal*
Billington,David.P. *A Response to* Giza:The Truth,
www.members.aol.com/davidpb4/lawton.html
Damasio, Antonio,Review of *The Feeling of What Happens: Body, Emotion
and the Making of Consciousness,*, Heinman:London 1999 by Bruce G
Charlton MD www.hedweb.com/bgcharlton/damasioreview.html